MARY AMAZON

BY JANINE CRIST

Copyright © 2019 by Janine Crist

First edition November 2019

Book design by **Carolyn Crist**

ISBN: 9781692361914

Front cover art painted by Wilbur G. Kurtz in 1958, provided for reprint courtesy of Pegram Harrison. The painting was first commissioned by DeSales Harrison Sr.

www.maryamazon.com

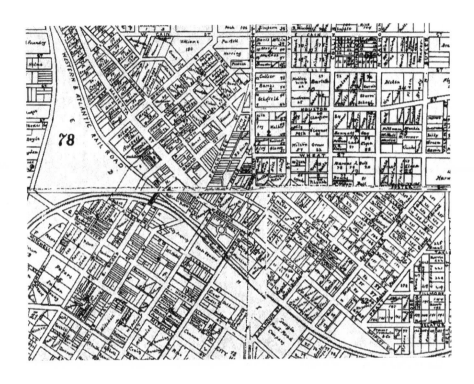

Downtown Atlanta in 1868

Image licensed from:
Kenan Research Center at the Atlanta History Center

In loving memory of
my mother, who never grew tired of telling the story,
and
my father, who taught me to persevere.

CONTENTS

AUTHOR'S NOTE

This story began as an exploration of my past. My mother used to tell me about my great-grandmother's birth on the Savannah River around the time of the Civil War, which captured my imagination. Curiosity about family letters and photos led to days flipping through card catalogues, spinning through microfiche rolls, and painstakingly pouring through old newspapers. My research took me to the Georgia Archives, Oakland Cemetery, Atlanta History Center, Augusta Historical Society, Maryland Historical Society and small towns in the Southeast, where along the way I found and used portions of Thomas Maguire's farm journal, John and Mary Mecaslin's letters, and John Mecaslin Harrison, Sr.'s articles published by the Atlanta Historical Bulletin. This novel in your hands is a decade in the making. I hope you enjoy the journey as much as I did.

Janine Crist
November 2019

PROLOGUE

1857
Atlanta, Georgia

The night guard at the train station heard something that jolted him awake around 7 a.m. He looked up from his post and saw the newspaper editor running toward the firehouse shouting, "Fire!" The guard ran over to the firehouse, and soon the fire bell sounded. The bells began to ring all over town.

Mack and Mary Mecaslin were having breakfast when they heard the chimes. Mary ran to the back porch and rang the dinner bell. Everyone who heard the bell would ring the dinner bell at their house with a distinct three rings and so on until everyone heard. Mack was out of the house and on his horse in no time.

Charles Rodes and Bill Barnes were on duty at the firehouse on Alabama Street. Several other men of Fire Company #1 heard the call and responded on horseback.

Not knowing exactly where the fire was, Mack headed down Decatur Street toward Alabama and Peachtree streets. People ran out of their homes and ladies waved their handkerchiefs, sending him in the direction of the flames. He saw the smoke straight ahead and his horse knew the way. He met with others as he arrived.

A freight car company had caught fire at the corner of Wadley Street and the Western and Atlantic Railroad. The fire had encompassed the whole building.

"Hurry, grab the buckets. Let's go!" yelled one of the firemen.

They ran a block away to fill the buckets, and a bucket brigade was formed immediately. The only accessible water was in the cisterns that were filled with rainwater by the gutters from the eaves of the buildings. There were only five of those, located at different areas downtown. Several men began hooking up the hand engine, which pumped water through a hose that was placed in a cistern. Then two men stood on each side of the machine, raising and lowering the bars, forcing the water through until it reached the fire.

"Push, push, push," they chanted as the bars moved rapidly at sixty times per minute. Their hands felt bitterly cold, and they had to switch frequently due to the strenuous activity. Four men took turns. At the sixty-second mark, they switched.

"You're up," said Barnes, a large, muscular man. Mack, a younger, shorter, but fit man, stepped up to the bar, and the switch took place seamlessly. The next fireman was waiting behind Mack to take his turn, chanting, "Push, push, push." The men relied on each other to keep the pace and motivate each other throughout the tough task.

Another section of the building caught fire, and the firemen switched their attention to a new challenge.

A crowd began to assemble, some cheering encouragement while others commented on the skills of the firemen and their teamwork.

"Let's go, boys!" the newspaper editor yelled.

Kidd filled the buckets. He knew exactly how much water should be in each bucket so it would transfer easily from man to man and get the optimal amount of water to the fire. He passed a bucket to the first fireman in line. That fireman passed it to the next, creating a quick, smooth movement, somewhat like passing a baton. A break in the action could mean death or destruction from the heat and the flames.

Just then, in the middle of the bucket brigade, a handle broke, and the bucket fell to the ground and lost all the water.

"Keep moving those buckets. No time to waste," Kidd yelled as he filled another one.

Rodes was the runner near the fire who ran the buckets back to Kidd. He was slender and fit and the fastest runner of the group. He took great pride in his position.

The flames grew higher and higher. The men worked harder and harder. When they doused the fire in one area, they moved to new fire outbursts. Hour after hour they toiled away, with new shifts and substitutions every thirty minutes.

"New shift," Barnes barked. The fresh firemen ran in to substitute for the exhausted crew. The first shift walked away, and the energy continued.

Finally, many hours later, the fire smoldered and the smoke rose to the sky. The climate was a strange combination of hot and cold. The firemen closest to the fire suffered from the heat, and those far away, passing buckets and pumping the bar, shivered in the winter air.

The men fought valiantly all day until the last ember was extinguished. They were not able to save most of the materials but kept the fire from spreading to the nearby buildings.

As Mecaslin, Rodes, Kidd and Barnes walked away from the smoldering ashes, exhausted, covered in soot and grime, wet and smelling of smoke, Mack said: "Well, men, we need more hands."

Barnes leaned over, put his hands on his knees to catch his breath and said, "Yeah, let's go to Kenny's Alley and talk about this. I'm thirsty!"

They joined a few more firefighters at the bar, and discussions led to the future protection of Atlanta. A few local citizens joined the conversation. Kidd spoke first.

"We need to either establish another fire company or recruit more men to the #1," he said. "We are not equipped to handle fires that are not near the cisterns. It takes too long for a few of us to get water to the fire.

"That's true, Will," responded Mack. "Even the hand engine can only do so much."

One of the local citizens stepped up. "How 'bout another station over by the Georgia Railroad? You could cover more of the city that way."

The mayor chimed in. "What do you think, boys? Can we recruit a few more hardy souls for the job?"

Mack nodded. Will patted Mack on the back and said, "Looks like it's time to start enlisting. We could use a little more competition on training days!" And they all roared with laughter.

CHAPTER 1

"There is, one knows not what sweet mystery about this sea, whose gently awful stirrings seem to speak of some hidden soul beneath."

~ Herman Melville

John "Mack" Mecaslin was born in 1825. Those were the days of new frontiers and vast ocean explorations. New worlds were being discovered. Little of North America had been settled. Native Americans still inhabited much of the eastern area of the continent.

Having grown up as a young boy running the docks at Baltimore, Maryland, John was enamored of the sea. Baltimore was one of the primary U.S. ports and close to markets, being inland on the Chesapeake Bay. His father, Thomas Mecaslin, owned a thriving flour mill on Pine Street, a few blocks from the bay. John also worked with his father and helped move the flour to the docks at Fells Points for shipping. He helped to load and unload the supplies. Then when the work was done, he met his friends at the docks. They would go swimming and fishing and play "walk the plank" like the pirates.

The boys spent hours talking to the sailors and learning the ropes of a life at sea. The stories were enthralling. They listened as the men told the tale of Lt. Charles Wilkes and his crew during the voyages of the U.S. Ex. Ex. (Exploring Expedition) and their discovery of new lands that would later be called Antarctica, the South Pacific and the Pacific Northwest. They talked about the gold in the Pacific Northwest of North America, which was some land on the other side of the world, he thought.

John dreamed of the days when he would go on long voyages to faraway lands and experience the great wonders and mysteries that lured him there.

One day when John was at the docks unloading the flour, a sailor came by and said, "Hey, lad, what's your name?" John told him his name.

"Last name, boy."

"Mecaslin, sir."

"Irish, you say?"

"Yessir!"

"Well, then, Mack, it is. Help me with these bags, Mack, and I will tell you a story about my adventures at sea."

Mack worked hard toting bags for the sailor. The sailor noticed how tired Mack looked and said, "Just two more bags, and then we'll take a break." Mack nodded eagerly and made his best effort before sitting down for a moment of adventure.

The sailor sat across from Mack and looked him in the eye and said, "There was a mighty storm, the likes of which you've never seen." His arms flew open. "The dark clouds rumbled and lightning was so close, I swear the hair was standing up on my arms. The waves were so tall that they were crashing over the deck. The crew held on for dear life, trying with all their might to get below deck."

"Where were you?" Mack asked, afraid to interrupt.

"I'm getting to that," the sailor grinned. "And then, with one mighty gust, one of the sails ripped, and there I was, in the bird seat, holding on. I knew I had to get down from there, but the wind was so strong, I thought it would cast me into the sea. Step by step, I lowered myself until I was almost on deck. Suddenly, crack," he slapped his hands, "the pole above me snapped, and it hit me on the head. I was out! When I came to, the sea had calmed, and the crew had to tell me what happened."

"What did they say? What happened?" Mack said with his eyes wide open.

"The sails were destroyed, and there was so much damage on deck that the ship had to ride the storm out."

"Then what did you do?" the little boy asked in wonder.

"We were rescued by a ship passing us. Our cargo was lost, and we had to say goodbye to our mate, The Mariner. It was a sad day," he said, looking down and away. "She was a grand vessel. Aye, she was."

Mack was speechless. He couldn't breathe. He sat there and stared at the old sailor.

After a moment of silence, the sailor spoke up, "You best be getting on your way, Mack. The sun is going down."

Mack nodded, jumped up and turned to go home. He looked back at the sailor and waved. The sailor nodded and waved. Mack knew he had just experienced a rare and special moment. *She was a grand vessel. Aye, she was*, he thought as he walked home.

✳✳✳

John Mecaslin and his father's family were from the northern Ulster area of Ireland. Hard-working and proud of their family, they endured many hardships and learned to fight and survive. Their clan often had a strong and sturdy build with a lively sense of humor. His mother, Maria Von Willis Mecaslin, had taught her son how to read and write at an early age and had given him direction in his education.

John traveled often with his father to different cities up and down the East Coast for business and pleasure. The sea was the way to go.

When he was a little boy, big news hit the streets of Baltimore. While states such as New York and Pennsylvania built canals, Maryland set the cornerstone for a railroad to be built from Baltimore to someplace on the Ohio River. The first train trip was in 1830.

During the same year, a steam locomotive was built in New York by the West Point Foundry and bore the name "Best Friend of Charleston." In 1833, the 135 miles of railroad opened from Charleston to Hamburg, South Carolina, across the Savannah River from Augusta, Georgia. In 1844, this company was consolidated with the Louisville, Cincinnati and Charleston railroads to form the South Carolina Railroad. The trains were able to enter Augusta across the new bridge that had been built over the Savannah River.

Many people thought of the railroad either as a fun novelty or a dangerous nuisance in those early years. Regardless, it allowed a new frontier to develop, which gathered interest and provided jobs for hardworking men.

Still, the most reliable form of travel was by water. Young Mecaslin learned about shipping and how to run the waters of the bay area. He understood the currents and how they affected travel. Learning about the types of sea crafts was his favorite hobby.

After high school in Baltimore, he was accepted at the Baltimore Technical Institute, which taught him the technical aspects of life at sea and nautical surveying. But his mother had cautioned him that life at sea was difficult, and she wanted a better life for him. She knew his degree at Baltimore Technical Institute would provide a good foundation for many types of jobs.

Plus, cloudy skies were looming for Irish Catholics in Baltimore. Irish and German immigrants, mostly Catholics, were arriving in droves at U.S. ports. The Irish were seeking relief from the potato famine and political upheaval. Baltimore was becoming overcrowded, and fear was taking hold that these new arrivals would take the jobs and change the lifestyle that citizens felt belonged to them. A religious objection to Catholics began.

Also, a new political party, the Know Nothings, had developed as a result of the nativist sentiment that had emerged. They wanted to prevent the immigrants from holding public office and extend the time required for them to become citizens and voters.

John passed a shop one day on his way to class with a sign in the window that read "NINA." *I wonder what that means*, he thought. Then another sign appeared on the other side of the street, then another. A businessman passed him and pointed at the sign. "No Irish Need Apply. This means you!" John was confused and felt sick. He had lived in Baltimore all of his life, and suddenly he felt unwanted.

Even though the Mecaslins were citizens, the atmosphere in Baltimore grew challenging, and overcrowded conditions led John and some of his friends to seek their fortunes elsewhere. After graduating from the technical institute, he and two of his buddies decided to head to Richmond to look for work.

While there, the men continued to hear about a new type of frontier developing in Georgia and decided they wanted to be a part of it. The railroad was being hammered across the east coast from Charleston to Augusta and further west into Georgia.

They took a ship from Richmond to Savannah and then up the Savannah River to Augusta. The Savannah River was bustling with boats full of cotton bales and other products being transported up and down the river from Augusta to Savannah and out to sea.

When they disembarked in Augusta, they were surprised at this bustling river town. Augusta was the second-largest city in Georgia and the center of cotton country. Cotton was the chief resource of the South, and Southerners traded cotton with Europe and the northern states. In 1830, America produced 30 percent of the world's cotton. In 1850, it produced 50 percent. Cotton was king!

Many in the industrial North profited from Southern cotton but turned a blind eye to the evils of the human machinery that provided it. There were many Northerners who owned plantations in the South, hired managers for their plantations, and visited seldomly but looked for the profits.

The first thing that the young men did was head to the nearby pub, where they inquired about lodging. The barkeep said there were several hotels.

John asked, "Whom do we see about employment here?"

The barkeep replied, "You and half this town are asking that question. Head over to the car shed. Over there," he pointed. "Follow the tracks, you can't miss it! You will see a lot of competition though."

John Cook said, "We are machinists by trade."

"Well then, boys, you're sure to find wages there."

"I hear that they need a new superintendent over at the Augusta Mills, the cotton mill," commented a man sitting nearby.

That sounded like an interesting position to John, and after applying, found that was the better paying job and accepted. The other guys found jobs at the railroad.

After a successful day of seeking jobs, they returned to the tavern to share their stories. An hour later, excited but exhausted, the comrades stumbled into the night to find lodging.

CHAPTER 2

"None of us will ever accomplish anything excellent or commanding except when
he listens to this whisper, which is heard by him alone."

~ Ralph Waldo Emerson

Mary Ann Mullin looked out the second story of her parents' house on Fenwick Street. She lived in a big house with two extra rooms that her mother had prepared for boarders, but she wasn't sure about these strangers. Father had told her that this might be possible since so many new workers were in town to work on the railroad and needed a place to stay. Her brother said he might bring home some workers, and she felt uncertain.

She pulled the curtain back and looked out her window as she heard the clippety-clop of the horses as the stagecoach approached. Once it stopped, she could hear the conversations of the men as they got out. Her brother hopped down from the front seat and welcomed the men in. John looked up and noticed Mary at the window, wondering who she was. She immediately stepped away and nervously ran to the mirror to check herself. She was wearing a dainty green and pink flowered dress with lace along the bodice. At the waist, the hoop skirt flared out and flowed to the floor. She smoothed her skirt, pinched her cheeks and brushed her hair. Convinced that she was presentable, she went downstairs to meet the new boarders.

Mary went straight to the kitchen to take directions from her mother as to how they would receive their guests. Her mother, Margaret Maguire Mullin, was a strong Irish mum who ran her household well. She was already preparing tea as her husband, James, received the guests. She instructed Mary to conduct herself well and to carry the tray into the parlor and place it on the serving table.

She wasn't an eager young girl. Mary was seventeen, mature, clever and calm. She entered the parlor. John looked directly at her with piercing blue eyes that took her breath away. They both looked away abruptly, and she took a short breath because a long breath was out of the question. She took another breath to try to regain her composure.

Don't look up. Steady your hand as you pour. Don't spill. Steady. Breathe.

She heard her father say something. She looked up at him.

James Mullin said, "Mr. Cook, Mr. Smith, and Mr. Mecaslin, I would like to introduce my wife, Mrs. Mullin, and my daughter, Mary Ann."

Mary's brother, James, introduced his wife, Amanda, and their daughter, Janey, who scurried up the stairs, turned around and hugged the banister.

Mary turned to face the new boarders. Mr. Mullin spoke again, "These gentlemen will be staying with us for a while. They work at the railroad, and Mr. Mecaslin is employed at the cotton mills as a superintendent."

Mrs. Mullin and Mary both curtsied. Mrs. Mullin greeted the men warmly and said, "Welcome to our home. I hope you find it comfortable."

Mary smiled, curtsied, and said, "A pleasure to meet you."

John studied every detail of her face, quite aware that her mother and father may be watching. He looked away in a timely manner, and yet his thoughts were a blur. Though he heard the other men speak to the ladies, all he could say was, "Ma'am."

Amanda poured and Mary served. The conversation became a calming influence for her. The ladies remained a while longer and then were off to the kitchen to fix dinner, consisting of a Georgia ham, biscuits and gravy and potatoes. John Mecaslin regained his conversational abilities and joined in naturally. He had found another Irish home.

✳✳✳

The following Sunday, Cook, Smith and Mecaslin were invited by the family to attend the service at the Church of the Most Holy Trinity on Fair Street. They were happy to accept the invitation. They walked to church because it was only a few blocks away.

The Mullin family loved their church. The Most Holy Trinity had been established before some members of the Mullin family had arrived in 1821. They were used to their highly attended church, but Mecaslin couldn't help noticing that there was standing room only.

After the service, the Mullin family introduced the newcomers to Father Barry, who was well-loved and admired for his untiring efforts in helping the sick and the poor. "So nice of you to attend our church, and I apologize that you had to stand," the Father said.

"No sacrifice at all, Father, and it is a pleasure to see such a large congregation," John replied.

"We have discussed enlarging the building and even constructing a new church, but alas, our abilities are still limited." Father Barry continued. "From where do you hail?"

"Baltimore, sir."

"Ah, I have visited there many times."

"I understand your dilemma with the church, but please allow me to be of service in any way that I can."

"Thank you for your kind offer. It has been a pleasure, young man. Please visit again."

The Mullin family and friends walked home for Sunday dinner.

✳✳✳

John was proud of his Irish heritage, and, being with the Mullin family who had lived in the old country, he loved to hear them speak of the Emerald Isle. Occasionally, he would hear himself sing an Irish tune or say something his father would say.

Mary had been reared as a devout Irish Catholic, and it showed. She was shy yet well-educated and well-mannered. She was able to uncover the truth about life through her humor and positive attitude.

At dinner the following evening, Mary listened as the boarders talked about their travels and home. She learned that Mecaslin had been born and reared in Baltimore County, Maryland, and went to school in Baltimore. She was intrigued that he had traveled extensively from New York City to Charleston for she had never been far from home, only once to her uncle's plantation.

After dinner, he asked permission to go for a walk with her. As they left the house, John began, "It is a wonderful evening, isn't it, Miss Mullin?"

"Indeed it is, sir," Mary replied.

After a pause in conversation, and a nervous look, Mary continued, "Do tell me more about your family, Mr. Mecaslin."

"I have two brothers and two sisters."

"And who is the oldest?"

"I am the oldest. My sister Rebecca is twenty, and then Catherine Marie is eighteen. My little brother George is six, and the baby Adolphus is five. They all still live in Baltimore with my mother and father."

John had stayed in Baltimore after high school and worked for his father at the flour mill. He felt it was his responsibility as the oldest. He went to technical school nearby and lived at home. Again, a pause.

"I am sure you miss them very much," Mary said.

"Yes, of course, but you know, it is an occasion such as this that finds me very happy that I am in Georgia," John responded, hoping to direct the conversation toward her. Mary smiled in return. Her heart became warm, and she felt extremely shy.

John was twenty-four years old, seven years older than Mary. She was taken by the kindness of his eyes and the strength in his demeanor. He had dark hair that curled softly around his face, showing off his blue eyes.

John found Mary to be quite lovely. She had bright green eyes that danced with a light that mesmerized him. Her long auburn hair flowed over her shoulders and down her back. The evening hadn't ended and yet he couldn't wait to see her again.

"I should go inside now. It's getting late," Mary said.

"Of course. Allow me to walk you to the door."

"Good night, Mr. Mecaslin," she said and curtsied.

He watched her as she opened the door. "Good night, Miss Mullin." It was the beginning of a whirlwind courtship.

John met with his friends outside and talked for hours after the rest of the house was asleep.

✳✳✳

John and Mary went on many long walks together, and John continued to join the family for church. One Sunday after the service, Father Barry talked about a town inland called Atlanta where he was doing missionary work. He would ride the train to this town and other small towns along the way, and sometimes parishioners would go with him. One day, he asked John, "Why don't you join me on a trip to Atlanta? James Jr. is going with me. We would enjoy your company."

So the men planned a trip that included James and the two other boarders, with a stop on the way to visit Thomas Maguire, Mary and James's uncle, at his plantation.

On their trip, John was amazed at the towns that had developed due to the cotton industry. Greensboro and Madison were alive and thriving. They were small towns due west from Augusta that blossomed as important supply stations along the railroad.

They stopped first in Greensboro for an exchange of supplies, and then on to Madison. By the time they reached the town, they had traveled 103 miles at an exciting speed of 10 miles per hour! The passengers were ready for a lunch break and looked forward to a visit.

Madison had a town square with places to eat and shop. It had developed as a quaint town with cultural highlights such as art, opera, theatre, and musical recitals. Travelers came from all around to enjoy the social atmosphere. Many of the residents were plantation owners who lived in town. Madison was flowing with wealthy landowners who spent money. They were in "high cotton."

The men dined at a small restaurant near the station and took a walk around the square. They enjoyed their break, but when the whistle blew, it was time to board. From Madison to Atlanta was sixty-eight miles, but they were going to make another stop on the way.

A few hours later, they arrived at the Lithonia station and unloaded. Thomas Maguire was waiting nearby with a horse and buggy and two more horses to take the men back to his plantation, The Promised Land.

He waved and walked over to the men. Thomas was an older man in his fifties, a hardworking farmer, and it was showing on him. His sunburnt face managed a smile. "Welcome, James! Welcome, Father! Glad to see ya, mighty glad, and who have ye here?"

"Thomas Maguire, this is John Mecaslin, John Cook and James Smith." He shook their hands and reached out and shook the hand of his nephew, James Mullin Jr.

"Welcome to cotton country! You young lads should make good use of it. How was your trip?"

"Long, but we're happy to be here."

"Well, let's get on our way. We have a short trip to The Promised Land, and it's getting late. Don't want the sun to set on us," he said. Father Barry and two men got in the buggy while John and James rode horses.

At sunset, they passed over the Yellow River and looked out at the massive Maguire plantation. He had rows of cornfields, cotton and everything he needed to sustain the family. He owned more than one thousand acres of land. Nestled amidst the rolling hills was a small farmhouse that he called home.

They stayed up late that night telling stories, and Thomas talked about his early years.

"Ah, yes, my lads, I remember the old country, the Emerald Isle. My brothers and I had heard about this 'Land of Opportunity' in the United States of America. We heard news from the sailors about the removal of the Creek from the wilds of Georgia and how they were setting up a land lottery to give land to upstanding citizens. We couldn't believe that there could be so much abundance and freedom and couldn't wait to set off on an adventure of a lifetime. 'We're going to America!' we yelled. We were dazed, I tell ya.

"We came over and settled in Augusta when we were about your age," he said, looking at Mecaslin. "I was learning everything I could about my new country and enrolled in writing school in Augusta back in '22.

"And then my dream came true! I won the first 250 acres on this gracious land in Rockbridge and named it 'The Promised Land' because we had finally arrived in God's country.

"It was wild back then, and there were problems along the way with the process that they used to remove the Creek and Cherokee. It was a bittersweet thing to see. I had to fight for my territory at times.

"Also, my brother, James, won the land lottery in 1827 and acquired ninety-nine acres in Muscogee County, which is now where LaGrange is. Then, when we were settled, my other brother John and I went back to Ireland and got the rest of my family — my mother and father, Catharine and John Maguire. And my sister, you've met Margaret, and her husband, James Mullin. Let's see, that was way back in 1828, it was. Boys, that was a rough trip and I remember it well. It was three months of turbulent and stormy weather. It brought me down, all of us down, to our very survival instincts. It took a mighty power to show us the way but was worth it all the same." He shook his head and took a deep breath as if reliving it.

"Well, I'm sure you've heard enough for one night ..."

Oh, no, his audience was fascinated by Maguire's stories, and after another round of drinks, he continued.

"My parents and the rest of the family settled in Augusta, and sadly, my father died from yellow fever just two years after we arrived, and my mother died a couple of months later. Those were hard times, they were.

"The Georgia government back then, around 1828 or so, took over the Cherokee territory and tried to abolish their laws and government, planning to take their land and divide it and do another land lottery. Big news and nothing else quite like it anywhere else.

"Andrew Jackson was elected president of the United States that year, and he immediately declared the removal of eastern tribes a national objective. In 1830, Congress passed the Indian Removal Act, which allowed President Jackson to begin negotiating with the Cherokee to leave the state.

"There was this great Cherokee leader, John Ross, who requested help from the government to fight Georgia and help them keep their land. The courts determined that Georgia had violated the treaty, but it was never enforced, and Jackson continued to pressure the Cherokee to leave. Gradually, they forced them to leave, as you all know, through blood, sweat and tears, and it wasn't a pretty sight. And not that long ago ..."

Mecaslin knew of the Cherokee and Creek removal but had never heard it explained in such a personal way. He had a new appreciation for the sacrifices that had been made.

"And your destination, the little railroad village of Atlanta, I've watched it develop over the last few years as they've laid tracks across the wilderness. Men buying up farmland and upsetting quite a few. You know, my neighbor Mr. Rutledge gave them quite a fight because they wanted to put tracks right through the middle of his two hundred acres. Can you imagine someone tearing through your very livelihood and money crops with a noisy, smoky machine? Strangers building on your territory? It's happening all over, but I'm sure you've heard the arguments. The railroad coming through and disrupting things. But many welcome it as an opportunity for faster travel and ease of moving products more quickly, and you get fresher produce that way. And certainly money to be made. All in the name of progress!"

Then he leaned in like he was going to tell them a mighty secret. "Land is sacred, men. Never take it for granted. It can be taken by the power and greed of men as if you were never there. I've seen it happen in Ireland, and I've seen it happen here. I've just been lucky so far."

Father Barry spoke up. "Well said, Mr. Maguire. May we all treasure our gifts and be thankful. And with that, I must bid you a good night. It has been a most memorable time with you, but dawn will soon break, and we don't want to miss that train!"

The men all stood up and stretched, shook hands and said good night. The younger men stayed up a little longer and fell asleep by the fire.

They continued on their journey the next day, caught the next supply train west, and arrived in a small pioneer town with rough roads of Georgia red clay. From the station, it looked as if three tracks met in the middle of town. Father Barry and John Mecaslin went to the Catholic mission house in town not far from the railroad.

John looked around and was delighted with what he saw. "It's beautiful here."

"It is that, John. I have work here. Why don't you boys look around?" said Father Barry.

✳✳✳

"This is a frontier town! Look around. Cows and pigs wandering around. Everything here is new, surrounded by forest. Trees everywhere," James Smith remarked with excitement.

They went to the livery to acquire some horses and rode around. As they were heading down Peachtree and Decatur streets, they were taken by the new homes being built in place of little cabins.

The men rode over to the Georgia railroad depot. They overheard someone saying that they desperately needed workers. John Cook spoke up, "We work for the railroad in Augusta. All of us except for Mr. Mecaslin."

"And you, sir, would you be interested in applying for a job here?"

"Oh, no, I have a job in Augusta as well." But John listened as they described the position. They began discussing his background and found that they had the perfect job for his qualifications. They hired him right away as a patternmaker at the shop with a hefty raise. Luck was with him! "Well, boys, want to move to Atlanta?"

"Not right now," Cook replied. "We have our jobs in Augusta. Why do you want to move to a one-horse town? Nothing much going on."

Smith agreed with Cook.

"I just have a feeling," John replied, looking wide-eyed at his new town. His mind reeled. Excitement was in the air.

When the men returned to the mission house later that day, they noticed that no more than a dozen or so members were present at the service. A very small town, indeed.

Mecaslin spoke to Father Barry. "It looks like another Irish boy is moving to Atlanta, sir. The Georgia Railroad hired me for a job here."

Father Barry reached out his hand. "Fine job, son. Good men are needed in Atlanta. They will be lucky to have you."

Cook mentioned it first on the train ride back to Augusta, "What's Mary going to say?"

"I don't know," Mecaslin replied, "but Atlanta is calling me!"

"Well, this is quite surprising news. The pack is breaking up," Cook said as he looked around at his friends.

"You have to take the breaks when you find them, boys," Mecaslin said as he passed around the cigars.

✳✳✳

When he returned to Augusta, Mecaslin left his notice at the Cotton Mills. Later that night, he took Mary for a walk after dinner and told her about his trip. "It was so wonderful to meet your uncle and see Atlanta. The strangest thing happened …"

When Mary heard the news, her heart sank. "Why don't you work at the railroad here in town?"

"The future is in Atlanta! The railroads converge there. It's a railroad town with endless possibilities, don't you see?" She could see how excited he was and knew there was nothing more to say.

"I promise to write you often," he said. "It's not that far away by train."

"It's very far away, John," she said. "So far away." She could feel her future becoming cloudy.

CHAPTER 3

"The universal brotherhood of man is our most precious possession."

~ *Mark Twain*

Atlanta was a small town that had begun to develop in the middle of Georgia due to the construction of railroads. It had only been there for about twelve or thirteen years and called Atlanta for a few years. Originally, it had been called Terminus and then a few years later changed to Marthasville, named for the governor's daughter. Three railroads had recently been built that met in Atlanta, making the town a central connecting point for freight exchange and passenger travel. The Georgia Railroad was completed first, connecting Atlanta to Augusta in 1845. The Macon and Western Railroad reached Atlanta a year later. Then the Western and Atlantic, which was started in 1842, was completed with its connection to Chattanooga in 1851. The Atlanta and LaGrange Railroad was still under construction and would run eighty miles from East Point through LaGrange to West Point.

The State Road was the Western and Atlantic, which was operated by the state under a superintendent who was appointed by and reported to the governor. It had been completed a year or so before in 1849, and the town expanded from 2,500, with more than 100 newcomers arriving per month.

In 1850, beautiful homes lined Marietta, Peachtree and Decatur streets in the center of town. Spacious brick mansions with classic porticos began to arrive. Old log cabins were torn down and replaced with cottages.

✳ ✳ ✳

When John first arrived in Atlanta, he procured a room at the Atlanta Hotel. It was convenient to his job at the Georgia Railroad "shop," where he used his technical skills to create parts for the trains. He learned every aspect of the trains, including the unique sounds of the whistles.

After work, he asked one of the guys where to go for a drink.

The fellow Irishman said, "Why, we go down to Humbug Square and Kenny's Alley. It's across the street, there. You can't miss it."

"Much obliged, sir," and he was off.

John opened the door to the smoke-filled saloon, and all eyes were on him, as everyone knew when a new worker was in town.

He walked over to the bar, sat down and the barkeep looked at him. John ordered a beer and gazed around. The man next to him said, "New in town?" and held out his hand.

John smiled, grateful to see a friendly face, and said, "Yes, I am, just started at the Georgia Railroad."

A tall man with a smile from ear to ear said, "Hello, I'm Barnes, Bill Barnes. Mighty glad to meet you."

A fellow seated at a table behind him said, "Yeah, and he sings like a lark." Everyone around them broke into laughter and John felt right at home. The gentleman got up from the table, walked over and introduced himself with a strong Irish accent, "William Kidd's the name, but everyone knows me as Will."

John shook his hand and replied with, "Nice to meet you, Will. John Mecaslin, but better known to my friends as Mack."

"Well, Mack, Bill here really does have a great voice. He entertains us at socials and the like," said the Irishman who had only been in Atlanta, and in fact the U.S., a few years himself.

Kidd was a burly man with reddish auburn hair, a full beard and a stocky build. He had a boisterous laugh and lively personality. He owned a tobacco store where Whitehall Street crossed the railroad tracks and worked for the railroad as a locomotive engineer. He had a firm grasp on the development of the small town. He was one of the major players.

He felt strongly about the need for paved roads and sidewalks in Atlanta, for travel was so difficult, especially after rain. Many of the roads were filled with potholes, gullies and ditches several feet wide and deep, making it impossible at times to move easily from place to place. Will asked the city council to pave the area around his store at Whitehall Street and they refused. He then requested permission to pave the area at his own expense, and they approved it. As a result, Whitehall Street from Alabama Street to the railroad tracks was paved with gravel. After seeing the improvement, the council built wooden sidewalks along all of the main

18

streets in town.

Bill Barnes was also an early resident of Atlanta, arriving from Charleston, South Carolina, about the same time as Will Kidd in the late 1840s, with his wife, Amanda Gullatt, sister of James E. Gullatt. Bill went into business with James in the tin and copper smithing business. He was interested in the fire protection of the young town and assisted in the organization of the Atlanta Fire Company #1, becoming one of its charter members in March 1851. The volunteer fire department had been established when a fire destroyed several stores on Marietta Street near Broad Street in 1850.

The fire building was located on the east side of Broad Street between Alabama Street and the railroad, and it took up the whole square. It was a beautiful property with shade trees and lovely flowers. It was a little one-story engine house and always remained the general headquarters. The first alarm bell of the town was put there.

"Hey, Mack, would you be interested in joining the volunteer fire department? It has just been established, and we sure could use a hand," Bill said, waving his hand around at Kidd and some of their friends.

"Absolutely, boys, where do I sign?"

John was excited about the idea of becoming a firefighter and jumped at the chance to become involved in the community.

"Ya know, everybody here is from someplace else," commented Bill. "Nobody has been here long. I have only been here for a couple of years, as well as Kidd there and our friend Charlie Rodes. I'm from Charleston and Kidd came over from Ireland about the same time."

"Over there," Will pointed, "is Mr. Hanleiter. He arrived in Atlanta in '47 as well. He's a journalist and quite an interesting guy. He's an editor, publisher, and councilman. He's from Savannah but started papers in Augusta and Madison. Loves Atlanta and will do anything for ya.

"And over there, Levi Richardson came from Philadelphia. He is a skilled machinist and planing mill proprietor."

A few minutes later, a man of stature in a coat, vest and top hat entered.

"Quite the collection of personalities joining us today. Richard Peters, there," Bill nodded at the gentlemen who had entered the room, "is the superintendent of the railroad and has lived here for about four or five years as well and hails from Pennsylvania. He met his wife, Martha, in '45 while staying at the Atlanta Hotel. He's been working the railroad since it began. Stagecoach chief, quiet and dignified, but he knows Atlanta. Even helped change the name from Marthasville to Atlanta. So you see, we were born somewhere else but call Atlanta home. It's exciting. It draws you in."

"Aye, that it does," Mecaslin said.

Will jumped in. "Well, Mack, Bill here really does have a great voice.

How about a little something now, Bill? Sing for us."

Bill thought about a popular Irish folk song. Then he said, "Here's one in honor of our new friend, Mack. God bless." And he began to sing a raucous rendition of "Paddy Works on the Railway …" And the fiddler knew what to do.

I-i-i-i-n eighteen hundred and forty-one
I put my corduroy breeches on
I put my corduroy breeches on
To work upon the railway.

Even the sleepiest of workers and those in conversation couldn't resist tapping their toes and clapping their hands. Everyone joined in as Bill continued.

I'm weary of the railway.

The patrons knew what was coming next as Bill picked up the tempo.

I was wearing corduroy britches,
Digging ditches, pulling switches,
Dodging hitches
While I was working on the railway.

Bill led the group through all of the verses and finished with the chorus, loud and strong. They thought the walls were shaking and the ground was quaking. They were stomping so hard that the dust was coming up through the cracks of the wood-planked floor. There were yells and pats on the back all 'round.

✳✳✳

That weekend, when Mack was leaving the Atlanta Hotel, he ran into Bill and shook his hand.

"Come by sometime and I'll show you around the firehouse," Bill said.

"Before you go, do you have a minute? Let me buy you a drink." Mack held out his hand, smiling and directing Bill back inside the hotel.

After they had been seated for a minute or two, Mack began, "Bill, I am looking for some property in the area to build a home."

"I happen to know of a place down the street a bit that I have had my eye on. It's not too far east of here and near the Georgia Railroad. Why don't we ride over there tomorrow and take a look?"

"Sounds good. How about two more right here, sir," Mack said to the bartender.

"Why, you've met Patrick Ennis," Bill said, pointing at the bartender. "His property is right next to mine."

"Mr. Ennis, nice to see you again," Mack said as they shook hands.

"Call me Patrick."

"Well, about time for the #1 to come rolling in," Bill said. "And there it is!"

The sound of the train whistle was right on schedule. The favorite Georgia Engine #1 had its own distinct sound, and everyone could hear it from miles away. It was a part of life to know what time of day it was by the sound of the trains coming down the tracks.

All three men smiled and raised their glasses.

"To the #1!"

When he left, Mack passed by the livery stables to take a look at the horses. A beautiful charcoal grey mustang stallion caught his eye. He had never seen anything like it. It had a shiny black mane and black legs. As he approached, the horse nodded his head a couple of times and moved forward. Mack reached for him and said "Hey, fella." He became immediately attached.

"He's a strong, spirited stallion," said the owner.

"What's his name?" asked Mack.

"Storm."

"I'll take him." Mack handed the man seven dollars and rode away with a new friend.

✳✳✳

The next day, Mack met Bill at the hotel and rode over to the property on the outskirts of town. They bought two lots next to each other on Butler Street. When they weren't working, the men were planning and building their homes.

Mack picked up extra shifts. He worked hard. It was miserably hot, humid and dirty in the summer, but it was the life of the railroad worker. He saved his money and, as time went on, began to establish himself as a citizen. He had found his home.

CHAPTER 4

"I find the great thing in this world is not so much where we stand as in what direction we are moving."

~ Oliver Wendell Holmes, Sr.

1851

The firemen were proud of their first uniforms. Red flannel shirts were adorned with a black "1" on the breast pockets with black pants. They completed their attire with firemen hats with "Atlanta," "1851" and the figure "1" on the front pieces. They wore black patent leather belts with "Atlanta" on the front. The hats of the president and foreman were white and the belts of the officers were white. Originally, they had positions available for thirty men, including four officers.

The members of that first fire department began training as soon as they could. They needed to be quick and fit enough to get to the water pumps to put out the fires.

After one of the training sessions, they all met at their favorite watering hole and began talking about the training.

"That was a lousy day for me, boys," Bill said, looking tired.

"No excuses there, Bill. You should have aced that last climb," Mack responded with a smile.

"True enough. I will whip you next time, for sure. How about loser buys the winner a drink next time?"

"You are on. I will accept that challenge anytime," said Mack, and the competition began.

The next weekend, Bill and Mack competed with each other. They challenged two other firemen to compete against them for the following Saturday. All agreed and the challenge grew.

The following Saturday afternoon, the members of the fire department met and began with only one event, running the water buckets to the place of the fire and back. They were to fill the bucket, run it to the destination and return it five times. The fireman who won would get a free drink.

The men continued competing in different events on Saturday afternoons.

✳✳✳

Mecaslin jumped off the train in Augusta and looked anxiously around for Mary. There she was with her brother James, looking absolutely gorgeous. She smiled and waved. He ran to her, picked her up and twirled her around with excitement. "It's so good to see you," he said as he gently set her down.

"I've missed you terribly," she said and hugged him.

"Welcome back," James said as he shook his hand. "How was your trip?"

"Fine. Just fine. I'll tell you all about it," he said as they turned and walked toward the station.

On that cool November evening, John and Mary went to a play in a horse and buggy. After the play, on their return to Fenwick Street, he said, "I miss you so much when I am gone."

"I miss you, too." She moved a little closer.

"I don't think I can take it anymore. I have to ask you …" He gulped. His nerves took over and he couldn't say anything.

Mary looked at him, worried. "Is everything ok?" He looked away. "What is it?" she touched his face tenderly and pulled him closer.

"Mary, I, uh … "

She sat silently. *This is it*, she thought. *It's over. He doesn't want to see me anymore.* She began to feel sick inside. She thought that they had been having fun.

They arrived back at the house, and John jumped from the carriage. He walked around to her side of the carriage and reached up to her. He grabbed her hand.

"Miss Mullin, I love you."

She was shocked. Now she nervously gulped, and her heart began to beat faster. He lifted her from the carriage and knelt on one knee.

"I can't live without you. Will you marry me?"

"Oh yes, oh yes, of course I will," she giggled.

Without saying a word, he pulled a ring box from his vest pocket, opened it and presented it to her. She smiled, and he removed the ring from the box and reached for her hand. He looked up to her and smiled with his blue eyes twinkling.

He slipped the ring on her finger. She looked at the ring, then at him. He stood up and pulled her close enough to kiss her and said, "I love you."

"I love you, too," she whispered.

Then he kissed her passionately and strongly and softly over and over again.

The coolness of the evening turned into a hot summer night.

✳✳✳

Mecaslin couldn't wipe the smile from his face on his train ride back to Atlanta. He remembered that Sunday stroll to church the week before.

"I wonder if I might speak with you, sir," he had said to Mary's father.

"Of course," replied James Mullin.

"I have worked hard and established myself well in Atlanta," he went on. "As you know, I am doing well at the railroad, have a home now, and work hard as a fireman."

"I know, John, and I am quite proud of you." He knew where it was going.

"Sir, I know that Atlanta is far away."

Mr. Mullin was silent.

"May I have Mary's hand in marriage? I promise to make her happy and love her dearly."

"I can't think of anyone who would be better for her. Have you talked with her about it?"

"No, I will soon with your blessing. And I hope she says yes. I know Atlanta is far away from her home, but I will protect her and cherish her."

"You have my blessing, son."

She said yes. She said yes. I just hope she likes Atlanta, he thought as he stared out the window.

CHAPTER 5

"Two souls with but a single thought, two hearts that beat as one."

~ *Freidrich Halm, Der Sohn der Wildness, Act II (1842)*

1853

John and Mary were married in 1853 at their own lovely church, The Church of the Most Holy Trinity in Augusta, by Father Barry, the newly appointed vicar general of the See of Savannah. What a wonderful honor for this Irish celebration.

Guests began to arrive a couple of days before the wedding. John's entire family traveled from Baltimore. Mary's uncle, Thomas, and his wife, Elizabeth, and their family rode the train from The Promised Land to attend. They stayed with the Mullins or next door at her uncle John J.'s house. A few of the neighbors offered to host some of the out-of-town guests and the family accepted gratefully.

The wedding took place on a Friday morning, not Saturday because it was market day, and not Sunday because it was the Sabbath. At sunrise that morning, neighbors and friends were at the Mullins' door, in a flurry of excitement, ready to pitch in and decorate the streets that led to the church. Her mother Margaret led them around to the shed, where dozens of floral garlands were waiting to be carried to their locations. James Smith and John Cook were decorating the bridal carriage and adorning the horses.

Mary's bridesmaid and girlfriends were in Mary's bedroom, doing whatever they could to help Mary on her special day. Margaret had waited patiently until this morning to put the final stitch on Mary's gown, which was customary to ensure a lucky marriage. The girls giggled and rushed around nervously, telling Mary how lucky she was to be marrying this handsome man. Mary was so nervous, thinking that this grand affair was much more than she could handle. She wondered how she could manage to make it through the ceremony, much less the rest of the day. *Where is John, and what is he doing,* she wondered.

John was in another house, pacing and waiting, waiting and pacing. Everyone had left him for the moment to run errands and take care of the final touches. He wished that he had someone to talk to. *Where is the ring? Does James have it?* He looked at his watch, waiting for someone to tell him it was time to go.

✳✳✳

At The Most Holy Trinity Catholic Church on Fair Street, guests were arriving in their finest. Excitement was in the air. Everyone oohed and aahed as they entered the church and saw how beautiful it was. It was already a charming church, but the flower arrangements and decorations made it truly special.

And then, John received the news that it was time to go to the church. He rode in a carriage with his best man and friends and took his place at the front.

Mary rode in an elegantly decorated carriage with a floral garland on each horse. Her father drove. As they rode to the church, Mary marveled at the garlands that were placed at the gate or streetfront of each home along the three-block ride down Fenwick. Then as they turned left, Mary had butterflies in her stomach. She saw the church with a few guests outside. *Someone needs to tell me what to do,* she thought.

Her father stepped down from the carriage and walked around to help his daughter. "Easy does it," he said calmly. She nodded and took a breath. He took her arm and escorted her from the carriage. All other members of the party found their places inside the church.

And then the organ sounded. Mary Mullin and her father stood at the entrance to the church. Mary was glowing in a stunning, perfectly fitted gown. Her mother was well-known as the finest seamstress in the neighborhood, but she had kept this a secret, and no one had seen it until now.

The wedding gown had a flounced skirt with fringe. It was made mostly of silk and cotton with a moiré finish. The bodice had a slight V-neck in the front and back with a V-shaped bodice that framed her body beautifully. A harp pin that she borrowed from her best friend was pinned at the V of the bodice. Mary was so grateful to have short sleeves with fringe because the skirt was so heavy. The dress leant a youthful, joyful appearance that matched Mary perfectly.

The entire congregation turned around, and some of the ladies gasped. Everyone rose to present the bride and her father. Mary smiled at her father as he held out his arm, and she placed her hand around his arm. She clutched her bouquet of orchids and Bells of Ireland with a delicately-placed green hanky within it for luck. They strolled down the aisle. John Mecaslin was grinning from ear to ear.

Father Barry began the ceremony. The bride and groom spoke these words:

> *"You cannot possess me for I belong to myself.*
> *But while we both wish it, I give you that which is mine to give.*
> *You cannot command me for I am a free person.*
> *But I shall serve you in those ways you require.*
> *And the honeycomb will taste sweeter coming from my hand.*
> *I pledge to you that yours will be the name I cry aloud in the night.*
> *And the eyes into which I smile in the morning.*
> *I pledge to you the first bite from my meat.*
> *And the first drink from my cup.*
> *I pledge to you my living and my dying, equally in your care.*
> *And tell no strangers our grievances.*
> *This is my wedding vow to you.*
> *This is a marriage of equals."*

Then Father Barry prayed for them and the guests. John placed the ring on Mary's finger, and Father Barry finalized the ceremony by saying, "You may now kiss the bride!"

John and Mary turned hand in hand to face the guests, and everyone clapped. They walk down the aisle and waited in a side room while the guests left the church and gathered outside. The carriage was ready.

Wedding bells were given to the guests, and they rang the bells as Mary and John left the church. Irish tradition was that they take one bell with them and place it on the mantel in their new home. When they had a fight, they would ring the bell to ward off the evil spirits or remind them of their love for each other.

John and Mary entered the adorned carriage. A fiddler led the wedding carriage back to Mary's house, playing a lively tune all along the way. It was as if he were announcing to all the world that this glorious occasion had taken place.

A while later, a casual lunch for the family was held at the Mullin home, and everyone prepared for an evening of celebration.

At four in the afternoon, John Mullin called for sherry hour, when guests would arrive for a bit of a drink before dinner. This was a casual time of chatting and relaxing. Then the dinner guests enjoyed a five-course meal with drinks and toasting.

Finally, the party began. More friends and neighbors were invited for drinking, music and dancing. Late night sandwiches were served and then more drinking and dancing. The party extended into the wee hours.

Early in the morning, most neighbors and friends staggered home, weary-eyed and full of fun. The kitchen was set up for hot coffee, biscuits, bacon and pastries for all who stayed as guests. A memorable time was had by all.

After an idle day of rest and relaxation, Mary and John began preparing for their move to Atlanta, and their guests were planning their departures as well. Mary was reluctant to leave home because she had lived there all her life. Because she loved John and knew her place was with him, she accepted the move to Atlanta. She began to pack her personal items: linens, silver, dresses, stockings, hats and books in three large trunks.

Mary's most prized wedding gifts were from her mother and things her mother had saved from her grandmother Catharine. Her mother gave her three silver candlestick holders and two lovely quilts that her grandmother had sewn many years before in Ireland. She and John also received family heirlooms from his parents, including a set of silver that had been handed down for generations and a set of china from Europe. Other family members gave them gifts that would send them to Atlanta in grand style.

✳✳✳

The train left for Atlanta at 7 a.m. the following day. The entire family arrived at the train depot to say goodbye. Trunk after trunk were loaded in the cargo section. They said their goodbyes.

John and Mary boarded the train and looked back, Mary a little longer, trying to take it all in — fixing her gaze on her family and friends, last looks, not knowing when she would see them again. Even though Mary was overwhelmed by emotions, nervous and sad to leave home, she felt a certain level of excitement as they left on their first adventure as a couple.

Mary had never taken a train trip. Years before the railroad was built, she had taken a trip with her family to visit her uncle Thomas at The Promised Land near the Lithonia stop, but they had traveled by wagon, not train. The trip was long and tedious for Mary for the most part with nothing but wilderness along the way. She had never been to Atlanta.

Once inhabited by the Creek and Cherokee Indians, the beautiful landscape was untouched except for the metal rails that forged their way across the state to Atlanta. Only a few stops along the way broke the sound of the engine chugging and the cars swaying. Mary felt secure with John's arm around her. Even though her heart was still tugging her back home, it gradually faded. She began to focus on what was ahead.

One of the stops along the way was, of course, the delightful town of Madison. As Mary stepped down from the train, she remarked, "Oh, how darling! I feel as if I have reached a breath of fresh air." She took John's arm and embraced the excitement of the town. They walked from store to store and stopped for lunch.

The farming industry flourished here with a strong cotton trade. There were beautiful homes in town and plantations in the surrounding countryside. Wealth and culture were abundant. All too soon, the whistle blew and they went back to the train, rested and ready for more adventure.

It took the rest of the day to reach Atlanta. The arrival time was 7:15 p.m. As they pulled into the station, Mary's head was spinning. She realized she was looking at the center of the railroads in Georgia. The general passenger depot was surrounded by trains and railroad tracks all around.

"This is the State Square," John said as they left the train.

"Quite pretty," Mary remarked as she looked around at the flowers and the park. She could see some hotels and stores in the evening light. Certain areas of town had wooden sidewalks. The streets were made of clay and dirt, and the buildings were no more than two stories high. Stores, saloons, and trains. No rivers near town, no lakes, not many houses. Not like Augusta.

"Why are pigs and cows in the street?" Mary asked.

John laughed. "I told you it was a country town."

However, Atlanta was a growing town and had a population of 6,000, which was quite an increase over the 215 voters that the first mayoral election had tallied five years earlier. Atlanta had outgrown DeKalb County, where Decatur was the public seat. A new county was formed, Fulton County, and Atlanta became its public seat.

The three railways joined to form a triangle near the center of town. Within that triangle was the Western and Atlantic freight and locomotive area. The center of town at the State Square would later be known as Five Points, and streets known as Decatur, Pryor, Ivy, Marietta and Peachtree branched off from that point. The city of Atlanta was considered to be a one-mile radius with the State Depot at Five Points as its center. Several stores and hotels lined the streets of the central area, and a telegraph in the post office was the only form of communication. Houses branched out from there.

Atlanta boasted several hotels, nine churches, Atlanta Bank, two entertainment halls, and three schools.

"I see several churches, John, but where is our church?" she asked.

"Just over the tracks." He pointed in the general direction. "But it's getting late. I will show it to you tomorrow."

John helped Mary off the train and located a horse and buggy with a driver who helped John to load up a few of their belongings. It was getting dark outside, and John was so excited about showing Mary her new home that he asked the driver to take them directly there. John asked him to store the trunks until tomorrow and take them to his house.

"I should be so very tired, but all of a sudden, I am excited!" exclaimed Mary as they rode down the streets. John smiled and put his arm around her. They passed a couple of blocks with stores, and then she began to see some houses. They traveled down Decatur Street about three more blocks and turned left on Butler Street, swaying as the driver swerved to miss the potholes and bumps in the road.

As they turned onto Butler, John pointed out where he worked at the Georgia Railroad, to the right over the tracks. They made the turn. *Just two more blocks*, John thought, but he didn't say a word. When the driver stopped the buggy in front of the house, John smiled. Mary looked first at John and then at the house on the right. She couldn't believe that it was her new home. She gazed in shock for a moment and then turned and hugged her husband warmly. Tears welled up in her eyes. John hopped down from the buggy, skipped around the back lightly on his feet, and lifted Mary up into the night air and down gently to the ground. They turned. John put his arm around his new wife and admired their new home.

It was a beautiful home: two stories, four large columns in front and a large balcony outside the upstairs bedroom, which overlooked the street. Two large oak trees provided shade for the balcony for most of the day and added an appealing entrance to their home. As John carried Mary over the threshold, she was caught up in the moment of excitement. He put her down gently and kissed her. She was in a daze as he took her from room to room, looking to her for approval.

A large entrance led to a parlor on the right and a library or smoking room on the left. In the parlor, Mary could envision her lady friends often sitting and visiting, sewing and reading. She thought that corner would be a fine place for a piano. She twirled around and ran over to the room opposite. The men would go to the library to discuss politics or the business of the day. A large staircase with an oak railing led upstairs. John pointed to the large dining room, which was through the hallway in the center of the house. A small guest room was located past the staircase on the left back section of the house. Outside the back door was a small walkway to the kitchen, separated from the house to protect from fires. Mary was thrilled with the kitchen.

"Oh, John, you remembered everything," she said.

The back door of the kitchen opened out into a large backyard perfect for a small garden and a place for children to play someday. Inside, a rear staircase led upstairs to three bedrooms — two smaller bedrooms and John and Mary's room, which was a great room where the French doors opened out onto the balcony. Mary ran to the doors and opened them breathlessly. She walked out onto the balcony, which extended the length of the front of the house, and looked out over the neighborhood.

"Oh, Mr. Mecaslin, this is pure heaven. I never dreamed we would have such a beautiful home."

John smiled with relief and satisfaction in knowing that Mary was so happy. He had furnished this room with a wonderful bedroom suite: a four-poster bed with a matching chest of drawers, side table and vanity with a red and gold upholstered bench.

"May I have this dance?" John reached out for Mary's hand and drew her closer to him. He began to lead her dreamily around the room. As she felt his arms around her, she knew that this was where she was meant to be, right here with her husband in this new home and this new town called Atlanta. He felt the same way. He had planned this moment for so long. It had turned out better than he had ever hoped.

He ran out to the balcony and yelled to the driver downstairs, "That's all for tonight, sir. I will pick up the trunks in the morning."

He twirled Mary out onto the balcony. He swept her hair from her face and, putting her head in his hands, pulled her closer and kissed her, leaving her breathless.

They didn't go back downstairs that night.

Hither, hither, hither,
Love this boon has sent;
If I die and wither
I will die content.

— *John Keats*

CHAPTER 6

"New thoughts and hopes were whirling through my mind, and all the colours of my life were changing."

~ David Copperfield

1853-1854

Mary's arrival in Atlanta took some adjustment — with a new town and a new husband. At least she knew Father Barry. Mack introduced her to his friend and next-door neighbor, Bill, and his wife, Amanda, who welcomed her new neighbor with open arms.

Mary found herself alone most days since Mack worked hard at the railroad and came home tired every night. He had regular meetings with the fire department and trained often. She spent much of her time working in her home or at the church.

However, she was not accustomed to society ladies "dropping by" for a visit without warning. A few days after she arrived, Mary was cleaning the floors in a housedress and apron with a kerchief tied around her head. She was on her hands and knees, scrubbing the floor in the foyer, up to her elbows in soapy water. As she reached in the bucket and squeezed the soap out of the rags, she heard some people talking outside, and then there was a knock at the door. Startled that someone was calling on her at this time, her sense of humor overtook her nervousness. She impulsively dried her hands and answered the door. Four ladies dressed in Sunday clothes and fine hats were standing there. The lady at the front of the group asked, "May we speak with Mrs. Mecaslin, please?"

Mary dropped a curtsy and lowered her eyes, answering in the speech of a servant in her thickest Irish brogue, "Yes, ma'am, she is most deftly at home. Please come in and be seated, and I'll tell her you are here."

She quickly ran upstairs and fussed over herself, removing her kerchief and taking off her apron. "This can't be happening!" she exclaimed. She searched frantically through her armoire for an appropriate dress and put it on. She ran to the mirror, looked at herself in horror, brushed her hair, pinched her cheeks, laughed and ran downstairs to present herself as hostess to some astounded callers.

"Why, Mrs. Mecaslin, how clever you are!" They all laughed. "We would like to welcome you to Atlanta and invite you to join our charitable group. Father Barry asked us to drop by and introduce ourselves. He told us that you recently arrived from Augusta and are the new bride to that charming Mr. Mecaslin. Welcome!" said Mrs. McFarland, the president of the group.

Mary doubted that Father Barry would say such a thing but maintained her dignity.

"Oh, well, you know how men are!" She shook her head and laughed. "May I offer you something cool to drink?"

"Oh, yes, thank you, Mrs. Mecaslin," said one lady, and the others nodded and smiled.

She excused herself and went to prepare drinks for her new neighbors.

✳✳✳

A small wooden church had been constructed on the corner of Lloyd and Hunter streets a few years before Mary and Mack arrived. It was on the northwest corner, two blocks south of the railroad tracks. It was called the Atlanta Catholic Church. As Atlanta grew, immigrants whose beliefs were of the Catholic religion often attended it. The church crossed over economic and racial boundaries to include anyone who sought comfort, help of any kind, or religious worship. Atlanta was a town of many cultures and people of many economic levels who hoped to find a home and opportunities in this railroad frontier.

Mary and Mack would walk two blocks down Butler, cross over the tracks and take a right one block further on Hunter Street. Then they would cross McDonough Street, and the church was another block away. The train traffic was increasing, so in 1853, a wooden bridge was built over Broad Street to provide safe passage for people over the railroad tracks. Broad Street was on the other side of town, so rather than go out of the way, they watched carefully and crossed over the tracks on Butler instead.

Atlanta was growing. A public school, a daily newspaper called *The Intelligencer* and Atlanta City Hall were all established that year. The Atlanta Medical College was also built that year diagonally from where Mack and Mary lived. It was a magnificent brick structure and a proud addition to the community.

Finally, some culture arrived upon the construction of a theatre called the Athenaeum, which had its performances on the second floor of a brick building on Decatur Street between Peachtree and Prior streets. Bill Barnes and Levi Richardson were two of the many talented people who performed premier roles on stage. Atlantans were proud of the Athenaeum and boasted that it was the best theatre between Charleston and New Orleans.

In addition, a three-story building, the tallest in Atlanta, was built at the corner of Alabama and Whitehall. The third floor was called Pace's Hall and was used as an opera house. On the bottom floor, William Kidd built a saloon called Alhambea, where everyone knew they would find their railroad friends after work. Kidd also became one of the directors of the Atlanta Gas Light Company, which was established later that year.

The frontier town where cows and pigs were allowed to graze wherever they pleased was changing. An ordinance was passed that restricted them from roaming freely. This change also allowed citizens to grow gardens in their backyards with fewer disturbances.

The city council agreed to extend the macadam paving to Mitchell Street, and wonderful brick sidewalks were placed on Alabama and Whitehall. It would be many years before the other streets would be paved. Kidd began the momentum necessary to create vast improvements and allow for growth in the little town.

The night guards of the town had increased to six members. Every evening, residents could hear the sound of the first watchman calling out, "Nine o'clock and all's well," from the council hall. Then the familiar sound was heard as each watchman called out in turn from each post to confirm the safety of the town. Mary's brother James Mullin was the chief of the night force.

Fire Company #1 was becoming more dynamic also. They continued working as a team and more members joined. More and more men felt the call to protect the community by being involved with the fire department. It was as if not being involved with the fire department meant that they weren't truly a part of the town.

"That's right," the chief said. "It's not about the wages, it's about family and community."

The firemen continued to train and work as a team each weekend. In August of that year, the firemen had a family outing and picnic to show their skills to the town. People of all ages came from miles around. They arrived early in the day to find a good place to see the activities. They placed their blankets and baskets on the ground to relax and enjoy the day.

The festivities began with the mayor introducing the firemen fully dressed in their uniforms. One by one, their names were called and applause filled the air. Then, the equipment that the whole town was proud of was introduced — a hand engine pulled by a beautifully-decorated, high-stepping horse. Everyone was standing and trying to see the sights.

Then it was time to prepare for the competition.

The first challenge was the traditional bucket brigade that everyone knew well. The rules and events were as follows:

1. Each team will assemble ten men in a line to carry the bucket from one person to the next. The men must race to their positions from fifty feet away. The men will not stand more than two feet from each other. The man closest to the cistern will be the key player and must be quick and strong. He will be responsible for picking up the bucket and gathering water from the cistern in the quickest way possible and passing it to the next man. The first team to pass ten buckets and fill their cistern on the opposite end of the line wins.

Everyone gathered around and cheered for their favorite firemen. Each man gallantly played his part to win for his team. Mack and Will were on the same team, and their team won the first event.

A short break was allowed before moving on.

2. Racing up the side of a building. The team shall run one hundred feet, hoist one man up the side of a building by the best means possible to show teamwork, and the first team to reach the metal rail at the top wins.

3. One-thousand-yard race for endurance.

4. One-mile relay race as the grand finale. Each team will have four runners, and each man will race one time around the park, which is a distance of one quarter mile. Each runner must pass a baton to the next player, and the team that finishes first wins.

Everyone gathered along the path to watch. Mack, Will and two others were on their team. Bill, Charles and two others were on the other team. They took their places at the starting line.

The gun fired and they were off. Both teams were neck and neck. Then Mack's team pulled ahead. The batons were passed with lightning speed. The race moved quickly and finally the baton was passed to Mack. He could feel the other runner right behind him. They burst into the final few yards and shoulder to shoulder, Mack pushed forward and won by a nose. The crowd jumped up and yelled and applauded.

The teams gathered around, shook hands and congratulated each other on a great race.

A tense moment passed as they waited for the final tally.

Finally, the mayor made the announcement:

"Ladies and gentlemen,

"What a wonderful event we have had today. A great measure of athleticism has been displayed. I would like to thank everyone who participated. I would also like to thank everyone who came out to enjoy the day.

"The final results for the day are:

"First, let me say that the score is very close.

"Team #1: 78 points

"Team #2: 79 points

"Team #2 wins! Congratulations! Will members from Team #2 please come forward!"

He waved over to Mack and Will's team to go to the podium, and they first turned to the other team and shook their hands before going to the podium. After the presentation, the firemen met with their families and friends for a picnic.

***

In March of 1854, Mack and Mary were blessed with a baby girl, and she was baptized Margaret, in the Irish tradition of naming their first daughter after Mary's mother. They called her Maggie. Mary had saved her green handkerchief from her wedding and made a bonnet to place on Maggie's head during the baptism ceremony. Maggie was a wonderful addition to this very happy marriage. She was the apple of her father's eye, and her mother cherished her. Mary's life had new meaning.

Family was of utmost importance in Irish families. It was the cornerstone of all that the Irish believed in. Mary had always dreamed of this wonderful daughter, and it seemed that everything was now falling into place with a strong and loving husband, a healthy baby girl and a beautiful home in a town in which she was beginning to feel very comfortable. Who could ask for more?

As the months went by, Mary delighted in working at home and caring for her baby. Maggie was growing stronger and healthier, and Mack and Mary delighted in her every new skill and noise she made. Neighbors brought gifts and toys for Maggie, and they could soon tell what her favorites were. She was particularly attached to a homemade doll that Mary's sister-in-law, Amanda, made for Maggie. It was sentimental and precious to Mary as well because Amanda made it. But her favorite item was a small, soft baby blanket. Maggie had to have it with her all the time, and as she began to crawl and walk, she carried it with her everywhere she went.

Mary and Maggie spent many enjoyable hours in the garden area. Mary loved caring for the flowers and vegetables. They took daily strolls through the neighborhood with Amanda. She introduced Mary to her friends, and Mary became involved in the social activities of the city. She was a member of the Ladies Altar Society of the Atlanta Catholic Church as well as several sewing and reading groups. She was also involved as a wife of a fireman. She and her husband enjoyed socializing in the evenings with Amanda and Bill and their other friends.

✳✳✳

A shocking book called *Uncle Tom's Cabin* had hit the press in 1852, and at the time, most Christian women in the South found it inappropriate to read such a book. It was being displayed in some bookstores but banned in others. Response books from Southern writers were being published in the same year to counter the beliefs that were established as a result of this book.

In 1854, however, copies were making the rounds. Ladies who were preparing for a hop were having a discussion one afternoon while their children were napping.

"You must read this book, ladies. It's startling what you will find. We must not be limited in our readings."

"Oh, surely you don't believe what you read in that book. It's fiction. Haven't you heard the outrage about our Southern lifestyle?"

"Oh, give it here! I will read it, on the sly, of course. We should each read it, and then we will see!"

"We shouldn't discuss it. Really, we shouldn't."

"We must let our gentlemen handle such nonsense."

As some eyes met with a mysterious glint, the conversation led to the dinner menu and dance list and what preparations needed to be made.

Mary received the book at the next sitting and began reading it that afternoon before Mack came home. He arrived a little early. She quickly hid it under the cushion of the chair and shifted the pillow. She greeted her husband as he came through the door. At the next meeting, she returned the book, believing that it was a cruel story. Propaganda? Maybe, but she knew in her heart that as a Christian woman, she would always help anyone in need. *There is so much more going on than I know*, she thought. She lit a candle. It would not be discussed.

The book outraged many Southerners, and it was considered abolitionist propaganda that had been stirred up by the Missouri Compromise of 1850, stating that runaway slaves couldn't find refuge in the North, that they must go all the way to Canada. Years of political turmoil continued.

***

The yellow fever had taken hold in the late summer of 1854, and the paper commented on how many lives had been taken by this demon. The churches were filled with patients, and homes were flagged and avoided. Mary didn't help at church for several weeks, as a mother with an infant had to be careful not to put her child in danger of catching the fever.

Although the paper reported only a few deaths the last week of October, the citizens were hoping for rain or maybe even frost to kick the final remnants of the fever out of town. Mary kept her infant close at home and, luckily, the fever passed over their home.

CHAPTER 7

"If there must be trouble, let it be in my day, that my child may have peace."

~ Thomas Paine, The American Crisis No. 1, 1776

1855

One Sunday afternoon after the fever had fizzled, while Mack and Mary were strolling down the street with little Maggie, they decided to take a break and sit down on a park bench. They sat near an old-timer who was reading the paper.

Mack politely said, "Hello, sir, nice day we're having."

The man replied, "Indeed. You have a lovely family there."

"Why, thank you."

"According to today's paper, it's not so grand elsewhere."

"Yes, I have read about the strife in Kansas and Missouri," Mack said. Mary gave Mack a look and reached for Maggie.

Mack changed the subject and continued, "Are you new in Atlanta? I haven't seen you before."

"Oh, yes, I am just here on business for a couple of days. I will be leaving for Augusta on the train tomorrow."

Mary chimed in, "Augusta, sir? Do you live in Augusta?"

"Oh, no, madam. I am on my way back to Virginia, my home."

"Well, you must come over for dinner tonight. We would love to hear about your home and travels," Mack insisted.

Mary agreed. "Oh, yes, please do."

"Of course. Thank you for the invitation."

They decided on the time, stood and shook hands. Mary, Mack and Maggie continued on their walk.

That evening, the visitor arrived promptly at 7 p.m. Mack had invited their neighbors, Bill and Amanda Barnes. They had a lovely dinner of Mary's fine cooking. They discussed their travels, and Mary asked, "Would you have time to visit my parents while you're in Augusta and, perhaps, take a letter to my mother?"

"Of course, I will, Mrs. Mecaslin."

"They live on Fenwick Street, not far from downtown."

"I'm sure I can find it. By the way, how do you like your new theatre? Everyone is talking about it."

"Our friend here, Mr. Barnes, is very talented and involved in the Athenaeum," remarked Mary.

"How wonderful, Mr. Barnes!"

"I do love to have a good time!" said Barnes with a grin. They talked about other events in Atlanta and Augusta.

After dinner, the men excused themselves to the library, and the women finished cleaning and went into the parlor.

Mack poured the men a brandy and offered them a cigar.

"Mack, get prepared, son. A war is brewing and has been for some time."

"I have been wanting to hear your point of view, sir, and I respect what you say. With everything we read and hear, there is considerable discontent in Missouri and the Kansas territory. But that's far from here."

"Gentlemen, I am an old man. I have seen how the government has glossed over the issue of slavery for too long. It goes back to the 1790s. We are at the mercy of the politicians. Year after year, new legislation is introduced that quiets the public for a while, but the same issues resurface again and again. The faces of the politicians become redder and redder, and the people wonder, how is this going to affect us now?"

Mack said, "I am actually from Maryland. I can see how political issues are tearing that area apart. My family is there now, and it doesn't look good. It's about power and independence. The government wants to tell the states how to run their states, and the states want to know that they can make their own choices."

The older gentleman replied, "The assumption argument about tore us apart before we even got started as a nation. Because of these sensitive issues continuing for all these years, bloodshed is occurring and will continue to happen there and, God forbid, elsewhere, and who knows what will happen? As they say, if you don't choose, the choice will be made for you — by the future. My allegiance is to Virginia, and you?"

"I am bound to honor my Maryland, and my home, Atlanta. I am a Southerner and will remain. As my father always says, 'What we have, we hold!'"

"Ah, a true Irish sentiment," the old man remarked.

Mack continued, "That it is. This current discord is in the territories and whether they will be slave or free." And he thought and hoped, *Surely, they will settle that in their own way in their own territories.*

"Heed my warning," the old man's eyes were piercing. "Prepare yourself. I've seen a lot in my life. I don't know what might happen next. I just hope the violence doesn't reach Virginia."

"Or Charleston," Bill toasted.

"Or Maryland," Mack held his glass up. "And never here."

"Hear, hear, a toast to peace," the visitor spoke up.

"To peace!" They all chimed in and raised their glasses.

Mack was pensive. He had an uneasy lump in his throat and tried to swallow. It was as if the truth had been spoken, but he didn't know what it meant yet. He offered his friends another brandy, but the visitor stood and held his hand up to decline.

"I thank you for your hospitality, kind sir, and a wonderful dinner. You have a delightful wife and child and dear friends in this quiet, friendly town. I must prepare for my departure tomorrow."

"Let me drive you," Mack insisted. They said their goodbyes to the ladies and left.

On their ride back to the Atlanta Hotel, their conversation lightened, and they spoke of the small town of Atlanta and how much they liked it. The town had a safe, peaceful and friendly atmosphere that was most enjoyable to the visitor from Virginia.

✳✳✳

Political conversations such as this had been occurring for many years and had become the talk of the day. In 1855, voting was attempted as a peaceful solution to determine whether Kansas would be a free soil or slave state, but it was tainted. Men were no longer just discussing what should be done. Unsavory political tactics were making people willing to take action and fight. The spirits of Missourians ran high, as men were enticed to go to Kansas and vote. They were being paid to slant the election, which resulted in thirty pro-slavery legislators and three free soilers.

In Atlanta, meetings were held several times that year to discuss their position in the Kansas situation. Many people traveled through Atlanta on their way to Kansas throughout the year, and citizens cheered them on as they made speeches to promote their case. Men traveled from Charleston and other areas of South Carolina, south Georgia and other states. Overall, Georgia made a huge push for the pro-slavery efforts in Kansas.

"The old man was right," Mack said as people in a crowd cheered on the politicians at the State Square. "We are being pulled into this, whether we like it or not."

***

The wives of the firemen began to plan the yearly charitable event to honor George Washington's birthday. It was to be held on February 22, 1855. It was decided that it would be held at the city hall and would be the social event of the season. Invitations went out in early January so everyone could begin to find their dresses.

"What do you think we should do for decorations?" Mrs. Rodes asked.

"Well, since it's Washington's birthday, everything should be done in red, white and blue, of course. All of the ladies will wear dresses in red, white and blue, and we will have banners and streamers in our union colors, too," Mrs. Barnes replied.

"Oh, how delightful, Mrs. Barnes, this will be fun. And maybe the men can wear wigs and suits like Washington did," added Mrs. Ennis.

"This will be wonderful! Let's wear masks and make it a costume party," Mary said with excitement.

The plans were set, and everyone looked forward to the grand ball, which would help the firemen buy more fire safety equipment for the town.

On February 22, Mary put on her beautiful red and white dress with a blue petticoat. Mecaslin was dressed in his finest, with a traditional wig. Mack wore a mask, and Mary had a handheld mask. They arrived in fine style in a horse-drawn carriage. Mack exited first, walked around and opened the door for his beautiful wife. He held her hand and helped her out of the carriage, and they floated into the hall.

"Well done, my dear," said Mack as he entered. Mary smiled proudly as she looked around and was pleased with the turnout.

The city hall was beautifully decorated in brilliant colors with a large banner across the ballroom that said, "Happy Birthday, George Washington!"

Everyone the Mecaslins knew was there. They danced the night away, and Mack even called a few dances. Barnes sang a song, and everyone joined in.

As the couple left, Barnes said, "Mrs. Mecaslin, you, my wife and the other ladies have done an outstanding job of planning this event. We congratulate you! Thank you for all of the contributions to a worthy cause. Well done, all!" And everyone applauded.

***

The event of the year, however, was on Christmas Day. The whole town was excited about the event that they had been talking about and planning for months. At around 6:30 that evening, when it was dark outside, the citizens of Atlanta began to leave their warm homes on a cold winter holiday evening. Some arrived by horse, some on foot, and others by carriage.

Mack decided to take the horse and buggy that night to make sure that Mary and little Maggie stayed warm. Mary held the candle. As they came closer to the center of town, they noticed that others also carried their candles and lanterns so they could see in the dark. They could see lights approaching from all around.

"What a wondrous sight!" Mary exclaimed.

Refreshments, such as hot apple cider, cookies and apple tarts, were enjoyed. Everyone was in good spirits and anticipating the great event. They began to form lines along Peachtree Street.

Then precisely at 7 p.m., an announcement was made for everyone to blow out their candles at the same time. On the count of five — 5, 4, 3, 2, 1 — and it was dark. The suspense was delightful. Suddenly, fifty gas lamps set atop beautiful ornamental lamp posts that lined the streets of the downtown area were lit at the same time. They were decorated with red ribbons. Everyone clapped and cheered. The sound of a piano filled the air as they began to sing "Joy to the World" followed by "The First Noel." Other carols rang through the town as the evening progressed. They finished the evening with "We Wish You a Merry Christmas" as they turned to each other to shake hands and hug. The true magic of Christmas that night was the closeness of the Atlanta families who shared this moment.

CHAPTER 8

"We cannot live only for ourselves. A thousand fibers connect us with our fellow men."

~ Herman Melville

1856

In Atlanta, the traffic of the trains had moved to twenty-four hours per day. A passenger bound for Augusta 171 miles away could buy a ticket for $5.50, board at 1 or 2 a.m. and arrive later in the morning. Transport to Chattanooga was less expensive at $5 one way, and one would board at 12:30 p.m. and arrive in Chattanooga at 8:18 p.m.

Mary and Maggie would often walk to town during these years and visit neighbors. They would stop and visit Mrs. Barnes next door and Mrs. Ennis, who lived on the corner of the same block. Mrs. Rodes lived across the railroad tracks by the church, but they had to walk out of the way through town to the Broad Street Bridge and cross the tracks there and double back. The passenger travel across the tracks at the Georgia Railroad Depot had ended for safety reasons due to high train traffic.

Everyone knew each other and their children, and keeping watch over others was part of life. It was commonplace to stop and visit and maybe sit on the porch and catch up on the latest news.

✳✳✳

A special portrait was being arranged with all of the firemen of Atlanta Fire Company #1.

"Come on, men, let's make this a memorable moment," Barnes said as they moved the faithful fire engine and hose carriage that they had used to extinguish so many fires to the open area between Alabama Street and the railroad. The area was called Holland's Square, better known as "Humbug Square." Everyone gathered around. Some stood behind the equipment, and some perched on the engine.

As was noted by one of the men that day, "That's right. Being a member of our fire department is not about wages. It's about community. It's about protection of our town and people. Pride and responsibility."

"Our fire equipment is the best around."

You could sense the camaraderie these men had with each other and the pride they had in their occupation as they posed proudly with arms around each other in a strong stance.

"Ok, ready? This one will hang in the Fire Station!"

Flash!

✳✳✳

On the cold and rainy evening of December 10, 1856, on the corner of Loyd and Alabama streets, ten to fifteen men, mostly employed at the Georgia Railroad, met in a wooden building to discuss the future of fire safety in Atlanta. The Masonic Order gave them permission to meet there.

The group agreed to create another fire company that they called the Mechanic Fire Company #2 because most of the members were skilled machinists, blacksmiths, and painters. Atlanta's new firehouse was built on the corner of Washington Street, overlooking the Georgia Railroad. They thought that was a good location in case any fires developed at the Georgia Railroad. The firemen would be easily accessible, and its location was farther east in the city than Firehouse #1, making it easier to cover more ground in that area quickly.

They were proud of their motto, "The Public Good Our Only Aim," and had a unique uniform — an oilcloth cape thrown over the shoulders with their company name and #2 on the helmet. They wore a different dress uniform for balls and special occasions, which was a gray dress coat with brass buttons displaying the company name and number on the front, finished with dress black pants, a belt and a helmet.

That night at the meeting, Bill Barnes was elected president of Mechanics Fire Company #2, and James Gullatt was named treasurer. Mack's loyalty was to the #1.

45

A few days later, the weather turned unusually warm and windy. A few blocks north of Five Points on Peachtree Street, someone heard a scream. A woman ran outside her newly-built house and yelled for help. A man jumped on his horse and started toward the fire station yelling, "Fire! Fire! Help!"

The neighbor next door grabbed a bucket, ran to the well and started to fill it with water. She turned around and the flames were out of control, leaping and dancing throughout the house, on the roof and dangerously close to her own house. She dropped the bucket and ran inside her house and said, "Come with me." She lifted her smallest child into her arms, grabbed the hand of her four-year-old and ran out of the front door just in time. The flames had leapt over to the roof of her house, and all she could do was watch it happen. She met her neighbor in the street, and the two women hugged.

The man on the horse, who had gone for help, had reached Fire Station #1, and the firemen rang the bell. Mack, Charlie, Bill and James Gullatt were at a meeting at City Hall when they heard the sound of the bell. They looked at each other, gave the signal to leave and excused themselves from the meeting. They met outside with some confusion because Fire Station #2 had just been established, and they had not discussed the exact territory they would oversee.

"Let's go to the fire station and find out where the fire is," Bill said.

Without delay, they hurried to the fire station, found the location, and Bill spoke up, "I don't want to interfere. We haven't defined the territories yet."

"We're firemen, sworn to duty," Mack said. "It doesn't matter where the fire is. Let's go!"

The other members nodded to each other, and the two departments became one again. The fire horse was attached to the hand engine, and they were on their way. The other members had left their businesses to tend to the fire, and the town seemed to slow to a crawl.

By the time Mack and his crew reached the fire, the evil demon, with the help of the gusty winds, had engulfed two houses and was well on to a third. Quickly, they went to work. The cisterns were far away, so they did a quick assessment for local wells. A few men searched all homes in the area to help residents evacuate.

"Push, push, push," the familiar chant was heard throughout the area, and the leaders barked out the change of shifts. The huge fire required two bucket brigades. All hands were working.

The fire spread to another house but more slowly as the firemen soaked the house with water.

If fortunate could be descriptive in this disaster, the fire was prevented from spreading to the other side because the house was on the corner. The wind tended to gust in the opposite direction.

Not soon enough, the fire slowed to a stop. Many residents huddled together and watched as their homes disappeared. Nearby trees, shrubs, and grass were burned beyond repair. Only two water-soaked homes were left standing on the block.

The firemen stood by while all final assessments were made. No loss of life. That was most important. Two homes, and possibly many more, were saved that day. Families lost their most cherished possessions, but they survived, and they would rebuild. The community would help.

The two fire companies realized that no matter the circumstance, they had an unbroken bond, a fellowship that would come together regardless of fire location.

Mack and Bill shook hands. No words were said. Gullatt and Rodes shook hands. Other members of the #1 and #2 shook hands and thanked each other for their help.

A lot of work was ahead for the men as they learned lessons and were determined to improve their skills, equipment and location of water. It seemed that every experience with fire presented new challenges. Sometimes they would prevent destruction, but sometimes they could only salvage. The best effort to improve their departments had shifts and setbacks. Through the most extreme situations, stronger bonds were built.

Atlantans loved their firefighters. They looked upon them with pride and accomplishment. Throughout the years, the two fire companies worked well together, supported each other in their accomplishments and became even closer through social gatherings and meetings. They were highlighted at gala affairs and social outings and often traveled to other cities in Georgia and other states to represent Atlanta. All of the men worked as volunteers, giving of their time freely and willingly to create a safer city.

1857

The presidential election of 1856 had been divisive, as people were learning quickly where their loyalties were, and there was only one political issue — slavery.

In 1857, the Dred Scott case, a landmark decision by the United States Supreme Court, determined that people of African descent brought into the United States and held as slaves were not protected by the Constitution and were not United States citizens.

The Supreme Court stated that Congress had no authority to prohibit slavery in federal territories and because slaves were not citizens, they could not sue in court. Furthermore, the court ruled that slaves as chattels or private property could not be taken from their owners without due process.

Well, that was that. The decision had been made. The issue of slavery had been settled. Or so some thought.

✱✱✱

As the new recruits trained as firemen, they began to compete more with each other. They continued to get together on Saturdays to hone their skills and have friendly competitions. Late in October, they had a family picnic day and the firemen had a fun competition. Earlier competitions were within the Fire Company #1, but today the firehouses would compete against each other.

The events of the day included an introduction of Fire Companies #1 and #2. The president of each company spoke in honor of his company as well as his competitor. The firefighters donned their uniforms proudly. And the games began.

The first challenge was the traditional bucket brigade. Ten men from each company lined up to prepare for the event. Ten buckets were lined up next to each water-filled horse trough. Each company had chosen their most experienced to lead their brigade and fill the buckets. Two more horse troughs were placed on the other end of the brigade.

"We've got this one," said Mack.

"Not a chance," said Gullatt, who was a member of the #2. "I'm feeling lucky."

A few cynical laughs were heard, and the starter pistol was fired.

The buckets were filled and passed on. The men chattered and cheered each other on. The sway of the buckets from one hand to the next had been perfected, and the slightest shift change could mean a win or a loss.

The last buckets were on their way down the lines. The crowd was cheering. The men were tired but focused on the moment. A second of uncertainty by the #2 allowed a smooth finish by the #1 as the last hand poured water into the trough. The #1 won the first event.

The ladder climb was the second event and easily handled by the #2.

A two-hour break was next, so everyone relaxed with their friends and families and enjoyed drinks and a picnic lunch.

The next event was exciting. Each company had chosen their fastest runners for the one-mile relay. Each runner would run a quarter-mile around the park and return to the starting line to pass a baton to the next runner.

Rodes would run the last leg of the relay for the #1. Levin Blake would compete with him.

All were set at the starting point. The crowd was on their feet. The starter gun was fired.

They're off! Everyone cheered excitedly for their favorite. The runners took their laps. As they rounded the turn and passed the baton, the crowd let out a wild cheer.

Finally, it was down to Rodes and Blake. Rodes was younger and thinner, but Blake had sprinting power. Rodes was ahead but was threatened by Blake coming from behind. Rodes stretched out for the final sprint and was victorious. The crowd broke the line and ran over to congratulate them both.

The most anticipated event of the day was here at last. The pride and joy of the fire departments was the hand engine that they called Blue Dick. The firemen attached a beautifully-adorned fire horse to the hand engine and paraded it through the crowd to the location of the grand finale. The firemen set up the event. Blue Dick was stationed in a permanent location next to a horse trough. By the toss of a coin, Fire Department #2 went first. They chose their strongest men to work the hand pump. The other members of the group were stationed next to the 350 ft. leather hose. Families and friends were crowded around. Some of the children climbed trees for a better view.

The judges checked their watches. The starter gun was fired.

The men began to unfurl the hose and extend it to its furthest position at the cistern. Then the first man at the hand engine began to pump. "Push, push, push," the firemen chanted, and they looked around and smiled as the crowd began to chant as well.

Everyone waited with anticipation as the judge at the end watched as the water filled the cistern to the designated fill line. When it reached the line, the judge called, "Stop!" They checked their watches and documented the time.

Then Fire Company #1 stepped up. The crowd roared. Watches were checked. The gun was fired. Rodes led the team to unfurl the hose. He waved to Mack to begin the pump. "Push, push, push," the crowd chanted with the team. The crowd's involvement motivated the team and increased their collective adrenaline. The atmosphere was dizzying.

Finally, the judge yelled, "Stop!" The judges checked and double-checked their watches. There was some concern, but the final decision was made.

Fire Department #1 won by three seconds. The crowd went wild!

The members of the #1 congratulated each other. Then, they shook hands with their opponents. "Well done, my friend," said Bill.

"Excellent competitors," Mack said.

After a short break, the mayor announced, "Ladies and gentlemen, your attention, please. The moment you have all awaited is here. We have thoroughly enjoyed the competition, and now it is time to announce the winner of today's events." He waited and heard the hush of the crowd.

"The winner is Fire Department #1! Congratulations!"

The crowd cheered wildly.

"We would like to recognize all of the members of Mechanics Fire Department first. All of the members of Fire Department #2, please step forward."

Bill led his group to the front to receive the runner-up trophy. The crowd clapped and families cheered.

"Now, congratulations to Fire Company #1! Please come forward."

Mecaslin and his comrades walked to the front of the crowd and received their first place trophy. Mechanics #2 applauded, as well as everyone in attendance. The mayor concluded the ceremony, "Thanks to all competitors. Enjoy this wonderful day!"

***

In December, some firemen who were traveling on the way to Charleston stopped off to have dinner with the firefighters in Atlanta. They were good friends and associates from Lumpkin, Georgia. The dinner was held at the Atlanta Hotel where they were staying. The men were having a drink before dinner, and one of the visiting fellow firemen said, "Gentlemen, you are establishing a fine company here in Atlanta. You should be proud of your organization and the work you do."

Barnes said, "We have been training and having small competitions among our companies. What would you say to joining us for competitions? We can also invite our friends and fellow firefighters from Nashville, Cincinnati, Augusta, Macon, Savannah and New Orleans. We will make it an annual event. What do you say?"

"What a stellar idea! We will discuss it further and contact you soon. Any man would be proud to be a part of such an up and coming town. You are protecting a town that is developing as the crossroads of our fine state of Georgia. Atlanta is the primary connection by rail in the Southland." He raised his glass and toasted, "I dub thee, Atlanta, the 'Gate City of the South.'"

CHAPTER 9

"It is in vain to say human beings ought to be satisfied with tranquility: they must have action; and they will make it if they cannot find it."

~ Charlotte Bronte, Jane Eyre, 1848

1858

John Mecaslin served in local government as the councilman for the Fourth Ward. The Fourth Ward was east of town in his neighborhood along Boulevard, the Atlanta Cemetery and beyond, and north of Decatur Street. The assignments for the councilmen were:

On Wells, Pump, Cistern: Rushton, Mecaslin and Blackwell
On Fire Department: Mecaslin, Rushton, and Hayden
On Lamps and Gas: Hayden, Mecaslin and Rushton
On Free Schools: Hayden, Collier and Mecaslin

Mecaslin also was elected as chairman of the first committee of the Fire Department. As one of his first duties as chairman in the new year, Mecaslin called a meeting to discuss the joining of both fire companies to protect and defend the proud city of Atlanta.

"Good evening, gentlemen. It is with great honor today that I open the discussion of an idea that was presented to us by our brothers of Lumpkin, Georgia. It is believed that we should combine companies and become the 'Gate City Guard' to honor and protect our Gate City of the South. All in favor say 'Aye.'" The room exploded with ayes. "All opposed," and there was silence.

"I would therefore like to formally dub our Fire Company #1 and Mechanics #2 as the Gate City Guards." All men stood and applauded.

January 10, 1858, was a special day to commemorate the bonding of the two companies. The ladies of the city had been preparing for two days for the hop that the firemen of Fire Company #1 were preparing to honor Fire Company #2. Mary had been working with the other ladies of the city to make a special presentation. That night, during the festivities, Mary and Amanda, on behalf of the ladies of the city, presented Fire Company #2 with a company flag.

These early days were spent developing friendships and bonding with each other through the work they did and social events that brought these men and families together. Another social event that spring was the party that Atlanta Fire Company #2 held for its inauguration and invited Atlanta Fire Company #1 and the city government.

At the next meeting, Mecaslin led the discussion of unifying the fire departments of many different cities in friendly competitions. Delegates were chosen, and they began writing letters to friends in Charleston, Augusta, Macon, Savannah, Richmond, and New Orleans, inviting all interested companies, including northern cities such as Cincinnati, Philadelphia and New York City, to a spring event. It was the social event of the season, and people would attend from all over to watch expert firemen compete individually and as teams to determine who had the best fire department in the country.

Members of the Atlanta Catholic Church were preparing for an exciting visit by their very own Father Barry, who had recently become the administrator of the diocese and bishop of Savannah. Bishop Barry was expected to administer the sacrament of confirmation to a class at the Catholic church.

✳✳✳

Mack and Mary were blissful in their marriage, and Maggie was growing up strong and healthy. Mack came home one day and Maggie saw him riding up on his horse. "Daddy, Daddy, here I am." She was waving. Mack's heart melted as he heard his little girl call him. He dismounted from Storm and ran over to her, picked her up and twirled her around.

"I see you, little Mags. How's my girl today?"

"Good, Daddy. I missed you!"

"I missed you, too, sweet girl," he said and hugged her. "Where's Mommy?" he asked as he put his little girl down.

"She's in the kitchen. Come on, Daddy." She grabbed his hand and led him to the porch and into the house.

"Hello, you two," said Mary with a smile and she met her husband and embraced him. "Hello, Mr. Mack. How was your day?" she teased.

"Mr. Mack, is it?" He drew his wife close and put his arms around her waist.

"It has a nice ring to it," she said as she put her lips on his and kissed him warmly.

Maggie was playing out in the woods one day not far from home. She spied a cute little puppy that was wandering along by itself. The black-and-white pup wagged its tail and approached her. Maggie smiled and stooped over and reached for the puppy. He ran into her arms and she giggled. She looked around for the owner and, not seeing anyone nearby, took the puppy home.

Mary warmed to the newcomer quickly, and after searching for the owner, concluded that it was a stray in need of a home. The puppy quickly became attached to Mack as well and followed him everywhere. Maggie thought that the puppy looked like her daddy, and they named him Mack, Ole Mack.

The fire bell of the #1 sounded. Mack kissed his little girl and jumped on his fire horse and headed back to town. As he rode, he saw citizens running out of their homes to ring their bells and look for the direction of the fire. Other members of the company followed the smoke to the Broad Street Bridge. The wooden bridge had caught fire. Pedestrians moved quickly off the bridge, and there were no injuries. However, many women and children were frightened, and some were crying.

Several firemen arrived on the scene, and two men quickly ran to the citizens and moved them far from the flames. Others comforted the distressed people.

All other firemen addressed the fire. A cistern was located and a bucket brigade began in no time at all. It was thrilling to see how they all worked well together.

Another team had arrived with the hand engine and set the hose in place. Mack began pumping. "Push, push, push," said the team. The water arrived at the burning bridge, but not soon enough. It was completely out of control.

Another safety and logistics factor was being assessed. Not only had the bridge traffic been halted, but trains entering and leaving Atlanta were stopped. No trains could leave Atlanta going west, and none could enter either.

The train depot was a transportation nightmare. From that point, any trains entering Atlanta from any direction were blocked from reaching the city. Only those already going south or east could leave. No train traffic could go through Atlanta, the central depot of the South.

The firemen worked their magic to the best of their abilities for hours and finally extinguished the fire. Barnes and Mecaslin inspected the area for remaining embers and assessed the damage. After an all clear signal, Barnes, Mecaslin, Kidd and other councilmen met with the mayor at the site to discuss the situation.

"All of this will need to be cleared and reconstructed," Barnes said.

"We need to get these trains moving as soon as possible," the mayor said with agitation. "The engineers and passengers are complaining. They have a schedule to keep, and you know how they are about their schedules. I have already ordered telegraphs to be sent to all stations to notify them of delays. Also, we need to contact an engineer to reconstruct this bridge."

A councilman said, "Our only engineer is in New York on a job."

"I know of someone," Barnes said, "but he lives in Charleston. He's a good friend."

"Don't we know of anyone else here? That's a day of travel, and we can't afford to hold up the trains any longer," Kidd said.

"Not that I know of," the mayor said as he looked around to the others for input. "Mr. Mecaslin, don't you have an engineering degree?"

"Yes," Mecaslin replied, "but I don't have the necessary experience to build a bridge. But I will be happy to provide assistance in any way possible."

"Thank you, Mr. Mecaslin. I'll ask around for further consultation, but we need to send your friend a telegram to see if he's available," the mayor said, looking at Barnes.

"I'll contact him right away," Barnes said. "Hey guys, let's get a cleanup crew to remove the debris. We need to clear the tracks and see what kind of damage we're looking at." All available railroad hands and firemen were put on duty to clear the tracks.

Meanwhile, two passenger trains and a freight train had been stopped and backed up on the tracks west of the bridge. After hours of waiting, the passengers were finally allowed to get off the trains and walk along the tracks to town. Atlanta had some unexpectedly disgruntled visitors to house and feed.

The Charleston engineer was on a train to Atlanta as soon as he heard. With the conundrum of train traffic issues, he had to get off the train when he reached Decatur and take a stagecoach the rest of the way.

When the engineer reached Atlanta, after a meal and some rest, he met with the mayor, Barnes, Mecaslin and other councilmen to discuss the reconstruction of the bridge. Within a couple of days, he designed a bridge the likes of which that small town had never seen. Mecaslin and other experts assisted him and helped with logistics.

The train depot manager worked around the clock to schedule delays and detours for the construction period so the builders could work on the bridge. Atlantans and travelers struggled for weeks, adjusting to the confusion, inconvenience and frustration.

Finally, the Broad Street bridge was finished. The chaos caused by the fire gave way to a safer, stronger bridge.

Bill and Mack took their wives for a stroll that afternoon. They stopped at the bridge and admired it.

"What a fine bridge," Mary said.

"This is a proud moment," Bill said as he hugged his wife.

"We will long remember the days that Atlanta stood still because of fire," Mack said to his friends. They nodded in agreement.

✳✳✳

It was three days before Christmas. The streetlights of the city were beautiful, and everyone was running around in preparation for Christmas. Suddenly, a woman screamed from a two-story frame house on the east side of Whitehall Street, south of Alabama Street. She was trapped on the top floor of a building. Somehow a candle had caught the drapes on fire, and she and her two small children were not able to get downstairs and out of the house. Citizens of the city gathered quickly, and the fire bell sounded. All of the firemen of both companies ran from their parties, dinners and businesses in town to fight the fire.

As soon as they heard the fire bell, Mecaslin and Rodes jumped on their horses and took off down Pryor Street, over the railroad tracks, and past the State Square. They could see the smoke from there. They took a quick right on Alabama Street and left on Whitehall Street. They couldn't believe their eyes. Some of the other firemen were arriving with the fire equipment. Citizens had begun to gather around. A bucket brigade was formed, but to no avail. Sadly, the fire departments were not prepared for second-story fires. They had buckets for a bucket brigade and the fire hose but no way to reach the woman and her children in time. The house went up in flames, and the townspeople could only stand by and watch in horror. Buckets of water and the fire hose were only sprinkles on a hotbed of flames, an incinerator.

The poor woman and her children lost their lives, and the horrible experience was the first recorded event in Atlanta in which lives were lost from fire. The citizens were outraged, and that evening, they gathered in the streets and demanded that the city council hold a meeting the next day to establish a company to save lives. Atlanta's first hook and ladder company was established as a result of this terrible disaster.

1859

Atlanta's train traffic continued to grow as Atlanta did. Forty-four trains arrived and departed daily. The population increased to 11,500.

In January, concerned citizens met to discuss the tragedy that befell their city. They continued to discuss the need for the new hook and ladder company. Finally, in May, they were able to get approval to build a new fire station on the east side of Bridge Street just north of the railroad. A fourth fire company was established within the year. Atlanta's fire department was growing to suit its population.

Tensions were building in Atlanta as the headlines of the newly-published *Southern Confederacy* read, "John Brown's raid on Harper's Ferry creates slave rebellion." Citizens of Atlanta were shocked and worried by the events that took place in Virginia and Maryland. Many Southerners became suspicious of Union sympathizers and were concerned that this event would lead to widespread rebellion among the slaves. More than ever, this event fed the idea of secession that would not die.

Mack sent a telegraph right away to his father to make sure that they were safe.

LADIES CIRCLE

One spring afternoon, the ladies met in their sewing circle to discuss a new article in the paper.

"Did you read the article in the paper? Those suffragettes in New York are causing quite a fuss."

"What did the article say?"

"Susan B. Anthony was quoted as saying, 'Where, under our Declaration of Independence, does the Saxon man get his power to deprive all women and Negroes of the inalienable right to vote?'"

"Hush that talk! You are so bold."

"Oh, my, they think she's so silly. People all over the country are laughing at her."

"Married women in some states can own property. And they are talking about women voting!"

"Oh, why? Why would we want to burden ourselves with such things? I am so happy to have a home and family to take care of."

"Still, we do have voices. Thoughts of our own."

"And to vote? Only a dream. Something to read about in books and theater. That's not reality."

"Still, it would be grand!"

"Stop that nonsense now, and someone read Shakespeare. I declare."

✳✳✳

In April, a fire broke out in a store on East Alabama Street. As always, the loyal and dependable firefighters answered the call. They first made sure that all citizens were out of the building. Then, while some firefighters were preparing the buckets and hoses, the runners desperately worked to remove all unsafe materials from the area. Levin Blake eyed some explosives in the back corner behind the counter and dangerously close to the flames.

"Levin, get out of there. Leave it!" he heard a partner yell.

"No, I can get it. It will cause too much damage if it explodes!" he shouted and ran to grab the keg of gunpowder. It was heavier than he thought, and it took longer than he anticipated to retrieve. The flames attacked the keg and his hands, and before he could drop it, the keg exploded. The sight was too much to bear for his colleagues as they rushed toward him, one grabbing another to save each other from the flames.

"I'm going for him. I need to get him out of there," called Mack.

"No, Mack, get back here. You can't help him now," Bill struggled while restraining his partner. They both heaved and broke down helplessly.

"Water, get the water over here," Mack said as they tried to save the body from further damage. Removing his partner from the flames became the priority. All else faded away.

Gradually, the billowing smoke was extinguished but not without claiming the most beloved life of an Atlanta firefighter.

The first recorded death of a fireman while performing his duties shook the townspeople. It was a difficult time for the Atlanta Fire Department. All firefighters of both companies felt the pain. Everyone in town was present at the funeral. Bagpipes were played and gospel music filled the air. The firefighters petitioned city council for money to buy a metal casket to send Blake's body to his family in Baltimore, Maryland. The request was granted.

As a result of Blake's tragic death, the firemen purchased a group of cemetery plots at the Atlanta Cemetery in the event of an untimely death of one of their own in the line of duty.

✳✳✳

As it became warmer and the dogwoods began to bloom, Atlanta was growing with opportunities. Already established as a firefighter and city official and working hard at the Georgia Railroad, Mack was ready for a business of his own.

He began discussing business options with a friend who was also a fellow firefighter, Mr. Rodes. Before the end of the year, they decided to open a grocery store together, and they couldn't resist a desirable storefront on Decatur Street between Pryor and Ivy streets. The space between the Trout House and the Masonic Lodge fit the bill.

The men were excited about their new venture. They made plans to put up their store sign, Mecaslin and Rodes – Grocery and Produce Dealers. The whole town turned out for the grand opening of the store on December 15 and celebrated another business in Atlanta.

CHAPTER 10

"But this momentous question, like a firebell in the night, awakened and filled me with terror. I considered it at once as the knell of the Union. It is hushed indeed for the moment, but this is a reprieve only, not a final sentence. A geographical line, coinciding with a marked principle, moral and political, once conceived and held up to the angry passions of men, will never be obliterated; and every new irritation will mark it deeper and deeper."

~ *Thomas Jefferson in a letter to John Holmes regarding the Missouri Compromise, 1820*

1860

In January and February, meetings were held by some merchants to consider withdrawing from some Northern trade due to the extra fees that the Northern merchants charged Southern merchants. The Mercantile Association was created for protection and solidarity of Atlanta businesses. They discussed how to build Atlanta trade, investigate the discrimination in taxing of freight at different ports, and highlight Atlanta as a port of entry.

In January of 1860, the Atlanta City Council asked that the four fire companies be combined into one single volunteer unit so they might work more cohesively under one command. Two weeks later, the firemen from all four companies met at Firehouse #1, where it all began. The presidents of each company were seated at the front of the room.

President Barnes of Mechanics #2 spoke first. "As you well know by now, the city council has asked the four companies to work as one unit to better serve the city. Do we all agree that this arrangement is the best for our city?"

The men discussed the proposal amongst themselves, and finally, Barnes interrupted: "I think it's time for a vote. All in favor say 'Aye.' I see all hands are raised. Therefore, a unanimous response allows us to combine all companies." As a result, a new constitution was developed, providing for a chief engineer and officers. Barnes was elected chief engineer of the newly formed Atlanta Volunteer Fire Department.

Following that, Mecaslin became the president of Fire Company #1. "Let us all welcome each other back to the fold," Mecaslin stated. "Reach out to the brothers who moved on from the #1 to create new companies. The newer members are now a part of one unit. Put aside any differences and work as one. Answer the call!"

An ordinance was passed that if a fireman called on citizens to help with a fire, they must do so.

Mecaslin, Barnes, and Rodes, among others, fought fires as a team against great odds and, lacking proper equipment, put their lives on the line to save their fellow Atlantans with no pay, only the satisfaction of knowing they did what they could to save the city and its people from fire. This group of men worked so hard and worked so well together. Little did they know that the bond they were creating would be extremely important in the coming years.

Another order of business that year was the purchase of property and construction of a new building for Fire Company #1. A lot was purchased on the west side of Market Street, but construction had only begun. Other events quickly became more important.

Mecaslin also joined forces with fellow firemen William G. Peters and William C. Moore to own and operate the City Flouring Mills. He felt confident about this decision, having the knowledge and background to create a successful flour mill as his father had done on Pine Street in Baltimore.

✻✻✻

As 1860 wore on, states discussed the upcoming election and possible secession from the union. Mecaslin picked up the newspaper daily to see what events had transpired. A political speaker, Senator Stephen A. Douglas, Democratic candidate for president, came to Atlanta to speak about popular sovereignty. Mecaslin, along with Thomas Maguire and his other friends and citizens of Atlanta, attended the speech, as they were interested in what he had to say. The speech took place in Market Square, and the railroad station was packed. The speech lasted more than two hours. Mecaslin and Maguire were not impressed. They agreed that he had some good points, such as not seceding, but they didn't agree with his other doctrines that seemed revolutionary. Douglas believed that, although it would enrage the South, territories and Congress had the right to elect legislatures and vote on whether or not they should have slavery. He stated, "If the people are opposed to slavery, they will elect representatives to that body who will, by unfriendly legislation, effectually prevent the introduction of it into their midst."

"Gentlemen, please join me at our home as soon as you leave here. I think we should take this opportunity to discuss today's events," Mecaslin said.

Barnes, Rodes, Kidd, Ennis and their other friends met at Mecaslin's home. In the library, the conversation became fanatical.

"Mr. Douglas does not have our best interest at heart, gentlemen," stated Barnes. "We should have the right to do as we please, according to the Constitution and states' rights."

"Now, I am not impressed with Mr. Douglas, but whether we should secede is another story," replied Mecaslin.

One man stood up and yelled, "To whom are you loyal, gentlemen, Union or Confederacy? Is it loyalty to Georgia or to your own dear Atlanta? This war will not be fought on Atlanta soil. It will all take place in and around the Capitol in Washington. However, we should protect ourselves."

"I think we should prepare ourselves against a government that tries to change our very way of living," a city council member retorted. "I think we should organize minutemen to be ready to second any attempt to secede from the Union and stand by our Southern neighbors."

"Aye, sir. All in favor say 'Aye!'"

The room was bursting with the feeling of unbelievable optimism as everyone chanted, "Aye, aye, aye, sir." The minute men of Atlanta were beginning to assemble that evening.

However, Mecaslin did not rush to join, as he could sense a foreboding sign and a difficult time if secession should begin. He hesitated as he thought of his family and friends in Baltimore. *What next*, he thought. Surely his home of Maryland would remain loyal as a Southern state. That evening, he wrote a letter to his father discussing the events of the day as he wondered what was going on in Baltimore.

At a meeting on October 31, an armory of Atlanta Grays was created and the Minute Men Association was formed.

November 6, Election Day, would determine the fate of the Republic. They would know whether its days were numbered or whether confidence would be restored between the people of the North and South.

***

After Atlantans voted for their presidential candidate on voting day, the results indicated that the majority (more than 1,000) voted for John Bell of Tennessee of the Constitution Union Party, followed closely by John Breckinridge from the Southern Democrats of Kentucky with 835 votes.

The Constitution Union Party was created in 1860, consisting mostly of the former Whig Party and Know-Nothings, whose platform was simply to follow the laws of the Constitution. They hoped that by avoiding the slavery issue, it would solve itself. The avoidance of the slavery issue had taken place during the making of the Constitution, and everyone during the time of the creation of the new Union in the 1780s knew that, if they had denied the Southern states limited slave trade or abolished slavery, it would end the union of the states before the new government had a chance to begin. Also, the states of the Union were so afraid that the federal government would try to put limitations on the states to the point that they would lose the freedom for which they had fought so hard to obtain during the Revolutionary War.

Breckinridge of the Southern Democrats wanted to keep the institution of slavery. As more states joined the Union, the question of whether the Union should allow those states to be free or slave states was a huge issue.

Abraham Lincoln of Illinois represented the Republican Party, which was interested in confining slavery to the existing states and not allowing it to expand to the new states. Abolishing slavery altogether was not their concern at that time.

Lincoln was elected on Election Day — without a single Southern state. Lincoln's name wasn't even on the Southern ballot. Everything changed as the Southerners felt that they were not represented properly.

Two days after the election, a meeting of the minutemen was held, and secession was discussed. Day by day, political speeches were organized, and on December 10, several Southern political leaders made speeches for secession. A torch-lit procession fired up the streets. At the Atlanta Hotel, more speeches continued.

On December 15, another political meeting took place at the Atheneum.

On December 20, South Carolina seceded from the Union.

Two days later, a large number of citizens gathered to listen to more political speeches at the Atheneum. The room was packed with standing room only. More were standing outside waiting to get in.

In the morning, former Georgia Gov. Howell Cobb addressed the Atlanta crowd. A fifteen-gun salute marked the event. Another speaker raised issues with the financial implications leading to this moment:

62

"Ladies and Gentlemen,

"A few years ago, as you know, Southern banks paid higher interest rates on loans made with banks in the North. Several economic panics occurred: One in 1857 that affected more Northern banks initially, but then affected Southerners when they were charged higher interest to help save Northern banks from their financial losses. Another item that has been affecting the South for years is that Northern insurance agents required extra fees against Southerners who traveled north during the summer.

"We also have news that New York City is considering secession due to the fact that they send so much of their revenue through imports to Washington, and they are tired of doing so. New York City's mayor, only last week, said, if the country is going to break apart, he would like his city to secede not only from this foreign power — New York — but also from the 'odious and oppressive connection' with the Federal government."

The crowd cheered with excitement at this thought. *Was it true?* They all looked around in amazement at what they were hearing.

"Jesus, Joseph and Mary, what are ye saying here?" someone commented from the crowd.

"As you know, no federal income or direct taxes required the government to rely on indirect taxes through revenue. Most duties are being collected at ports. We believe that the Southern ports pay most of the revenue. Why, in the past few years, the tariffs have been raised to 90 percent of revenue, and the South has paid most of it. Our Southern ports paid 75 percent just last year. We can't stand for this!"

The crowd jeered and looked around and shook their heads.

"I don't need to remind you of our darling sweetheart port at New Orleans, the largest city in the glorious South and the grand center of cotton and sugar exports. Raw products of the Mississippi Valley are all shipped to New Orleans. Thousands of seagoing vessels and river steamers are working their magic at that port."

Secession was considered an economic boon for the Southerners, and they thought that keeping more of their money would allow the independent control they desired.

The ceremony continued. At 2 p.m., one hundred rounds were fired. Rallying continued throughout the day.

Finally, after dark, a breathtaking torchlit procession paraded up and down the streets of downtown Atlanta with a mob of excited supporters looking for a fight.

CHAPTER 11

"It is well that war is so terrible, or we should grow too fond of it."

~ *Robert E. Lee, December 1862*

1861

Many Atlantans did not favor secession at first, but before Lincoln was inaugurated, South Carolina had begun the division from the Union and created the Confederates States of America. A fury had begun. In January of 1861, Mississippi, Alabama and Florida all seceded within three days of each other. Atlanta was in a state of excitement and idealism.

Georgia was in a difficult position, being between the states that had already seceded. It would be tough to have a united Confederacy if Georgia did not secede. The citizens of Atlanta could feel the inevitability, and they waited daily for the newspaper to see what would happen at the state capital of Milledgeville. Then, on January 19, men came running out of the telegraph office yelling, "Georgia has seceded!" Soon after, the news came by train. An engineer was yelling from the train and waving his hands.

"We've done it. Georgia has seceded from the Union! Hip, hip, hooray!"

Yells were heard throughout the town. Before long, citizens, shop owners, firemen, city councilmen, and ladies at market crowded together in the square, caught up in the excitement of the moment, saying, "Hip, hip, hooray. Glory to the South!" Men jumped on their horses and began riding through the town, calling out to their neighbors, "Georgia has seceded. Glory to the South!" Still others looked on shocked and confused at the impact that this news would have on their lives.

Later that day, cannons could be heard all the way to The Promised Land near Lithonia. The people of the countryside assumed that the sounds of the cannons meant that Georgia had seceded.

✳✳✳

As the Southern states seceded, war became imminent. Lincoln believed secession to be unconstitutional. Events transpired that led to preparation for war between the Northern and Southern states. The Confederacy began to organize its government.

That night, Mary said to her husband, "What is going on? What will happen now with the Northern states? What about our friends in New York and other Northern towns, and your family? This can't be happening."

"There's no need to worry. It's going to be fine."

"Mack, don't treat me like a child. The tension is so thick you can cut it with a knife. I can't walk out of this house without hearing something about war and secession. Please talk to me."

He put his arm around her. "It's all very uncertain right now. If we do go to war, it won't take place near here, near Atlanta. It will likely be in Virginia or Maryland. I am worried about my family so close to Washington, D.C. We must have faith and patience. You and Maggie will be safe. Please don't worry," he hugged his wife for a long time and tried to calm his mind.

LADIES CIRCLE

Amid the daily political excitement, the Ladies Circle was planning the annual celebration of George Washington's birthday in February.

"A parade and hop must be planned. Who would like to make the arrangements for the parade?" asked Mrs. McFarland. Three ladies raised their hands.

"Excellent, and who would like to prepare for the hop?" Two ladies on the front row looked at two of their friends, and they all raised their hands with excitement.

"Wonderful, now is there any further discussion before we break into groups for planning?"

"Who will be giving the hop this year?" asked Mrs. Rodes.

"My husband said it would be the Tallulah Fire Company," replied Mrs. McFarland.

"There is so much political excitement right now that it makes me nervous," Mrs. Stone, Amanda's neighbor, whispered to her.

"Oh, you shouldn't worry so much. My husband says it's for the best," Amanda replied quietly.

A lady behind them overheard and added, "We should let our men handle such affairs."

"Ladies, please. We must plan the hop," Mrs. McFarland said, seeming annoyed by the side chatter.

"My sister is in New York. Does secession mean that we can't travel and visit our friends?" Mrs. Ennis whispered to Mary.

"Of course you can. And you can shop and do all of the things you want," Mrs. Rodes jumped in. "I overheard my husband say that New York City may secede as well. Then you surely will be able see your sister."

"Ladies, please! We must complete our business."

The meeting continued.

✻✻✻

An already inflamed tax policy became worse. Before President Buchanan left office in March, he signed the Morrill Tariff into law, making powerful changes in how tax duties were assessed on incoming supplies to the ports. The industrial workings of the North were favored. This greatly outraged the already dissident South. England opposed the Morrill Tariff as well.

Mack walked out of City Hall and heard two men talking on the front lawn.

"Did you read in today's paper where President Buchanan signed the Morrill Tariff?" one councilman said.

"Raising tariffs, yes," replied his coworker.

"The only reason it passed was because our representatives resigned from Congress," the first man said.

"That would really affect New York City, but if they side with the Confederacy, then the Union will be defeated. They will go bankrupt!" the second man said with excitement.

Mack continued on his way. Political conversations like this were common in Atlanta every day now.

✻✻✻

After South Carolina had seceded, the U.S. government was told to remove all of its operations at Charleston Harbor, but it didn't happen. President Buchanan had attempted to resupply and reinforce Fort Sumter before he left but was unable to complete that operation. Charleston seized all federal property in that area except Fort Sumter.

Lincoln was pressured to take action to supply Fort Sumter. He was warned not to send in a supply ship and to evacuate, but he made the attempt to send one. Confederate shots began a fight for Fort Sumter, and it fell without casualties. Decisions about who would be for the North or South rippled across the country. New York City backed away from its strong Southern stance and sided with its state due to overwhelming Union sentiment.

On April 4, the Virginia legislature took a measure of secession, with 89-45 against. Then Lincoln called for 75,000 volunteers to end the insurrection. Days later, the Virginia convention voted to declare secession.

✳✳✳

One state in turmoil due to the split loyalties between the Union and Confederacy was Maryland. Thomas Mecaslin's flour mill shop was on Pine Street, three doors north of Franklin Street. It was only a few blocks from Pratt Street and just north of Camden Station, the train depot.

He had delivered flour bags to the dock in a horse-drawn flatbed trailer and was on his way back to his shop when he heard some terrible commotion ahead of him on Pratt Street. A large crowd was following Union troops who had abandoned their horse-drawn railcars to head toward what he guessed was Camden Station. He was at the shop when Union volunteers coming from the North had traveled the same way the day before, in an effort to cross through Baltimore to get to Washington, D.C. The secessionists were outraged and determined to prevent them from passing through.

He witnessed the whole scene. The mob forced the horses of the railcars to stop on their way from one train station to another. The troops got out of the cars and began walking toward Camden Station. The crowd went wild, throwing things at them. Chaos ensued. The Baltimore police tried to control the crowd and allow the troops to get to their destination, but a riot soon led to the death of four soldiers and twelve civilians. The war had produced its first casualties. Shocked that the anger had led to such violence, Thomas Mecaslin closed his shop and headed home to East Monument Street, about a mile away, to check on his family.

Because Maryland controlled the access of northern traffic to Washington, more dissension was bound to occur. The governor of Maryland requested that no more Union troops be sent through Maryland after this horrific event. Lincoln later commented, "Union soldiers were neither birds to fly over Maryland, nor moles to burrow under it."

After that, the railroad bridges going into the city were destroyed, preventing troops from coming into town.

On April 27, Lincoln suspended the writ of habeas corpus in Maryland due to the defiance of his orders. The suspension of habeas corpus was declared unconstitutional, but Lincoln and the military ignored the ruling. It took place only in Maryland at the time.

Orders in Washington stated that a route must be provided from Annapolis, Maryland, to Washington, D.C. The governor and mayor of Annapolis fought it, but they were forced to provide the route.

Major protests called for Maryland to secede from the Union, and a legislative meeting was held on April 26. Again, against protest, the meeting was held in a strongly Unionist part of the state and, by a large number, secession was denied.

A state that had only submitted a small percentage of votes for Lincoln found itself secured by the Union, and Baltimore was under martial law by May 13. Troops entered the city.

Confederates found their way south as quickly as they could to escape the Union hold. They left by land and by sea.

ATLANTA

Atlantans prepared for war. A new thrill was in the air.

The Atlanta Amateurs, a group of volunteer musicians who performed for charitable war efforts such as the Soldier Relief Society, began doing concerts for the Confederacy to raise funds for the soldiers. Bill Barnes, as manager and chief singer in the group, was known by many as "quite the genius in his line and certainly the life and soul of the company."

People loved to hear the Amateurs sing "Come Where My Love Lies Dreaming" by Stephen Foster. Bill Barnes and his band traveled to several cities around the South, including a Macon performance on April 19.

Mary held Maggie's hand as they walked downtown. Recruitment stations were bustling with excited young men waiting their turn. Barnes and his band of brothers were playing a lively tune. He waved at Maggie and Mary.

"War, Mommy, is that fun? Can I go?"

"No, honey, little girls don't go to war. It's not fun. Soldiers fight each other. We won't see the fighting here in Atlanta. Our boys will win the war in just a few weeks, and all of this will be over. We will probably never see a Yankee. Don't you worry. The war will be far, far away from here."

On April 20, all fire companies offered their services for military and patrol duty. During the summer of 1861, the city council equipped all four fire companies with guns and ammunition. These were strange times for the Atlanta Fire Company because they were trained and prepared to save lives from fire. Yet now they were protecting the citizens of Atlanta in another capacity, willing to kill the enemy as soldiers to defend the people and property of their town.

After a victory for the glorious South at the First Battle of Bull Run, military brass bands played at patriotic rallies to encourage men to join the army. The reality of war hit home as one of the Atlanta Fire Company #1's own Lieutenant Smith appeared on the list of casualties. A great sorrow filled the air amidst the sound of victory, a paradox that would continue.

By August 11, companies of Atlanta and Fulton County were volunteers in the Confederate military service. The Confederate infantrymen looked sharp and proud as they were outfitted with a slouch hat or kepi, gray or brown woolen jackets, woolen trousers and high ankle leather boots.

Mack observed the recruitment process. He recognized a boy he had watched grow up in the streets of Atlanta, who was now a young man about George's age, excitedly waiting in line to enlist. The lad stood proudly and saluted an officer. A band nearby was playing "Dixie."

Mecaslin received a letter a few weeks later. It read:

George enlisted in the Maryland volunteers under the Federal commanding officer of George B. McClellan. We hope for the best during these troubled times. Please keep him in your prayers.

Love,
Mother

He sighed and shook his head as he flipped the letter over and over in his hand. His thoughts went back to the innocent young man saluting an officer. The North against the South became real to him as he contemplated how the twists and turns of fate had placed him on opposite sides of war with his seventeen-year-old brother.

In Baltimore, Maryland, on September 18, 1861, George Mecaslin joined the Maryland Volunteers 480 Purnell, Legion Regiment Infantry Company H. The legion was raised under special authority of the Secretary of War to serve three years. The H Company was recruited in Baltimore City and organized in Pikesville, near Baltimore City, between October 31 and December 31, 1861. The companies were recruited by William H. Purnell, postmaster at Baltimore. The command was assigned to Dix's division, Army of the Potomac, until May 25, 1862. They became a part of General Lockwood's brigade that drove the enemy out of the eastern shore of Virginia. Then they were sent to Harpers Ferry, Virginia, to prevent further advances.

THE PROMISED LAND

Thomas Maguire received two letters. Both letters had news of his son, Thomas Jefferson Maguire. Since the postal service had been delayed for weeks, Maguire carefully checked the dates and opened the earlier date first. It was from the W. Master of the Traveling Lodge in Arkansas. Dated August 2, it stated that his son had been very sick but that he had improved greatly over recent days. The second letter, from Mr. Joseph Daniel, dated August 5, stated that his son had died of typhoid fever. Enclosed was a lock of his hair. *Poor Jefferson is no more,* he wrote in his diary.

Thomas sent word to Mary and Mack about Jefferson. They insisted that he come to visit them as soon as possible. They met him at the train station on August 26. Thomas looked so tired. Mary gave him a big hug and said, "I'm so sorry, Uncle Thomas."

"How are you holding up?" asked Mack as he shook his hand.

"I've seen better days, I'm afraid. It's such a comfort to see you both," Thomas said with a shaky voice.

"Let's go home and get something to eat," Mary said to Thomas but then looked at Mack with a worried expression.

When they reached their home, Mary led Thomas straight to a chair. They sat down for a visit, but soon Thomas drifted off to sleep.

Mack picked up the newspaper and read the headlines:

Union imposes blockade on Southern ports
Confederate ships taken by surprise and destroyed

The ships they are using are too large and easy to spot, he thought, remembering his days at the docks. *They need to streamline their vessels and make them smaller and only run the blockade during high tide and dark of the moon.* He put down the paper.

The Confederates began holding meetings to discuss the needs of the South and strategies of sending cotton to Europe and other areas.

✳✳✳

Even though war was taking place, life in Atlanta was in many ways still going on as normal. On December 19, Mary and Mack had tickets to a sold-out concert at the Atheneum. They were so excited to see the amazing talent of Blind Tom. He was the most talked about pianist from New York to Charleston to Savannah, and now he was going to be in Atlanta. People had long awaited and anticipated the performance of this young twelve-year-old boy who was born as a slave on the Wiley Edward Jones Plantation in Harris County, Georgia.

Everyone arrived at the Atheneum in their finest. Excitement filled the air as citizens milled around inside and outside the theater. Mary and Mack connected with one friend after another as they headed for their seats. Then the show began.

The young man was led onto the stage, and the audience exploded with applause. The youngster, who had no visual perception, became one with the piano. He danced his way perfectly through every symphony of sound.

Blind Tom mesmerized the crowd, and audience members gasped in amazement throughout the auditorium. He received a standing ovation from the crowd.

After the concert, the Mecaslins and others were invited over to the Rodes' for a nightcap. The conversation continued about the concert. The favorite of the evening seemed to be the piece called "The Rainstorm," which was inspired by a storm that young Tom experienced when living in Alabama. He created such unique and haunting sounds from the piano that sounded just like a storm.

Mary commented, "That was one of the most exciting and eerie events I have ever witnessed."

"He was remarkable, indeed," Mack replied.

As they headed home in the horse and carriage that evening, Mack and Mary enjoyed the festive decorations that lined the streets and houses. They talked about the upcoming events of Christmas. Mary looked forward to picking up Maggie at the neighbor's house and holding her tightly.

DECEMBER 28

The fire bell at the Fire Station #1 awakened a sleepy town at dawn. Mack awoke to the alarms and dinner bells ringing throughout the area. He ran outside and could see smoke in the distance. Right downtown! "Mary, ring the bell!" he yelled as he jumped on his horse and headed to town. No time for changing clothes. Other men began to head that way.

"Let's go, boys. Where is it?" He headed straight for the smoke and a sight gripped him that sickened and terrified him. His store was going up in flames. "What the devil?" Others were at the station across the railroad tracks preparing to deliver Blue Dick, but they couldn't move fast enough. Mack saw Charlie, his partner, and yelled, "Grab a bucket! We can't wait." Both men grabbed buckets and headed for the cistern. They kept looking back over their shoulders in disbelief. Their feet seemed to be in slow motion, even though they were moving as fast as ever. Their training took over.

Blue Dick arrived, and they hooked up the hoses. Finer men couldn't have worked on the fire. People came from everywhere to help. For hours, they attempted to salvage some part of the store, but it was of no use. They lost everything. Their gallant efforts turned to preventing any collateral damage. The Trout House and Masonic Lodge on either side were carefully monitored and suffered little damage.

Mack and Charlie spent most of the next day searching through the ashes for a sign of what caused the fire. Nothing.

"What happened? What caused the fire?" he questioned his fellow experts.

"Could have been arson," a policeman said.

"Did you leave your cigar burning when you closed up?" Mack asked Charlie.

"No, you know I am careful about that sort of thing," Charlie responded defensively.

"Of course," Mack said quietly.

That evening, Mack asked several friends and city officials to join him at his house for a meeting.

"We need to investigate more thoroughly to determine what caused it. It may take some time," the sheriff said.

The mayor jumped in, "When was the earliest train this morning? Six a.m.? Could someone have deliberately torched it as some sort of political statement?"

"Surely that type of arson has not reached our town," said Barnes.

The mayor looked at the sheriff and said, "We have forty-four trains going through here all day and night. It could have been anybody. Look again for some kind of explosive or remnants of a torch."

Later they discovered part of a jar while sifting through the rubble.

"This doesn't look like something from the store," Charlie noticed.

"Greek Fire! It must be. Damned Yankee," Barnes exclaimed.

"Joseph, Mary and Jesus, what are you saying here?" Mack said in shock.

"Greek Fire is an incendiary concoction of sulfur, naphtha and quicklime. All you have to do is throw it, and when it hits something and breaks and is exposed to air, it bursts into flame," explained Barnes.

"Why do you think they would target my store? Or was it an attempt to take out the Trout House and Masonic Lodge — the entire street? And Mecaslin and Rodes was the central location?" Mack asked.

"Maybe. We may never know," his trusted friend replied.

"We must be vigilant and report anyone who looks suspicious," Mack said to his comrades.

It became difficult to tell who was friend or foe in Atlanta after that, and caution led to fear and mistreatment of citizens, even among those who had lived in Atlanta for years.

CHAPTER 12

"Duty then is the sublimest word in the English language. You should do your duty in all things. You can never do more. You should never wish to do less."

~ Robert E. Lee

1862

At city hall, councilmen crowded around to congratulate the newly-elected mayor and Mecaslin, who was appointed as city treasurer. "Congratulations, Mr. Mecaslin, on your appointment. You are the man for the job," the mayor said.

"And to you as well, sir. It is providence that has led me here. I am most grateful for this opportunity," Mecaslin smiled.

"Pardon the interruption, gentlemen, but I heard that the Yankees are off the coast of Savannah. It appears that the Union navy has positioned a fleet along Georgia's most prominent port city," said a councilman who had just arrived.

"What action are we taking?" asked the mayor. He looked around for an answer but didn't receive one.

"If they take Savannah, our blockading efforts will become extremely limited," said the councilman.

The Confederates desperately needed the support of Britain and France to challenge the United States. Britain and France depended on Southern cotton. Southern planters temporarily withheld cotton against the British in 1861 and 1862 to try to get them to side with the Confederacy, but Britain and France were reluctant to do so unless the South was winning. Britain and France were able to get cotton elsewhere, and the Union made it clear that joining with the Confederates would be war with the United States. Britain and France would lose grain, exports and investments with the Union otherwise. The Europeans monitored the situation and had many diplomatic talks during that time.

THE PROMISED LAND

In February, folks at the plantation received one disappointing report after another about the war. Fort Henry, Kentucky, was taken by the Yanks. Then more bad news from the battlefields in Kentucky and North Carolina. The Army of the Tennessee at Fort Donelson delivered good news. Only days later, Fort Donelson was taken by the Federals. Five thousand Confederates were killed and ten thousand were taken prisoner. Good news and bad news.

Soon after, the Yankees marched on Nashville. Confederate telegraphic reports from Nashville said, "*We cannot hold it, all our guns and ammunition lost.*"

Yet farm life at The Promised Land carried on as the workers shelled corn and spun cotton until the rain stopped. Idle hands are the devil's workshop. Always clothes to mend or wood to chop.

As soon as March began, Maguire went to Lithonia to see the muster. A couple of days later, after an early breakfast, Maguire and nearby plantation owners David Anderson and B.P. Weaver drove to the nine-mile post from Lawrenceville, the place of rendezvous for the Confederate volunteers. Fifty-four men were assembled and lined up. B.P. was elected captain without opposition, Andrew Ford as first lieutenant and W. P. Donaldson as third lieutenant. The men paraded back and forth for a short time and received a stand of colors from Thomas P. Hudson. The time and place of muster was appointed in town the next day. They were then dismissed.

Maguire went by the post office on the way home and saw a letter from Mrs. Mecaslin. Mary reported that all was well in Atlanta and little Maggie was growing fast.

Everyone was preparing for the big send-off of all the soldiers, including Maguire's son John E., who had volunteered from the Lithonia district. On March 10, Maguire went with Captain B.P. Weaver and David Anderson to Hudson's store. They rambled along in the flatbed wagon through rough roads in the pouring rain. They arrived at the store to find lots of folks crowded around listening to a speech from one of the representatives. After that event, they headed for the mountain through the heavy rain, and each downpour created more potholes and washed out roads to navigate. They finally arrived at the mountain around 2:30 p.m. At the train station, freight trains arrived that were packed with soldiers from Newton County, and another one arrived from Gwinnett County. Eight boxcars were hitched to the passenger train. Then Maguire, Weaver and Anderson helped to load all of the baggage on board the cars. Everything and everybody was drenched. The soldiers boarded the trains and were off amidst the shouts of a large crowd. The volunteers were on their way.

Captain B.P. Weaver left with his company for Big Shanty. Maguire and Anderson headed for home in the torrential rain. Anderson said, "What a terrible day for sending our troops to the battlefield. They certainly have courage and a great sense of duty."

✷✷✷

Glorious news was reported as April began. The Yankees were badly whipped at the Battle of Shiloh. General Johnson was killed, however. Then good news came from the Battle at Corinth, Mississippi.

As the reports filed in that the Yankees occupied New Orleans, Maguire and his staff continued life as usual. Busy hands beat out peas in the old house while men prepared a roof for shingles. Back in the garden, a farmhand hived a swarm of bees that settled up in the big oak.

In early May, Mary and Maggie took the train to Augusta to see her family, and Thomas went back to Atlanta with Mack and stayed the night. The next day, they both ate breakfast at Mr. Gullatt's house. Thomas spent much of his time wandering around town and visiting with friends. Many of his meals were eaten at the car shed. He headed back to Lithonia and stopped to get the mail. He overheard someone say that the only news was that Stonewall Jackson has it all his own way. He grabbed a paper and read an excerpt from the *Richmond Daily Dispatch*:

"Somebody said John Randolph was mad! The late Wm. R. Johnson said: 'I wish he would bite me.' If folly can be taken by inoculation, we wish Jackson would inoculate some others of our generals. There is a thing as being too smart, and persons who labor under that misfortune never do anything in this life. Jackson has gone on, blundering from victory to victory, until he has at last driven the Yankees entirely out of the Valley [Shenandoah]. A series of similar blunders in this neighborhood, with a similar result, would please the inhabitants better than all the profound calculations that are keeping them here."

✷✷✷

Mack went to pick up his mail at the Atlanta Post Office and heard the chatter about Stonewall among the locals. He heard which Union troops were there and knew immediately that it was George's troop at Harpers Ferry against Stonewall Jackson's ragtag group. *What an odd state*, Mack thought, *to cheer for one side and yet hope for safety for the other.*

He stopped by to visit his good friend Will Kidd at his cigar store. Will saw him as he entered, waved and nodded, and continued working with his customer.

"Thank you, sir. Come again," he said and looked at Mack.

"New customer," he said and nodded at the door toward the man who left. "What brings you by?"

"I was picking up my mail and thought I'd say hello," Mack said.

"Glad you did, friend. Business is booming, and I don't mind that at all."

"Just heard that George's troop is up against Stonewall at Harper's Ferry," Mack shook his head.

"That's unbelievable! How is this happening?" He looked at his friend in shock.

"I don't know. Nothing makes sense."

"Listen, George will be alright. He's a Mecaslin! Tough stock!"

Mack laughed. "I hope so. I know it's about time to close up, but I'd like to buy a couple of my favorite cigars. You know the ones."

"Indeed, I do. The best," Kidd flashed his signature grin. "On the house."

"Thanks, buddy. See you tomorrow."

"You bet," Will waved as Mack walked out the door.

As he headed down the street, Mack ran into Mr. Samuel Taylor, a freeman who had bought his freedom a few years earlier. They said hello under the gas lamp on Peachtree and began to chat.

"Care for a cigar, Mr. Taylor? Fresh from Mr. Kidd's store."

"Why thank you, Mr. Mecaslin, don't mind if I do." Mack gave him a light. "What do you think of all of this business in Atlanta, sir?"

"We have new citizens every day, and it does make it difficult to know your neighbors these days."

"Indeed, it does. Why, I remember when you knew everybody on the street. How are little Maggie and your fine wife?"

"They are well and how is your wife?"

"She's doing dandy, and I bet she'll be looking for me soon. I mustn't be late for supper." Mr. Taylor grinned. They shook hands and Mack nodded. Taylor held up his cigar as if to thank Mack and then turned and walked up Peachtree Street toward his house.

Bill Barnes and Mack had been discussing for days their strong concerns about the war, and Bill finally told Mack that he was going to volunteer. Being from South Carolina, Bill had long believed that he would be more useful fighting at the front for the South. Mack told Bill, "I am torn about whether to enlist and fight."

Bill said, "Mack, we need you in Atlanta. You are a remarkable councilman and leader in the community as well as a top-notch firefighter. You know the financial aspects as the treasurer and have a command of the railroad functions. We need you here."

Mack had a strong desire to stay in Atlanta because he loved Atlanta so much and remarked without question that he would defend her with his life should war reach that far south, unlikely as it seemed. Mack considered volunteering to go to the field as well, but many councilmen and friends insisted that they needed his backbone and dedication, guidance and leadership in Atlanta.

"Mack, my friend, the only one I trust, I need to ask a great favor from you."

"Anything, brother," said Mack.

"It would give me great peace in the field if you and Will would take care of my share of Tomlinson and Barnes Smithing and Metalworking business while I am gone."

"Absolutely, you don't even have to ask."

"Look, I know that Amanda is strong, but I would feel better if you and Mary would look after her."

"I will make sure that she has everything she needs, and she can count on us at any time."

✳✳✳

A private council meeting, held the evening after Bill talked to Mack, discussed the options for the city. It was important to the leaders of the town that they hold a strong front and continue to do their part as the central point of the railroad and other businesses that were vital to the success of the Confederacy.

The population of Atlanta was growing daily as refugees headed south, and changes were being made faster than anyone predicted. The hub was becoming the primary location for organizing and moving military supplies as well as making them. Factories were making railroad cars, revolvers, cannons, knives, saddles, buttons, belt buckles, tents, canteens and ammunition. Atlanta was a thriving city, and they needed strong leaders. Mecaslin was one of those leaders.

On May 30, Barnes informed the mayor that he would resign from his post of chief engineer of the department to join the army. First Assistant Chief Sherwood was chosen to succeed him.

On June 2, a celebration to honor Chief Barnes took place at the City Hall. The following article written by W.L. Scruggs was in the *Intelligencer* the next day. It was entitled "Sword Presentation."

"On Saturday evening last, at the City Hall, we witnessed the ceremonies of the presentation of a magnificent sword (cost $100) by the Fire Department of Atlanta to Lt. Wm. Barnes, their previous Chief. The Fire Companies and Hook and Ladder Company were out in full costume, all looking as bright as a 'new pin.' It was an imposing sight, and it made our heart glad, that, notwithstanding so many of those who, in days past, were members of these companies are now absent in the tented field, so many are yet left to do the patriotic duty of fighting an enemy as much to be dreaded as a foreign foe. We have on former occasions said much in commendation of our Fire Department. We have nothing to take back. In the loss of Wm. Barnes the former Chief of this Department, we have much to regret. We witnessed his fidelity and skill on many occasions. Our consolation is that he has been transferred to another field of labor and peril, in which we feel no doubt he will be equally efficient and useful. His successor, Mr. Samuel Sherwood, is in every way worthy and well qualified to follow in the footsteps of Bill Barnes. He is always ready, when our peaceful homes and families are exposed to the fiery enemy. All praise to the firemen of Atlanta.

"The meeting consisting of the several Companies of the Fire Department, a large number of ladies and gentlemen, was called to order by the Chief of the Fire Department, Mr. Samuel Sherwood, who, in a few appropriate remarks, explained the object for the meeting, and introduced Mr. J. H. Mecaslin, who made the sword presentation. Lieutenant Barnes made a reply. The addresses of Mr. Mecaslin and of Lieut. Barnes will be found below. At the conclusion of the ceremony, the celebrated Wm. H. Barnes was loudly called for, and responded in a song, which none but Barnes could have done."

Mr. Mecaslin's address: "Through the kindness of the Fire Department of Atlanta, it becomes my pleasing duty, upon your retiring from the honorable position which you have so gallantly sustained, to appear in behalf of the Firemen of this city, and present you with a slight token of their esteem for you as a gentleman, and their admiration for you as an officer. To your unflagging energy and untiring zeal is this city mainly indebted for its present effective Fire Department. Your motto has been 'EVER READY.'

"And when flaming scenes have surrounded us, your voice has inspired the corps, and your judgment has ever pointed to the path of success; and it is with pride that I and those around me, from the time we first linked ourselves together as a band of Firemen, have watched your energetic and successful efforts to organize and build up an efficient and well working Fire Department.

"You are now leaving us for another sphere of action. To say that you will be successful is superfluous. Believe us, Chief, you carry with you the warm affections of the Firemen, the esteem of the community in which you live, and the regards of all who know you.

"Accept this sword — 'tis an emblem of our feelings toward you 'EVER READY AND TRUE.' May it ever strike for the cause of Liberty, and never be sheathed until our land is redeemed and disenthralled from the chains in which vandals would bind her.

"Accept it, Chief, as a token of love from your brother Firemen and may God, in His mercy, bless and protect you and return you in safety to your home and friends."

Lieut. Barnes' Reply (in song): "Mr. Mecaslin and Gentlemen of the Atlanta Fire Department:

"I accept this handsome present from your gallant body, and it is with pleasure that I attempt to return my grateful acknowledgements to you all for your kindness shown, and gentlemanly deportment toward me on all occasions in days past and gone, at which time I had the honor of presiding over your gallant band. Whether it was at your meetings, parades, or to fight the demon of destruction, I have always found you ever ready for duty, and giving your time, your money and risking your lives for the public good. Your motto has ever been 'To the Rescue, Boys, to the rescue,' and it has always been a great source of pleasure to me to meet you on all such occasions.

"Although I have laid away for the time being the 'Machine,' the pride of the fireman, and taken another field of action, the remembrance of the past will ever be dear to me; and now, in conclusion, let me return you my sincere thanks for one of the highest tokens that could be given a soldier. When, on the battlefield, rest assured, I will try and defend your rights and avenge our country's wrongs."

Lieutenant Barnes left the next day for the fields of battle to defend his Southland. A grand ceremony took place and many loved ones and admiring citizens gathered. Maggie ran up to her favorite "uncle" and Barnes hugged her. Other children gathered around him, jumping up and down and waiting for a hug goodbye. With his bandmates playing "Dixie," he hugged Mary, and she said, "May God bless you and bring you back to us safely."

He looked over at Mack and shook his hand. "Take care of her." He nodded at Mary.

"I will. Look out for stray bullets." They both smiled but their eyes did not. "In fellowship, love and trust, brother — F.L.T."

Armed with his shining sword, he kissed his beautiful Amanda. When the whistle blew and the conductor yelled "All aboard," he boarded the train and stood on the steps and waved. His fellow band members played until the train was out of sight.

THE PROMISED LAND

During another trip to town, Maguire heard more news from the front. In the meantime, Stonewall Jackson was busy in Virginia. The Union sent three armies to the Shenandoah Valley to meet Stonewall Jackson's small band of brothers who turned the battles into victories. One of the stories was that John Palmer wrote about Jackson's success in Garrett County, Maryland, while the guns were still roaring in his ears. Maguire had heard many versions of the story but only knew that it made him feel alive as he headed back home on his horse, whistling the tune and occasionally shouting out the lyrics to Palmer's song:

Stonewall Jackson's Way
John Williamson Palmer (1825-1906)

Stanza 2

We see him now — the queer slouched hat
Cocked o'er his eye askew;
The shrewd, dry smile; the speech so pat,
So calm, so blunt, so true.
The "Blue-light Elder" knows 'em well;
Says he, "That's Banks – he's fond of shell;
Lord save his soul! We'll give him — well!
That's "Stonewall Jackson's way."
Stonewall Jackson has it his own way!

When Thomas arrived home, Elizabeth had cooked a wonderful meal of ham, biscuits, gravy, corn and peas and they enjoyed a family dinner together. Then Maguire set out on this June evening to walk around the plantation. Everything was green and full of the smells of summer as he looked out over the rolling hills of the countryside. He began a sojourn through the Trail Field, then the Ford Field. He followed the creek to the little bottom and looked down to the big bottom where the hands were working. He walked down and talked with them for a while and relaxed with a drink. Continuing on his walk, he traversed the hill to the new ground through the Ford Field and over the Farmer Field. *What an abundant space this is*, he thought. Indeed, The Promised Land. He looked around at

80

all of the oak trees and pines. The livestock grazed gratefully in the warm night air. A cool breeze picked up on the top of the next hill, and he stopped to gaze across the vast land once again before heading across the Moore Field on his way back home.

On July 4, Thomas learned that his son, John E., was wounded. Thomas immediately left for Atlanta to get a passport. His boy was in Richmond, and the travel was going to be tough. David Anderson said that he would go with him, and they were on the next available train to Augusta. When they arrived, they hunted down Thomas's brother and next-door neighbor to the Mullin family, John J. He immediately made arrangements and went with two other men to the South Carolina depot. They hopped on a crowded train that took them to Weldon, North Carolina. They missed the next connection to Richmond and had to wait twenty-four hours to get the next train out. They finally arrived at Richmond at eight o'clock at night and slept all night on the floor of the station. They rose early the next morning to search for Christian and Lee Hospital. When they approached the hospital, they found they could not get in until eleven o'clock. After waiting around for hours, they finally found John E. He was happy to see his father, uncle and friend. It felt like home again. He was wounded but soon able to walk about. A few days later with proper care from the hospital and comfort from family, he was discharged and able to go home.

The train depot was terribly crowded, but on the train to Lynchburg, they were fortunate to find a spot on the floor for John E. to relax. David and John J. were left hanging off the steps of the train as they drove off.

Their travels took them over the mountains through Bristol, Virginia, Morristown, Tennessee, and further south through north Georgia. They began to see familiar territory as they passed through Dalton and headed south to Atlanta.

When they finally arrived in Atlanta days later, they made plans to stay at the Atlanta Hotel, but the Mecaslins insisted that they stay with them. By the time John E. and family arrived in Atlanta, he was not feeling well from a tedious and difficult trip. Mack immediately called for Dr. D'Alvigny to check on him. Mary and Maggie spent the greater part of the day looking out for her cousin. He was in good hands as his aunt Margaret, Mary's mother, had made the trip to see him.

When all were sure that he was in good health, Maguire and the rest of the family went home to Lithonia and saw Margaret and John J. off to Augusta from there.

✳✳✳

In July of 1862, Abraham Lincoln called for three hundred thousand volunteers to fill the ranks of the Union army, which were rapidly fading. The "Battle Hymn of the Republic" was at first the warring cry of the Union, but a new song was written at that time called the "Battle Cry of Freedom," which quickly made it to the Union battlefield.

Lieutenant Barnes was in the field when he heard "The Battle Cry of Freedom" and quickly retaliated with his own version of the song for the Confederacy. He created his own lyrics to the song by composer Herman Schreiner:

Our Dixie forever! She's never at a loss!
Down with the eagle and up with the cross (albatross)!
We'll rally 'round the bonny flag, we'll rally once again,
Shout, shout the battle cry of Freedom!

Chorus

While our boys have responded and to the fields have gone.
Shout, shout the battle cry of Freedom!
Our noble women also have aided them at home.
Shout, shout the battle cry of Freedom!—

LADIES CIRCLE

Mary hosted the Ladies Circle at her home on Butler Street. All of the ladies were seated in the parlor enjoying tea and pastries.

"Did you see the article in the *Southern Confederacy* today?" Mary began and looked around the room.

"Please read it, Mrs. Mecaslin," Mrs. Ennis replied.

"It states, 'Much has been said about the pure waters, salubrious air, and the delightful climate of Atlanta. These great blessings which Heaven has favored us with are about to be put to practical use in a line not heretofore attempted.' Mary looked up from the paper.

She continued, "'The Medical Director of the Confederate States Army is here to establish a mammoth hospital at this place, which for convenience, natural advantages, and the warm sympathies of our citizens, is not equaled by any place in the Confederate States. It is equally convenient to the coast and the West, and it is probable we will be the last to feel the tread of invasion...'"

"My goodness, I wonder where they will build it. Or will they use one of our current buildings?" Mrs. Barnes asked.

"I don't know. Maybe it will be a temporary shelter of some kind," Mrs. Ennis replied.

Within a few months, several hospitals had been declared open. The concert hall and the medical college across from the Mecaslins were just two.

The Ladies Circle had created the Ladies Soldier Relief Society, the Atlanta Hospital Association and the St. Philip's Hospital Aid Society. Mrs. Mecaslin worked at the Catholic church as well. Later in the summer, a smallpox hospital was constructed to deal with a smallpox epidemic in the city.

At the weekly meeting of the Ladies Soldier Relief Society at the Atlanta City Hall, someone outside the meeting room heard the following:

"Will the secretary please take the minutes and write an article to be submitted to the *Southern Confederacy* tomorrow?"

"Donated anonymously from Fulton County, GA: 10 dz. eggs, 2 lbs butter.

"From Washington, GA: Paper, soap, 1 mattress, 1 quilt, 1 pillow, 1 sheet, 1 pillow slip, 5 towels, 3 pair socks. Several other contributors donated similar items and money.

"A summary of the Society's distributions from April 1 to April 8: 68 shirts, 75 pairs drawers, 18 pairs of pants, 6 vests, 9 collars, 72 pair socks, 25 towels, old clothes, 15 bottles of wine, 4 bottles of cordial, 5 bottles of brandy, 8 doz. eggs, hams, beef, butter, milk, coffee, tea, sugar, dried fruit, corn, starch, meal, grits, flour.

"Please submit this information to the *Southern Confederacy* office by tomorrow morning. To continue with other business, please note your schedule for cooking dinner for the soldiers each night next week."

Monday: Mrs. Lynch and Mrs. Stone
Tuesday: Mrs. McFarland and Mrs. Gates
Wednesday: Mrs. Mecaslin and Mrs. Barnes
Thursday: Mrs. Peters and Mrs. Rodes
Friday: Mrs. Ennis and Mrs. Richards

"Please volunteer for the following week when you can. We really need and appreciate your contributions to the Cause. This concludes our meeting for today. You are dismissed."

The Relief Society also sent shipments to the field. Items included twenty bottles of wine, two bottles of catsup, two bottles of cordial, ether, honey, pepper sauce and castor oil.

In addition to these organizations, the Ladies Circle met weekly to make quilts, socks, and other items for the men in the hospitals and the field.

On August 8, a general order from the Secretary of War exempted firemen of the state from the conscription act of that year. Many gallant and brave firemen enrolled anyway because they felt their call to support the

Cause.

Three days later, Atlanta was placed under martial law by General Braxton Bragg.

CHAPTER 13

"Yet in my dreams,
I'd be Nearer, my God, to Thee,
Nearer to Thee."

~ Sarah Flower Adams

1862

The Mecaslins and Maguires spent much of their summer traveling to visit each other. Thomas visited Mack and Mary in Atlanta, and the Mecaslins went on short trips to The Promised Land. Thomas insisted that they have a much longer stay and Mary agreed. Mary and Maggie would come to stay for at least a week, and Mack would visit when he could. Maggie was looking forward to a fun time with her cousins.

On August 22, Mary, Mack and Maggie took the train to Lithonia Station. Thomas was there to pick them up. They traveled by horse and buggy to The Promised Land. The family had a nice dinner and stayed the night. The next day, Mack had to return to Atlanta for business for about a week, and Mary and Maggie stayed to visit. Mack was seldom gone from Atlanta because of his dedicated involvement with his work as a councilman, fireman and city treasurer. Now, he was also a partner in Barnes' metalworking business located at Whitehall and the railroad.

He read in the paper the next day that Lockwood's brigade, George's troop, had been in a battle at Catlett's Station in Virginia.

Several days later, Maggie became sick while still at the plantation. She was up all night with a fever. The next day, they called Dr. Bond. He came to see Maggie that night. He said she had a cold, and Mary covered her with cold compresses for the rest of the evening. Mack arrived late that evening and heard that Maggie was sick. He went in the room to visit with her and read her a story. Maggie finally fell asleep and slept most of the night. The next morning, she was up early, ate a hearty breakfast and was running about. Seeing that Maggie was feeling much better, Mack went back to the Lithonia station to return to Atlanta.

For several days, Maggie seemed to improve, until she started coughing and complaining of a sore throat. She seemed to be getting weaker, simply lying on the sofa and finding it difficult to raise her eyes. Mary and Thomas called for Dr. Bond to come again. He arrived to check on her that evening. Her nose had been bleeding all evening, but the doctor thought that her sinuses were dry and congested and that she was no worse off.

After Dr. Bond left, Mary became concerned about Maggie's lethargy. Her nose continued to bleed, and she was miserable.

"Send for Mack, Thomas," Mary said.

Thomas called out, "Dick, saddle up the horse and get to Atlanta quick."

Dick hustled to the Lithonia station. He jumped on the next train to Atlanta. The train had to make a few stops, so by the time it pulled into the Atlanta depot, Dick was standing on the platform of the caboose. He jumped off the train while it was still moving. He ran over to a man that he knew would know Mack, and said, "I need to see Mr. Mecaslin right away. It's an emergency, sir." The man pulled Dick up on his horse and headed to the city hall. Dick hopped off the horse, murmured, "Much obliged, sir," and ran in yelling, "Mr. Mack, Mr. Mack, hurry, it's your Maggie. Come quick."

Mack and Dick hurried to the station and took the next train out. They got back to Lithonia station, and Dick gave Mecaslin his horse and borrowed one from a friend. They arrived at the plantation and ran into the house. Maggie was bad off, and Mack became concerned. He called again for the doctor. When the doctor arrived, he didn't know what to do. He checked her vital signs and walked out to talk to Mack and Mary. They could see the concern on his face, and they hurried in to be with her.

Both parents were in the bedroom, by her side, holding her hand, when she passed away at ten minutes past ten o'clock that morning. The doctor looked at the parents, reached out and put his hand on Mack's shoulder, hung his head, and walked out of the room.

Mary began to sob violently. Maggie was her life, her love, her everything. Mack was in shock as he stood by Mary, his arm closely around her. He came to realize that he didn't know how to comfort his wife. He was in such distress that he felt like he was losing control of his life. It was his place to always care for and protect his family. He tried helplessly to reach out to Mary, and she wanted desperately to reach out to him, but she couldn't. The pain was too overwhelming to do anything.

Elizabeth entered the room and tried to talk to Mack and get him to understand that they needed to take care of Maggie and prepare for the funeral. He nodded in shock and tried to move Mary, but she wouldn't budge. She held onto Maggie and cried.

Finally Elizabeth asked, "Mack, will you let me talk to her?" He nodded again, kissed Maggie, looked at Mary and left the room.

Elizabeth put her arm around Mary and said, "Dear Mary, Maggie is in a better place now. God is with her; our angel is with God. Now let us prepare for her final resting place."

"I can't leave her, Elizabeth, she's my only child."

"Know that she is not suffering. We must trust that she is better off."

Elizabeth knew that Mary needed to take a part of Maggie with her, and she asked for a pair of scissors. She held Mary's hand as they clipped a golden lock from Maggie's hair. Elizabeth placed it in brown paper, carefully folded it and gave it to Mary. Mary held it tightly in her hand. The two women wept for some time, and Elizabeth finally escorted Mary from the room.

Meanwhile, Thomas, David and some of the slaves constructed a temporary pine box for Maggie's little body.

By one o'clock, they left for Lithonia. Mary and Mack rode in David's buggy, with David in Thomas' buggy, and Thomas drove the carriage with Maggie's coffin. They arrived in Atlanta at 5:30 that afternoon. At the train station, Mack acquired a buggy to take everyone to his house. He stopped to telegraph Mary's family to come to Atlanta at once. Many neighbors heard immediately and rallied around to support them. Several ladies stayed all night. Everyone passed the next day mournfully.

Mary's mother and James, her brother, arrived the next day on the evening train. Everyone moved in carriages to the Atlanta Catholic Church and then from there to the Atlanta Cemetery. Father O'Reilly spoke to a devastated crowd.

Mary returned home that evening mourning terribly for her little Maggie. Mack was also sorely distressed, and although he tried to be strong for Mary, his eyes showed that his heart was broken.

Everyone reached out to her, but no one knew how she felt — she was numb. She nodded and smiled meekly in social courtesy. She looked around and realized that she was alone in a room full of people. *Why are all of these people at my house?*, she wondered. She smiled and nodded.

She sat with her mother for some time without saying a word. Then she reached out her hand and gave her the innocent golden lock of Maggie's hair wrapped in paper. With tears in her eyes and a tremor in her voice, she said, "Will you please make a brooch?" Margaret took the paper and held it close to her heart and hugged Mary.

As the days went on, Mary continued to mourn and wander from place to place in shock. Her pain was so great that at times she could not speak or do the daily chores. Mack and Mary became more distant. Mack felt helpless because he thought he knew how to be a man and protect his family from harm. He didn't know how to make it right.

A few days later at The Promised Land, more gray skies ensued as the neighbors reported that their children were deathly ill, and every day another child died from the symptoms similar to Maggie's, beginning with a sore throat. No one ever knew what caused the mysterious disease.

Death was happening across the countryside although the war had not reached Georgia. Sons, brothers and fathers were dying at war, and babies were dying at home. Would they have no relief from the never-ending sadness and grief? Prayer was their only hope.

Little one, sleep!
Dear withered bud! We will not weep,
For God, in His wise providence,
Knew best and took thy spirit hence.
And where His angels' vigil keeps,
Little one, sleep!

Little one, sleep!
Thy memory in our hearts we keep,
Striving to turn the joy we miss
Into a hope of holier bliss,
When these dimmed eyes no more shall weep-
Little one, sleep!

~ Montgomery M. Folsom

CHAPTER 14

September 1862

It was quiet. Mack picked up a paper from a few days earlier. He had not felt like reading the paper lately as he did every morning. More shocking news had occurred. Somehow it was far away from the devastation that was occurring right here at home. No more.

HEADLINES FROM THE WAR:

Aug-29-30 Battle at Manassas, Virginia

A Victory for the Glorious South

Mack felt nothing. No excitement over the victory. Numb. He gazed out the window. As he always did without thinking, he glanced down the list of the fallen and saw only a few people had been identified at this early date. It often took weeks before soldiers were identified. Sergeant Hulsey was on the list. Mack's good friend and comrade, a member of the Atlanta Hook and Ladder Company, a soldier of the Atlanta Grays, had died at Manassas. He had volunteered on August 8 with many of the brave firefighters who had been exempt from going to war. He thought of Bill and George. There was no way to know if they were alive. He put the paper down. Not now. Even with victory comes death. He went to check on Mary. She was still in bed. He kissed her cheek and left.

He went outside and looked around. *Peace in our town — but our souls?*

His horse was tied to the post. He numbly headed in his direction. He reached out and ran his hand across his neck and mane and grabbed the rope and untied him. He jumped in the saddle and headed toward the edge of town at a gallop, fiercely holding the reins. *Oh, the comfort of a horse,* he thought. *Familiar, alive …* He knew exactly where to go. "Let's go, Storm."

He took Marietta Street and didn't stop. For miles he rode north, then west, until they came to the Chattahoochee. The beauty, the serenity of the rushing river. Mack jumped off, ran into the river and didn't stop until he was submerged in the cool, flowing water. He stayed underwater as long as he could hold his breath, feeling the peaceful relief that only water can provide. His thoughts went to the ocean, the waves. He burst up and out of the river and back to reality.

Why? Why? Why wasn't I there for her? I'm so sorry, Mags. So sorry for my little girl.

CHAPTER 15

"Abandon all hope, ye who enter here."

~ Dante Alighieri, between 1306 and 1321

September 1862

NEWS FROM THE FRONT:

September 15- Harper's Ferry, Jackson Gains for Confederacy

September 17- Battle of Sharpsburg/Antietam

The Bloodiest Day of the War

Terrible Casualties Both North and South

Lee Withdraws to Virginia

Sharpsburg? Maryland? Mecaslin read the headlines and knew it well. That's where he was from. His brother fought for the Union out of Frederick, Maryland. He read quickly and looked for any news of

George's unit — third brigade, second division, twelfth Army Corps of the Army of the Potomac. They wouldn't provide the list of the Union troops who were injured or fallen. He looked anyway for any hint that he was there. No news. Mack began to write a letter to his father and then stopped. He couldn't risk it.

On September 24, President Lincoln issued a proclamation suspending the right to writs of habeas corpus nationwide. He had suspended these rights to Maryland back in 1861, but now he extended it across the country. Suppression set in even as the courts declared the measure unconstitutional, but Lincoln and his cabinet ignored it.

News of the aftermath of Antietam trickled in at The Promised Land. On September 25, Maguire heard that the news was far from satisfactory. Two days later, ten days after the Battle of Antietam, the talk of the countryside was that the news from Maryland was dark and mysterious. No one quite knew what was going on. It was a confusing time.

Meanwhile in Atlanta, more and more trains arrived daily loaded with passengers, surgeons and hospital cars containing bunk beds stacked with wounded soldiers.

Atlanta became a home to refugees and funerals, and the bagpipes continued. It seemed as though the funeral processions to the Atlanta Cemetery became a daily way of life, and yet each procession was just as meaningful as the last. Black and deep blue became the colors of the day.

Widows were supposed to go into mourning and wear black for two and a half years after the death of their husbands. Jewelry and veils were often worn. After the grieving period, they might wear grey and sometimes lavender or burgundy. Some women wore black for the rest of their lives.

✳✳✳

Mary wore a black dress every day and would continue to do so for years. She sometimes wore a veil when going out. Her lively personality had disappeared. Amanda and Mary became closer. Still, Amanda could not coerce her into getting out a little bit.

Mary carried Maggie's favorite blanket with her throughout the day, sometimes sitting for hours in grief. She began going to church every day.

Father O'Reilly saw Mary sitting quietly in the pew. He walked over to her with a serene presence and sat down. Mary began to cry, and he sat quietly next to her. After some time, he reached for her hand and said, "Give yourself time."

"Father, I don't know what to do."

"Sometimes, in our time of grief, if we can find a way to reach out and help others, we somehow begin healing through giving and doing for someone else."

"Thank you, Father."

Gradually, she was able to start sewing again, making clothes and socks for the troops, and was convinced by Father O'Reilly that she was needed at the hospital where the wounded soldiers continued to arrive. She carried her rosary beads with her and kept Maggie's blanket in her pocket.

She and Mack were still having trouble communicating and comforting each other. Mack stayed busy with his civic duties to bury his sorrow. When he came home in the evening, he and Mary hardly spoke.

Finally, one evening Mack could not hold in his frustration any longer.

"Mary, we need to talk about this."

"We've tried and I feel so lost."

"I do, too, but we must move on and maybe we can try again. Let's have another child. I know that no one can take the place of Maggie, but we can still love and raise other children."

"I am just not ready." She sighed and looked away.

He knew that the conversation was over.

They sat there in silence for a moment, and then Mary rose and left the room. Mack remembered and quietly began to hum the sweet song by Stephen Foster that Bill often sang at social events that captivated everyone's attention:

Come where my love lies dreaming.
Dreaming the happy hours away.
In visions bright redeeming
The fleeting joys of day;
My own love is sweetly dreaming
The happy hours away.

Mary didn't hear a thing.

While true feelings are suppressed and inexpressible, we soldier on in our attempt to find relief from the pain. Our search continues for ourselves, our identity, and our happiness, including independence, comfort and joy.

✳✳✳

Mary found herself at the hospitals almost every day after church. Not only did she help the doctors with triaging, making bandages and bathing, she spent time talking to the soldiers as well. She looked for men that she knew, but many came from Antietam now and were far from home.

One young man said, "Ma'am, would you read to me just one more time, the letter from my sweetheart?" And she did. She offered to write a letter back to her.

"Mrs. Mecaslin, please assist me," Dr. D'Alvigney called out. She ran over to help.

"Mrs. Mecaslin, we need more bandages," another assistant called out. Mary ran over to the storage space to find out that there were no more bandages. She frantically tore off a part of her skirt and handed it to the aide.

A soldier nearby heard someone call her Mrs. Mecaslin and reached out to her. He whispered, "We must be discreet. Please ask your husband to visit me."

She held his hand confidently without speaking and ran out of the hospital to honor this strange request. She ran to a friend nearby and asked him to take her to the city hall in his carriage. She found Mack there. "Come with me," she said urgently. "Don't ask any questions."

Mack could tell that Mary was serious, and when they were alone, she said, "A soldier in the hospital is asking for you."

He honored her wishes and when they arrived, she pointed to the soldier and let him go alone.

"Sir, you wish to see me?"

The soldier was having difficulty breathing. "Mr. Mecaslin?" Mack nodded. "Sir, what is your brother's name?"

"George," Mack said. "What do you know of him? Do you have news?" He looked around to see if anyone was listening.

The soldier reached into his pocket, took out a letter and partially stuffed it into Mack's pocket. Then he dropped his hand and fell back and stopped breathing. Mack looked around, pushed the letter into his pocket and called for help. It was too late. He helped to cover the man's body and asked for his name. No one knew him.

Puzzled, Mack left the hospital and saw Mary waiting for him. She said, "What is it?"

"He wanted to tell me that Bill is fine." He couldn't tell her anything without knowing what was in the envelope.

When he was alone, he took the letter out of his pocket. He noticed that it was sealed and wasn't addressed to anyone. It had no writing on the envelope at all. He opened it and saw that it wasn't addressed to him. It wasn't addressed to anyone and had no signature, yet he recognized the handwriting immediately and an anxious feeling came over him.

Hope this finds you well. The young one is a caged bird in the first city you lived in after you left.
So glad you're in a safe location.
Burn it.

Mack understood. George has been taken to a prison in Richmond. The handwriting was his father's. He burned the letter immediately.

Mack had read about the conditions of the Richmond prison. Many soldiers were crowded into tiny rooms. They suffered from hunger and disease and were exposed to the elements. Mack had read that the prisoners were often shot at for standing too close to the windows or when violating rules. *He'll die in there*, he thought.

He tossed and turned in bed that night. The next day, he told Mary that he had to go to Richmond for business. He should be back in a few days. He left the next day.

He traveled all day from Atlanta to Augusta in overcrowded conditions. He caught the next available train through South Carolina and North Carolina. He had to wait twenty-four hours to get the next train to Richmond.

✳✳✳

When Mack arrived in Richmond, he went to the Richmond Fire Department and was able to locate an old fellow firefighter who used to live in Atlanta but had moved to Richmond before the war. He saw his old friend and said, "Well, aren't you a sight for these tired old eyes of mine!"

"Likewise, my fellow Atlantan. How's your family?"

"Let's go have some lunch, and I'll tell you everything."

Mack shared how Maggie had died and how he and Mary were struggling. He talked about losing the produce store, how providence stepped in and he was elected city treasurer, and how he was still active in the city council and most devoted to the #1.

"Oh, what great times we had then. Remember the time that we had those competitions in the park? Great times! We sure beat the #2 badly that time, didn't we? And Blue Dick? So proud of our Atlanta Fire Departments. How is Ole Mack, the dog? He still around?"

"Oh, yes. He goes with us on the runs usually," Mack said. They laughed and remembered fondly.

His friend shared his adventures and challenges as well, and then said, "What brings you to Richmond?"

"Business, really. I'll tell you all about it as we're heading out."

As they walked down the street, Mack looked around to be sure he wasn't heard. Mack hesitated, then knew he could trust his dear friend from the old #1.

"I need your help. I had a bizarre experience when a wounded soldier brought me a letter from my father informing me that my brother is in prison here."

His friend listened quietly. "Not now, Mack. Continue walking."

They stopped at a small park and lit their pipes. No one was around. "You know I will do whatever I can for you, but this is dangerous business," his friend said.

"I know, but I fear for his life and want to do whatever I can."

"We are family and your family is mine, brother. I am going to make this visit short because I have business." He looked at Mack with a sparkle in his eye and shook his hand. "I will do what I can. You should go home now."

"Thank you, brother. This means the world to me." Mack headed out on the next train south.

He was afraid. Afraid for his brother, his friend and himself, but he had to take a chance.

What have I done, he thought. He didn't realize that he was holding his breath. And he couldn't tell anyone, not even Mary.

CHAPTER 16

"'Hope' is the thing with feathers -
That perches in the soul -
And sings the tune without the words -
And never stops - at all -"

~ Emily Dickinson, 1861

November 1862

NEWS FROM THE FRONT:

November 7 - Union General Replaced,
Burnside Takes Command

December 11-15 - Battle of Fredericksburg,
Amazing Victory—Our Boys are on the Move

The South is Jubilant and Richmond is Alive

Casualties and losses:
Union - 12,653
Confederates - 5,377

Mack walked out of the fire station and felt a level of excitement that he had not experienced in a while. People seemed to be more energetic. Some were waving Confederate flags, and he heard someone say, "Haven't you heard? Lee whooped Burnside at Fredericksburg." Mack grabbed a paper and saw the headlines. Looking at the number of wounded and killed, he wondered about George and if he were better off in prison than on that familiar ground near home. He thought about all of his friends and family and hoped that they were well. His thoughts went to Bill and the soldiers of Leyden's Battalion and hoped that he was safe.

"Look at this place," Mack said, having trouble getting through the crowd. "Just when you think that no more people can move through here, more arrive."

Every train was packed with as many people as it could handle. Schedules were no longer accurate due to the extra time needed to work the ticket line and board so many passengers. People were moving through Atlanta, moving to Atlanta, and visiting friends in town, and the hotels were not able to keep up with the crowds. Some people were getting sick due to unsanitary conditions.

With the cramped conditions, safety became a factor. Desperate people were stealing anything they could. Passengers learned quickly to guard their valuables by hiding them in their socks or clothes while they slept, especially if traveling by freight train — that is, if they were lucky enough to get on board.

Despite difficult conditions, severe casualties and crowded hospitals, the momentum was with the Confederacy and spirits were high. Atlantans felt the danger of the war itself was distant, and they would defeat the Yankees soon.

$$***$$

Mary continued to mourn and have difficult days. She looked in the mirror and didn't recognize herself anymore. *What has happened?* she thought. *When did I change?* She longed to see her family.

That night after dinner, she said, "Mack, can we go to Augusta for Christmas? I miss my family and I think it would do me good."

"What a great idea. I will get the tickets."

"I will send a letter to my mother." She smiled for the first time in a while.

When he went to get the tickets, he picked up his mail and found a letter from his good friend in the field, Captain Weaver, informing Mack that he would be passing through Atlanta with his troop before Christmas. "I know it's a great imposition to ask of you, but may I give you some money to deliver to my wife?" he wrote. "If the mail is delayed and I don't receive a response from you, I will wait at the gate for fifteen minutes for that is as long as my stopover. I hope that you and your family are well and hope to see you soon."

Mack wrote him right away. "I will be waiting to meet you. It will be my pleasure to carry out this important request. All is well. See you soon."

Mack was running late that day, but as promised, Weaver was waiting at the gate. Weaver saw him from a distance and waved. Mack ran toward him. "I am so sorry for the delay. How are you, B.P.?"

A battle-worn soldier replied, "Well enough but always moving, it seems. Thank you so much for meeting me. I knew I could count on you. This takes a load off my shoulders."

"Glad to help in any way that I can. How are things in the field?"

"Just left Fredericksburg. Next destination, I'm not sure, but we're preparing for the cold weather. Mack, I don't have much time. Here is the money for Mrs. Weaver. I'm grateful."

"The train is boarding; you better get going. I'll take care of everything. Anything else I can do for you?" Mack asked.

"Pray that we are victorious and come home soon," Weaver said as he shook hands with Mack.

"Stay out of harm's way, friend. We hope that you will soon be home for good."

Captain Weaver rushed toward the train, jumped on the steps, turned around and waved at Mack as the train headed north. Mack raised his hand to his forehead and saluted.

Mack sent a note by messenger to Thomas at The Promised Land, "Please meet Mary and me at the Lithonia Station at 12:30 p.m. tomorrow. We are going to Augusta for Christmas, and I have a favor to ask."

They saw Thomas as they approached the station the next day. "Look, Mack, he is holding presents," she smiled. "How sweet!"

Mary and Mack disembarked from the train and walked over to meet him. "Merry Christmas, Uncle Thomas," Mary said and hugged him for a long time, until tears welled up in her eyes. It was the first time she had seen him since the devastating losses that they had all endured.

"Merry Christmas, lassie. How have you been?" Thomas smiled.

"Hello, Thomas," Mack said as they shook hands, "Thanks for meeting us."

"My pleasure, as always."

"We don't have much time, and I hate to be so abrupt in my request."

"Go on, Mack. You know you can ask me anything."

"B.P. stopped in Atlanta yesterday and asked me to deliver this Christmas money to Mrs. Weaver. As you can see, we're on our way to Augusta …"

Thomas broke in. "Let me help you. Where is Mrs. Weaver? At home?"

"No, she is actually coming back to Atlanta from Charleston in a few hours, and we will just miss her. Will you make sure that she gets this?" Mack held out the money.

"Oh, say no more! We won't let him down!" Thomas took the money from Mack and put it in his pocket.

"Thank you so much, Uncle Thomas," Mary said. "This will mean the world to Mrs. Weaver." She handed him Christmas gifts for Elizabeth and the family.

"All abooaarrd!" the conductor announced.

He gave his presents to her and Mack. "Merry Christmas! There are some presents there for Margaret and James and the kids. Your train is boarding. Get going! Safe travels!"

Mary hugged her uncle again. "Merry Christmas to everyone!"

"Thank you, brother. Let's go, Mary! The train!" Mack grabbed his wife's hand as they headed toward the train.

That afternoon, a grateful Mrs. Weaver received the $200 that was intended for her. These acts of favor, brotherhood and community were a normal part of life among the Atlanta family.

THE PROMISED LAND

It was an abundant time at the farm because Maguire was able to kill twenty-two hogs and have them prepared, stored or delivered where needed.

Everyone at the plantation enjoyed a holiday dinner. The families of the countryside had lost so much this year but gained as well. In the spirit of Christmas, they came together with gifts and decorations and celebrated their friendship with a feast of potatoes, corn, beans, cakes and pies. Thomas remarked, "We pitched in and made the turkey squawk. He was worse cut up than Burnside at the Battle of Fredericksburg."

On Christmas morning in Augusta, Mack delighted Mary with a tiny bright yellow canary in a beautiful birdcage. It sang so sweetly. It chirped and relieved Mary some, and she smiled. "Look at those wings," she said. "Bright yellow with white tips. How beautiful and delicate." *Like the wings of an angel*, she thought.

"What shall we name him?" Mack asked her.

"He sings so beautifully. Let's name him after our dear friend, Bill. Should we call him Billy? William? No, Will. That's it. We will call him Will."

She was afraid to let Will out of the cage at first. She didn't want him to fly away. The canary gave Mary much comfort, and before long, she began to train the bird, taking it out of the cage and teaching it to perch on her hand. *He is good company*, she thought.

They returned to Atlanta after a safe and comforting Christmas with her family and friends. When Mary arrived at her home on Butler Street in Atlanta, she went into her room, found an heirloom jewelry box in the closet, neatly folded Maggie's blanket and placed it in the box. As she did, she said a prayer for her little girl and wept silently.

✳✳✳

The Atlanta telegrapher received a message for Mr. Mecaslin that day and, knowing that he was back in town, put it in his pocket. When Mack walked by on his way to the station, his old friend the telegrapher waved and ran out to say hello. He shook his hand and asked about the family. Mack did so in return and went on his way. As he walked away, he put his hand in his jacket pocket and discovered a piece of paper. As he turned the corner and walked up Peachtree Street, he pulled the paper from his pocket and read.

The bird has been set free.

He released a breath that he had been holding for weeks, tossed the note in a nearby fire bin, and kept walking.

CHAPTER 17

"I am no bird; and no net ensnares me; I am a free human being with an independent will."

~ *Charlotte Bronte, Jane Eyre, 1848*

1863

On January 1, Lincoln issued an executive order, the Emancipation Proclamation, which freed all slaves in the Confederate states. By January 10, Lincoln's Emancipation Proclamation was honored with salutes and other demonstrations at Pittsburgh, Boston and other places. On the 21st, a spokesman for the Lincoln administration advised that the slaves would remain on the plantations until their rights were definitely established. "Whatever benefit the Government intends shall be secured," he said.

Still, the days moved slowly in Atlanta as the overcrowded city experienced a smallpox outbreak. Homes were quarantined if someone who lived there contracted smallpox. Red flags were placed over the homes to signal a quarantine. Symptoms such as fever, body aches, headache, backache and chills — especially a rash — would be alarming enough to send for the doctor. Mary spent much of her time in February giving aid to the doctors as an epidemic spread.

Mary put a five-cent stamp on a letter to The Promised Land to inform her uncle that smallpox was spreading all over Atlanta. She urgently requested that he allow vaccinations to be given to all members of the plantation. Thomas agreed and the doctor arrived to vaccinate sixteen family members and twenty slaves.

The dreary winter marched on and the injured soldiers continued to be transported into the city. Time was taking its toll. The soldiers were in need.

LADIES CIRCLE

"What a wearisome time we're having."

"Smallpox has taken hold and the soldiers are in need of items and food. We can't seem to meet the demand."

"I have never seen so many red flags on homes."

"We must do something. Citizens are donating what they can, but it's not enough."

"I know what we can do. Let's have a benefit for the Confederacy."

"A glorious ball would fit the bill!"

"Keep sewing, ladies, we must keep sewing."

"We must invite everyone, including the finest families and wealthiest business owners."

"Precisely. We need donations to refill our storage rooms and comfort our soldiers."

"For the Cause!"

"Stand strong, ladies of Atlanta! For the Cause!"

The Ladies Circle met later to discuss the details. It would be held in February, and Independent Fire Company #4 agreed to sponsor it.

It was below freezing the night of the ball but exciting nonetheless. The firemen such as Kidd, Rodes and Mecaslin and the policemen arrived in their finest, and all the movers and shakers of the town showed up in droves. The ladies wore their best and most glamorous winter wraps with black dresses to show solidarity because most in Atlanta had been touched by the war. Still, it was an uplifting and spirited affair. The decorations were delightful, and the Atlanta Amateurs who were in town provided the perfect music for the joyous event. Everyone seemed to forget their troubles at least for the night.

As the evening progressed, different members of the community were recognized. Mayor Calhoun was first and all applauded him. He spoke to the attendees: "It saddens me that many of our fine citizens are not here tonight. We wish they could be with us to dance and share this time. But let us remember to give what we can so that we may help them wherever they are, and Godspeed in bringing them back to us safely." The crowd clapped in fond agreement.

Next, the councilmen, policemen and firemen were acknowledged. They all received rounds of applause from the proud city. Finally, the devoted and beloved Dr. D'Alvigny surprised everyone by arriving just in time for the waltz. Mayor Calhoun introduced him, and he received a standing ovation and an emotional hurrah! Dr. D'Alvigny then called his favorite dance.

Members of the Fire Department and city council took turns calling the dances, and everyone was in great spirits and danced the night away. A successful charity event continued into the early morning hours.

THE PROMISED LAND

An old Irishman stopped at the plantation after walking ten miles, and Thomas welcomed into his home someone else who hailed from the Emerald Isle. He felt so proud to be the host for this weary traveler. They stayed up half the night sharing stories and reminiscing. They enjoyed watching the little children playing ghost and having fun. The old man continued on his journey the next day. Thomas didn't charge him for the stay, as he did with some travelers. *I believe that did me some good,* he thought.

Thomas took the next train to Atlanta to sell the forty-three pairs of socks that he and his wife had made. Lots of people were traveling around town in a hectic pace that he wasn't used to on the plantation. He took care of business and noticed that few red flags adorned the homes. Smallpox had moved on.

In early May, Thomas received news at Lithonia Station that there was an amazing victory at Chancellorsville, and General Lee was the champion of that event. However, a cloud hung over the victory because Stonewall Jackson was wounded, and after days of confusing rumors, it was reported that he had died. Thomas sang his favorite Stonewall song in remembrance, yelling out, "Lord save his soul! We'll give him hell, well! That's Stonewall Jackson's way."

People loved Jackson and always cheered him on. He had led the South to many great victories. Special tributes were made to "Remember Jackson." Many shook their heads and said, "It's all up to Lee now."

A train arrived at the station and the conductor waved and yelled, "Yankees in Georgia! Yankees in Georgia!"

"Stop yelling that, Sam, you're giving me a fright," commented a ticket agent.

The conductor jumped down and ran over to him. "Really, you think I am kidding? I hear that the Yanks were trying to take Rome, but we took fifteen hundred of them prisoner. Then the Yanks retook all of them and claimed Rome, Resaca and Calhoun. You don't have to believe me, but I'm telling you the truth."

"That can't be true. That makes no sense. No way the Yanks can be here."

"I don't know what to believe anymore," said another.

✳✳✳

Yankees in Georgia? Railroad Cars Spread the Word!

In the paper the next day, a possibly more accurate account of the events was displayed. Confederate General Nathan Bedford Forrest, who was monitoring the situation at the Tennessee line, had learned in late April from a scout that Yankees were heading east from Alabama. He moved south to cut them off and chased some weary Yankees for a few days. He had the aid of some locals to keep him sharp and finally captured seventeen hundred exhausted Yankees at Rome.

Forrest was hailed as a hero by the sleepy little town. The celebration could have gone on for days, but Forrest sent his prisoners on the next train south and moved to the next task.

"Holy Mary, mother of God. Forrest is taking care of business! That will tell those Yanks a thing or two. Send them on out of Georgia," said Maguire, waving his paper in the air.

ATLANTA

While more wounded were sent to Atlanta, the arsenals and factories churned away, making weapons and clothing as fast as they could. More men went to war and more died. Women were left to take care of their children. However, Southern women didn't receive a pension when their husbands died as Northern women did. They were forced to go to work in the factories and arsenals.

"Ma'am, you can't go to work in that arsenal, it's too dangerous," said the pastor.

"Father, I have no choice. I have no money and no food. Many women are in my place. We are losing our husbands, sons and fathers. We can't sit at home and grieve and knit. We must rise to the challenge as our fine men have done."

"This is an outrage, our women working like this," one businessman said.

"This is war, man," said another.

One young mother had not been receiving her husband's letters and had no money. She went to work in the factory to get a small wage. Her children were kept in the church's care.

Word came a couple of weeks later that her husband had been killed. She left her job to take care of the children and make funeral arrangements.

One day, she got out of bed, took the children to the church and went to work. As she entered the factory, the women and slaves looked around and couldn't believe that they saw her back at work so soon.

"You shouldn't be here!" the supervisor said. "Please go home. You need time to grieve."

"I have no food for my children, sir. I will not receive a pension." She sat down at the table and picked up a casing to make a minie ball. Everyone stood and cheered her on.

It was uncommon for women to receive their own paychecks. Bold moves of independence for women occurred by necessity. New voices were heard.

CHAPTER 18

"There are some catastrophes that a poor writer's pen cannot describe and which he is obliged to leave to the imagination of his readers with a bald statement of the facts."

~ Alexander Dumas, The Black Tulip (1850)

1863

July 1-3 Battle of Gettysburg

The Great Victory
The Rebel Army Totally Defeated
Its Remains Driven into the Mountains
Its Retreat Across the Potomac Cut Off
Twenty Thousand Prisoners Captured
118 Guns Taken
General Longstreet Killed
Details of Three Days' Fighting
The Most Terrific Combat on Record

"Another scene in the great drama of the war was being enacted twelve hundred miles away. At the very moment when the Confederate column started upon its march to death two guns were fired from the confronting lines at Vicksburg. They were the signal that Grant and Pemberton were approaching to confer upon the terms of surrender for that stronghold. During that hour in which two armies were struggling upon the heights of Gettysburg, those two men, seated apart in the shade of a great oak, were debating upon the conditions upon which the great western prize should pass from the hands of those who had so long and stoutly held it into the hands of those who had so long and stoutly sought to win it. At the moment when the fragments of the southern army streamed back in wild rout from the northern cliffs, the great river of the West was permitted to run unvexed to the sea. The same shadow of the dial marked the time of defeat at Gettysburg and the virtual surrender of Vicksburg."

— *Harper's Magazine* in July 1863

***

The Mississippi River at Vicksburg had been blockaded by the Confederacy. On July 4, Grant entrapped the Confederate army and Vicksburg surrendered. Grant completed a successful siege at Vicksburg, which had been in the works since May 18 or as early as December of 1862. This victory cut the Confederacy in half in the western theater.

Although a victory at Gettysburg was claimed for the North, casualties were severe on both sides. It took weeks before an accurate count of casualties could be assessed. Dark and nervous days went on and on as people waited for news.

More than two weeks later, the *Southern Confederacy* published a newspaper so shocking that no one wanted to read it, but they needed to know if their loved ones were still alive.

Throughout Five Points in Atlanta, people waited for the paper to hit the streets. Mary and Amanda walked into town to go shopping and wondered what was going on. Mary stopped someone and asked, "What is the news?"

"They released the casualties from the Battle of Gettysburg!" said the passerby.

Amanda looked at Mary in shock. "Bill," she said.

"Was he at Gettysburg?" Mary asked.

"I don't know, I don't know. I haven't heard from him. Quick, let's get a newspaper," she said. Mary grabbed her arm and led her to the nearest paper stand. They waited anxiously to buy a paper. Finally, with the newspaper in her hand, Amanda said, "I don't want to read it. I don't think I can manage."

Mary took the paper and nervously looked down the list. "I've passed the B's. He's not there."

Amanda reached out for the paper. "Let me see. Let me see." She saw with her own eyes that her husband was not on the list of wounded. "Mary, what about deaths? Look again." They bravely checked the other list and, "He's not there. He's not there," Amanda said with tears in her eyes. Mary hugged her and they jumped up and down together.

They felt relief only for a moment because as they stopped and looked around, they could see that others were not so lucky.

✳✳✳

Mack sat at his desk at Atlanta City Hall, stared at the front page of the paper and shook his head, "Jesus, Joseph and Mary, what happened?" The pages were covered with letters printed from soldiers sharing news both personal and public so Atlanta's citizens could connect with more than the rumors that they had heard. List after list named casualties: shot in the arm, lost a leg, missing and captured. His head was swimming. He looked for his comrades on the lists. He didn't see any familiar names. He couldn't take it all in, so he focused on one letter:

Letter from Soldier Jim
Casualties of the Atlanta Greys at Gettysburg
Camp 8th Regt Georgia Vols
Near Hagerstown, MD
July 6, '63

Dear Cousin:
Before this perhaps you have heard of the great fight we had at Gettysburg on the Baltimore Pike, in Pennsylvania. It was probably the most desperate fight that ever was known on this continent.

After we had arrived in Pennsylvania and advanced some distance before Chambersburg, our column was halted for a few days rest, which time was consumed with washing, foraging, &c. The country is beautiful and well supplied with the necessaries of life. The boys generally lived high. They paid for what they got when the people would take Confederate money, but when they would not, they pressed for such things as needed. In walking through camps you might have found at the soldiers' table, such things as chicken, butter, eggs, preserves, jelly. &c—but we did not have many days before we had orders to march.

Our column was turned and marched off on the Baltimore Pike. We had marched two days and nights, passing many sour looking faces, when our column began to move more slowly—We wanted no better evidence that Yankees were ahead, and very soon we could see the signs of battle, for the gallant Ewell was ahead of us, and had driven the Yankees two or three miles. Our lines were soon formed and we moved forward driving the cowardly fellows back to a small mountain where they had rock fences for breastworks and their batteries planted on the mountain. Their batteries were soon charged and a number of their pieces, with about seven or eight thousand prisoners, were captured. Their dead were left in heaps on the field. I suppose they sustained the greatest loss of any engagement during the war. Our loss was also heavy but we drove them away from their position, and on the 4th we found that they were moving away towards the Capitol. Our army was very soon afterwards in motion: The wounded who were in a condition to be moved were sent across South Mountain, but those who were seriously wounded were left in charge of our Surgeons and nurses. Though they have doubtless ere this fallen into the enemy's hands.

The next day we moved off in a direct course for Hagerstown, our cavalry driving a force of Yankees before them. Since crossing the mountain we have captured about 300 prisoners and will probably take in a few more of the blue coats.

Before closing I must say to you that the few "Greys" that are left are "good grit" and will stand to blue coats as long as there are any of them left. One of the Greys, viz: George Grambling captured ten prisoners and brought them out by himself.

The casualties of our company are listed below. This is a correct report from the Greys,

Yours, &c

J. A. Adair

The paper that day was filled with letters from other soldiers and officers, telling their story and listing their casualties, dead and wounded. The people of Atlanta were in shock and mourned terribly for their people. It was enough for a day of prayer.

George Mecaslin was at Gettysburg, fighting for the other team, and Mack was tortured by the unknown.

✱✱✱

After the losses at Gettysburg, Jefferson Davis called for more soldiers, as did Lincoln. Riots in New York were caused by Lincoln's demand for more soldiers through the Conscription Act.

The New York Daily News
Tuesday, July 14, 1863

The Conscription Resisted
Terrible Scenes Throughout the City
The Telegraph Wires Cut
The Second and Third Avenue Railroads Torn Up
The Cars Used for Barricades
Several Public Buildings Demolished
An Armory Burned

Burning of Eighth and Ninth District Draft Stations
Police and Marines Beaten with Stones and Clubs
The Provost Guard Fire Upon the Citizens
The Colored Orphan Asylum Cleared and Burned
A Negro Hung and Burned
Over Three Hundred Killed, Wounded and Missing

ATLANTA

The gossip column of the *Southern Confederacy* didn't have much gossip because nobody cared to hear or read it anymore. It was, instead, calling on all men to fight.

Even though far from Georgia, the war overwhelmed Atlanta.

More soldiers were sent by train every day, and they didn't have the hands or materials to help them all. The ladies couldn't seem to do enough.

LADIES SOLDIER RELIEF SOCIETY

Mary couldn't stand it. "This is intolerable, really. We need more bandages and supplies, and I have these petticoats and hoops that I just don't need as much as the soldiers need them." She reached under her skirt and tore the bottom ruffle of her petticoat. "For the Cause!"

"Oh, my, Mrs. Mecaslin!"

"Our hoops and crinoline that attaches them will be much better used by our military as they see fit. Certainly for bandages, but with our shortage of material, perhaps they can use it to bind items for shipping. Indeed, I shall donate my hoops. Amanda, help me remove this crinoline." Amanda jumped up and helped her to take off the hoops and throw them on the floor. "For the Cause!" they shouted.

Two other young women giggled, jumped up and did the same thing. "For the Cause!"

The next day, Mary and several other women proudly dressed with less clothing than they had the day before. The hoops were gone. More bandages were available. For the Cause!

In November, an article was published in the paper about Southern women who refused to wear crinoline. They considered it a badge of "secesh" principle in support of secession. Rebel women agreed not to wear hoops. It had become their secret sign, their badge, their Rebel flag.

✳✳✳

Blockade Runners unite!

On the Southern coast, the Union was relentless in its pursuit of Confederate ports. The blockade runners were becoming more creative in their attempts to travel in and out of ports. Many vessels were being destroyed, and along with them, large amounts of valuable cargo, including gold. Risky business was the order of the day.

Late one hot and muggy August night, a secretive meeting was held in a small office at the cotton mills on the outskirts of town. Members arrived on horseback and entered through the back entrance so as not to make their presence known. High profile businessmen and plantation owners gathered to discuss their businesses and the impact of the blockade on their livelihoods. They spoke quietly.

"With the frenzied activity at the Charleston Harbor, we may need to make some changes to run the blockade. We did well in the first couple of months, but they are tightening and closing in."

"Wilmington?"

"Yes, I would agree."

"This war will be won by sea. If Lincoln cuts off any more of our ports, we're done."

"We need more investors to keep our runners happy and moving. We must have supplies as well."

"Our cotton is sitting at the railroad stations and ports waiting to be moved. It's in high demand if we can get it out," one of the local plantation owners remarked.

"Ok, who's in? Most of you know the drill. We will move our exports, mostly cotton, by rail to Wilmington. I have contacted the captains who will run the blockade. They are excellent masters of running the gauntlet. Investments are not guaranteed, but not investing will surely sink the Confederacy."

"You will have high returns on a successful journey as well as excellent return cargoes of the captain's best choices, usually coffee, beef and other essentials. I don't have to tell you that you are a select group of trusted men who must keep this meeting and all information confidential. All it takes is one tip-off to lose it all."

The capitalists of Atlanta worked their magic, and the money came pouring in. Blockade runners were in business.

Two weeks later, at the dark of the moon, supplies were loaded onto sleek vessels on the dock at Wilmington. The best of the best prepared to run the gauntlet.

The news spread throughout town that the Yankees were heading toward Atlanta. A councilman in the square spoke up, "This can't be true! Nothing could be further from the truth. Our courageous soldiers will never, ever allow the Yankees to get anywhere near Atlanta."

That same day, an article in the *Intelligencer* read:

From Headquarters Military Post
Atlanta, GA
Sept. 1, 1863

Gen'l Orders #2

I.   *All absentees from the Provost and Atl. Fire Battalion are hereby ordered*
        to return and report to their commands immediately.
II.   *All furloughs and leaves of absence heretofore granted are hereby revoked.*
III.   *The Atlanta Fire Battalion is hereby ordered into camp at 3 o'clock this*
        inst. at Walton Spring with blankets.

By Order
G.W. Lee
Maj and A.A.G. Comd'g Post and
Lt. Col. Comd'g Fire Battalion

"Atlanta Fire Battalion report to duty. No more leave. Return immediately," Mack said, turning to Rodes. He had recently been commissioned as major and became the mustering-in officer.

Ten days later, political discussions were held throughout Atlanta, addressing an article that was written in the *Intelligencer* that morning about prominent Northerners discussing the fate of the South. A rally was held at the passenger station.

"Gentlemen, we must address the information that has reached our hands via the *Intelligencer* today," a local politician began.

"I am outraged at the idea that these Northern characters are suggesting," yelled a man in the crowd.

"Indeed, that they think they can determine the fate of the South through their supposition that we will lose, and they should therefore prepare for subjugation and reconstruction of our lands," continued the politician.

"Having written a letter on the subject, Mr. Whiting, Solicitor of the Federal Treasury to the Union League of Philadelphia, which is semi-official but nonetheless a valid discussion from a prominent Northerner. And the other, kind sirs, is none other than General Alvea Hovey. He presented his letter to a Democratic meeting in Indianapolis. Known as the 'hero of Champion Hill,' he claims to represent nine-tenths of the Yankee army.

"Mr. Whiting's letter states, gentlemen, that a consequence of subjugation should be the abolition of Southern state lines and the reduction of the seceded states to a territorial condition, admitted back to the Union as the Northern states may designate.

"He seems to think that should the Confederacy reenter the Union, as if we would, that Civil War removes the lines of states, and the only boundary is that from its enemy."

"And please, discuss with us the second consequence proposed by Mr. Whiting, should reconstruction take place," called out another man.

The Atlanta politician went on, "The emancipation of all blacks throughout the Southern states, which was sanctioned by the President at the beginning of this year.

"He then urges that to fail to accomplish this end thoroughly and effectually would be to break the nation's faith with Europe, and the colored citizens and slaves in the Union — a depth of unfathomable infamy from which he earnestly hopes they may be saved, despite whatever disasters may befall their arms, or humiliation be in store for them.

"As for General Hovey, who claims to represent the sentiments of nine-tenths of the army, his proposition forms the third and closing scene, the finale of our subjugation. It is the partition of our lands among Northern soldiers. We will let him speak for himself, for his language is as explicit and unambiguous as it is possible for us to employ."

He waved the newspaper in the air and then read a section of Hovey's letter from the paper:

"'A word in regard to the property of Rebels. In my opinion they have forfeited all, and their wealth should be so used as to prevent a repetition of their crime. Their personal property should be used in defraying the expenses of the revolution. Their slaves must be released and liberated, and their lands, as far as practicable, divided among our soldiers who have nobly sustained the Government in the hour of its sorest trial.'

The speaker then asked, "May I continue with the sentiments of the editor of the *Intelligencer*? For he speaks for us well:

"'These three propositions then, namely, the obliteration of all State lines and the reduction of the whole country of the South … partition of the lands of the South among the soldiers as rewards for their services, fill up the entire programme, which, to use a figure of speech, has been published and placed in the hands of every soldier now fighting in the Northern army.'

"This, they will have a right to expect, would be faithfully carried out by the Northern government in the event of the subjugation of the South, and even if Lincoln and Seward had the disposition to depart in the least iota from it, of which they have never given us the slightest reason to suppose, then that army, already consolidated and thoroughly infused with those grand ideas which have been served as their beacon in all their mad schemes of invasion, would have it in their power to *demand* that it should be carried out to the last jot and tittle of the record.

"'We lay this brief statement of the designs of our enemy before the people of Georgia, to let them see for what they are fighting and what they are fighting to avoid.'" He glanced up from the article and looked around.

The crowd became excited and panic ensued. The shocking discussion opened the eyes of the Southern community to the consequences if their Cause was lost.

"And now we have heard of Yankees in Georgia, our finest Fire Battalion has been called back to the city's defense, and then we read such news from the Northerners who have received this one and all," the speaker rallied the group.

The crowd began to yell and shake their fists. "We will not be defeated! They will not take our homes! Victory to the South!"

"Let us rally and fight. Spread the word!"

The troops soon engaged in a great fight along the northern area of the Tennessee/Georgia line at Ringgold and Chickamauga.

This series of events prompted a succession of political speeches discussing the future of the South followed by a grand visit by the president of the Confederacy on October 8.

As President Davis arrived in Atlanta by train, a celebration was waiting for him. The band struck a chord with "Dixie."

Oh I wish I were in the land o' cotton,
Old times there are not forgotten,
Look away, look away, look away,
Dixie Land.

The passenger depot was covered in red, white and blue. The Stars and Bars were draped throughout the town. The celebration took place at the Trout House.

The firemen took part in the celebration. They were in their finest uniforms, and when Davis got off the train, the firemen were lined up on both sides, creating a pathway for him to the stage where he was scheduled to speak. The citizens were everywhere. They were on every corner and at every store entrance. The passenger station was consumed with citizens. Men and boys had climbed on top of the trains so they could get a better look. Boys were perched in trees nearby. Mary beamed with pride as she watched her husband in service to the city.

Davis' speech rallied the crowd, and it was well received. He left the stage and entered a buggy. The firemen led the way, on horse and on foot, down the streets of Atlanta. People were lined up all along the way, waving their flags of hope. The parade continued around the town and returned to the Trout House for a celebration. A new blast of energy and urgency filled the air.

Davis continued on his southern tour but came back through Atlanta two more times that month from Marietta. His travels would bring him through Atlanta often because it was a common connecting point.

At the end of November, Lincoln gave his Gettysburg address, and in the South, the Federals won the Battle of Chattanooga near the Tennessee/Georgia line. A few days later, the Confederates won the Battle of Ringgold in North Georgia.

An Ad in the *Intelligencer* in November showed an abundance of goods for the holidays:

For Christmas
Old Whiskey, lemons and sugar
Sugar cured hams, wine and coffee
Pepper, spice, ginger and soda
Bacon, flour, rice, lard and butter
Genuine Windsor soap, wax and tallow candles,
Liverpool washing soap and potash,
Chewing and smoking tobacco, the latter cheap to soldiers

— *For sale by Edwardy*

Christmas at The Promised Land found the children up early, excitedly looking to see what Santa Claus brought them. They were delighted to find candy in their stockings. They soon woke up the entire house. Maguire watched the children play while his thoughts turned to the threat along the state border.

CHAPTER 19

"Poor boy! I never knew you. Yet I think I could not refuse this moment to die for you, if that would save you."

~Walt Whitman, Drum Taps, 1865

1864

The winter of 1863-64 was the coldest in Atlanta's history. The temperature was eight degrees every day since Christmas. On New Year's Day, it was six degrees. Zero degrees at night. Cows and pigs that were left outside were found frozen. People started to bring their livestock into the house to keep them alive. Bringing animals inside also prevented looters from stealing.

It became more difficult to stay warm, as there was a shortage of firewood because the arsenal needed it.

Paper was also hard to come by. The newspapers used a variety of types of paper as newsprint. They began using paper of less quality and eventually even brown wrapping paper and straw-colored paper.

On January 10, John Mecaslin, president of Fire Company #1, was elected chief engineer of the Fire Department.

From February 22-27, a number of skirmishes were reported around Dalton, Georgia, but the Northern troops withdrew, another reminder during the cold winter that war was knocking on Atlanta's door.

In the spring, the state legislature passed a bill that created the "Atlanta Fire Battalion." This organization came under command of Lieutenant

Colonel G.W. Lee of the post of Atlanta. On April 12, Chief Mecaslin was commissioned as major in command of the Third Battalion Georgia State Guards, Thirty-fifth District GA Volunteers. The Thirty-fifth District included Clayton, Fulton and Cobb counties, a large area that swept from the northwest to the southeast of Atlanta, including Marietta and Jonesboro.

In early May, General William Sherman began moving his troops out of Chattanooga along the railroad route toward Atlanta.

On May 7, General Sherman took Tunnel Hill, which is named for the tunnel that was completed in 1850 and was the first railroad tunnel to be completed south of the Mason-Dixon line. It linked rails from the Atlantic to the Mississippi River. The construction was 137 miles long, took thirteen years to build and cost $4 million.

Sherman was housed at a three-story hotel located nearby called the Austin House until May 12. While there, he received news about nearby battles. One important activity was that his commander McPherson wasn't able to cut the railroad lines at the nearby town of Resaca, which would have cut General Joseph E. Johnston's supply line to Atlanta. After going through the unguarded Snake Creek Gap on May 9, the Union secured that area. Johnston retreated.

All attention turned to Resaca.

✳✳✳

Battle of Resaca on May 14 and 15

Confederate General Johnston sent word to Atlanta via telegraph that he urgently needed supplies and hospital cars to take back wounded soldiers. Major Mecaslin, chief of the Atlanta Fire Department, received the telegram and ordered firemen from each unit to load guns, rations, magazines, and medical supplies on the boxcars at the Western and Atlantic Railroad to be transported north to the front.

Members of the fire departments immediately loaded supplies on the W&A going north and arrived in Resaca late on May 14. Soldiers were there to take supplies, and the firemen went into rescue mode. They went out into the field wherever the wounded were and helped with triage, wrapping wounds and providing help as needed. They carried the wounded back to the boxcars that were designed for hospital care and placed them anywhere a bunk was available. After those were occupied, the wounded were placed on the floor. They made a hasty retreat back to Atlanta hospitals that same night.

This battle was considered the first of the Atlanta Campaign. Johnston retreated south toward Adairsville during the night of the fifteenth. The number of wounded were high on both sides.

Confederate officers Hood and Polk wanted to attack, but Johnston retreated again at Cassville. Rumors were that he didn't want to stay and wait for the enemy to attack. Soldiers could hear the Feds cutting timber in the distance in preparation. Confederates moved on a by-road to Cassville station on the main road to Cartersville.

Meanwhile, back at the Atlanta Hotel, Patrick Ennis, the bartender, asked one of his customers, "Where are our boys now?"

"They keep falling back. From Adairsville to Cassville and Kingston. They're heading our way!"

"Don't worry. We'll stop 'em," he said as he poured another drink.

On May 17, Sherman's army was victorious at the Battle of Rome, Georgia.

An ad in the *Intelligencer* called for eighty good men who were not under conscription to report and receive good wages for being guards for the businesses in Atlanta.

MARYLAND

Prisoners filed in and infirmaries were numerous, especially after Gettysburg. A serious discussion of the abolition of slavery took place.

ATLANTA

In June, Mecaslin put a notice in the paper to call all available firemen in the city to meet with him. He had hopes that they would show up in large numbers so they would have a strong troop to defend Atlanta. They trickled in, but after an hour of waiting, he looked around. Eighty souls showed up.

Mack was discouraged, but he couldn't show it. He held his head high and carried on with his instructions. He could not falter. Strength and focus were required at this time.

He discussed the current status of Atlanta and prepared his men for battle. He encouraged them to spread the word to all men of Atlanta to answer the call.

✳✳✳

Mary woke up one night and had a strange feeling. Mack wasn't beside her. She called his name. No answer. She was beginning to get nervous and crept downstairs. "Mack?" No answer. All was quiet in the parlor and library, so she tiptoed quietly to the back of the house and looked outside.

She saw light in the kitchen window and wondered if she should go out or stay in and wait for Mack. She summoned her courage and opened the door and went outside, barefooted. She ran over to the window and looked in and saw her husband with a shovel in his hands. The floor planks had been removed, and he was digging a hole.

Relief followed by confusion. *Has he lost his mind?* She opened the door. "What are you doing?"

"Oh, you scared me!" He was sweaty and dirty. He wiped his forehead. "Go back upstairs now and stay there. Go back to sleep."

Confused and scared, Mary understood the urgency of the moment, and suddenly nothing else mattered. She looked at her husband with determination, grabbed a bucket and started filling it with dirt. Shortly after, Charlie showed up with a horse-drawn flatbed to load the dirt.

"We should be finished by morning. No word to anyone," Mack said to them both. They worked all night, and an hour before daybreak, the men took a trip out of town and dumped the dirt. While there, Charlie and Mack found a remote location to hide some supplies should the need arise.

***

After holding at Kennesaw Mountain for 30 days, the worn and weary Rebs packed up and marched across the Chattahoochee River toward Atlanta. Sherman quickly followed and moved over to Peachtree Creek to approach Atlanta from the north. Some of his troops were ordered to Decatur with the strategy to destroy the railroad tracks going east.

***

Mack traveled back and forth to the City Hall, the Fire Department, and out to the troops, watching out for businesses, and when needed, checking on friends and neighbors.

He also helped to run the businesses of many of his friends who had gone away to war, including his best friend, Bill. He, Rodes and Kidd worked diligently to hide or destroy any valuables of the company. The men of the town were closing shops, picking up their weapons and going to fight.

Mary spent her days at the medical college across from her house, aiding the doctors with the wounded soldiers. She ran errands for the doctors and used whatever she could at home that might help anyone in need. She ate what she could when she could and slept at the church. She didn't sleep at home unless Mack was there.

***

On July 17 and 18, a major change of command happened overnight. Hood became the Confederate commanding general, and Johnston headed south to Macon. Hood was unaware the next day when he officially received orders that a Union line was being formed at Peachtree Creek and railroads were being destroyed seven miles east of Decatur.

In the blink of an eye, the Feds were at Atlanta's front door.

On July 18, an emergency city council meeting was called to discuss preparations to protect the city. The truth lay before them. The long-denied enemy was breathing nearby. The woods were filled with mystery and illusion. The leaves were shaking and the eyes of the hunter were piercing.

"How do we protect the innocent from slaughter? How much longer can we endure the unknown? We must use every measure within our means to defend our people, property and finances. We must destroy our records so the opponent doesn't gain the advantage." These thoughts were addressed by the councilmen at the City Hall that day.

***

The lights burned late in Major Mecaslin's office that evening. As city treasurer, he finished the books that showed a $1.64 balance. He followed orders. He would never forget the balance and would do what was necessary. He gathered the books and all files, extinguished the light, looked back at his desk and sighed, turned around, walked out and closed the door. The lock in the door echoed. It was so still and quiet. He realized that this might be the last time that he saw this place. He consciously felt the weight of the items in his arms. All of the documentation of his work and that of his colleagues would be erased in history. He proceeded to the fire bin at the back of the building and set it all ablaze.

On July 19, Hood quickly formed a line of battle at Peachtree Creek, a left line at Pace's Ferry and the right covered Atlanta. Hood felt that with the Union troops at two different locations, he could divide and conquer. He called Hardee, Cheatham, Stewart, Major General G.W. Smith of the Georgia state troops and Major Mecaslin together at his tent on Decatur Street to prepare for orders.

Meanwhile, the Feds were building bridges over Peachtree Creek and beginning to cross. The other Union forces in Decatur were not able to help Union Major General George H. Thomas at Peachtree Creek without detouring several miles.

Mack sent word to Mary to find Amanda Barnes, Sarah Rodes and Mary Ennis, who lived on the same block, and go to the shelter. They knew what to do. She had already discussed with Mack what the emergency

121

arrangements would be. *Go straight to the church*. The shelter had already been supplied with all necessities. Lanterns, candles, food and blankets. *Be ready*.

Mecaslin went to his meeting with his troops who were standing by.

Having rallied the Third Battalion in preparation, Mecaslin was discouraged by the eighty men he was able to pull together out of eight hundred that were originally listed. Most of the listed Fire Department of Atlanta had gone to war in other places, and some had perished. He thought of Bill and some others and how he wished that they were here now to be with him to fight. So few men were left to defend Atlanta.

He knew that now was the time that all courage must take over, and dedication to life and property was more important than ever. He looked over at Captain Rodes and Captain Kidd and the other men he had worked with so closely and knew that all of their training and dedication would soon be put to the test. All of the bright and shiny uniforms that so impressed the town, as well as parades, socials and trips to visit and compete with other fire companies, were a distant past. The training done for all of the competitions to represent Atlanta would now come due. They had worked as a team for years to extinguish fires that threatened to destroy their town. Now it was more important than ever to use all strength and training to protect Atlanta. A serious state of mind was now ever present among this group, a readiness that he knew would represent Atlanta well. Credit would be given for each deed done and each fire extinguished. Credit belonged not to one fire department but to all men who called themselves firemen here.

He spoke to the group: "Gentlemen, I don't have to tell you that the position we are in is a grave one. We must continue our motto of 'To the Rescue' and 'Ever Ready' as we fight not only as firemen but also as soldiers to protect our families and property. Be 'Prompt to Action' as we vow to assist in every fire, never leaving until the deed is done."

One man said, "What's the point? We are all tired, hungry, and our families are either gone or suffering."

"Let me tell you something," Mack said. "Atlanta is our home. That's exactly why we must continue even harder to defend Atlanta, for our families and our friends. Most of us have been a part of its development since the beginning and have created lifelong relationships with each other. I look around at the men who built the very foundations of some of our buildings, who have established churches and fought to save lives and buildings from the evil flames. We must remember the men who have lost their lives or are in prison, and the others who still fight every day, all around us to protect and preserve our town and our families. So now, regain your strength and your faith.

"Let us follow the gallant General Hood and join with your brothers to fight for victory. Use your weapons as needed. Defend to the death if necessary. Never surrender!"

With that, the men jumped up and applauded, patting each other on the back and shaking hands. They saluted Major Mecaslin and waited for instructions. They had renewed faith in themselves and their cause. *Onward!*

CHAPTER 20

"Let Chaos storm!
Let cloud shapes swarm!
I wait for form."

~ Robert Frost, *"V. Pertinax"*

"The Yankees are comin'!"

So rang the words throughout Atlanta. The troops moved into place, and the town shifted into panic. On July 20, the Battle of Peachtree Creek began. When the shots were heard north of town, the townspeople were shocked and scared, trying to dodge the shells and run for their lives. They packed their things, attempted to board overcrowded trains or ran away. Those who had shelters hid as quickly as possible.

Mary ran to Amanda's house and saw her frantically throwing clothes into a trunk.

"What are you doing?"

"Mary, I'm afraid. I can't stay here any longer without Bill. I need to go home," said Amanda, talking about Augusta.

"Amanda, you can't take the train. Look at this place. I heard they are cutting the lines going east. You can't go yet. Stay with me. Go with me to the church, and we can talk about it later," Mary urged her dear friend. She couldn't dream of her friend leaving in this chaos. She grabbed her hand and said, "Come on, it will be alright." Mary called to Ole Mack the dog.

Amanda said, "Don't forget Will," and she smiled. Mary was alarmed that she almost forgot and ran back to her house.

"I can't let anything happen to you." She grabbed the cage and hustled back to Amanda's, with Ole Mack right beside her.

They ran from their homes on Butler several blocks through the wild crowds, passing piles of rubbish and boxes of personal items that people abandoned all over the road. The stench at the hospitals was horrible, and the sweltering heat made it worse. They reached Sarah Rodes' house beyond Five Points, ran into the house and yelled, "Let's go, Sarah, to the shelter!"

Sarah hurried to get her three children and grabbed some clothes, and they moved as well as they could through the streets. Someone bumped into one of the children and knocked her down, but Sarah picked up her crying child, and they kept moving through the muggy heat of the day until they reached the Atlanta Catholic Church.

Father O'Reilly waved them in and said, "Welcome! To the cellar, ladies. Take your dog and bird with you. You will be fine there."

"Safe at last," sighed Amanda as she sat down to catch her breath. The cellar was cool and dark except for a small window near the ceiling of one wall that looked out on the street level. They could only see shoes and legs scurrying from one place to another. The women calmed the children and animals and settled in.

✳✳✳

Hood went on the offensive to try to stop the Union before they could completely pass over Peachtree Creek and build defenses. There was a delay in his orders by three hours. Hood kept listening and wondering what the delay was, and at his tent headquarters on Decatur Street, he knew when he finally heard the firing that the attack was too late to be effective. Adjutant Claudius V. H. Davis of the Twenty-second Mississippi was killed while carrying the colors and was still waving the flag as he hit the ground. At the end of the day, casualties for the North were nineteen hundred and for the South were twenty-five hundred. The North was not able to break through the line, or they would have moved on toward Atlanta.

The next day, the town waited quietly, not like the excitement of the day before. Most of those who were leaving had left, and the others were hiding. Businesses continued to close, and the last newspaper moved south to Macon. The post office closed, and the workers joined the fight. The pressure was intense as they prepared for battle.

A Confederate strategy was developing around Atlanta. Hood kept the Second Corp along Peachtree Creek while five thousand Georgia state troops, including Smith's and Mecaslin's troops and militia, were to defend Atlanta on the east side along the railroad at Decatur against 106,000

Federals with the mobility to move more troops into position at any time. The band of Confederate men included old men and boys with limited arms and ammunition.

Wheeler had received orders to move south at dusk along the McDonough road and cross Entrenchment Creek at Cobb's Mill. At daybreak, they were to turn left and attack McPherson, who was a longtime friend of Hood's from school days.

Mecaslin's group under Smith and Cheatham had received instructions to move east out of Atlanta and hit the Union front.

Major Mecaslin was excited and thrilled in a strange way, not at all what he had expected. But he was here now in the moment, preparing for a fight for his life and the lives of his family, friends and way of life, just as his father and grandfather had taught him. Exhilarated and proud, he stood alert. He looked around at the small group of men in his care. A strong bond of fellows who had grown up together in so many ways, who had built a city and protected and cared for each other and their families. Older men, boys too young to fight, and older boys were in his care now. He thought about Mary and his Maggie and how much he loved Mary and missed his daughter. He wondered if he would survive this battle — as well as his friends. He held Mary's daguerreotype in his hand. He cleared a lump in his throat as he focused on the task at hand. He waited quietly for battle with his comrades inside the city limits, not far from his own house.

He heard two soldiers in front of him. "Hey, Johnny, you might want to use your sharpshooting skills to hit two of them Yankees with one bullet, seeing how we are so low on bullets."

The other one snickered, and said, "Yeah, I might be able to take out three." And they rolled over and started laughing and a few more soldiers laughed and broke the tension.

On July 21-22, while Hood was preparing his strategy, the Feds destroyed the railroad along the Augusta line, completing thirty miles of damage in that direction. They began to head south to cut off the Macon rail.

"Charge!" The rebel yell commenced — "Yeee yippyiiiaawwwwww!" — and companies of Confederate soldiers surprised McPherson's troops from their rear. A mighty fight began.

Major General Smith and Major Mecaslin had waited all morning for directions to move. Finally, they heard the mighty Rebel yell from Decatur and knew that their comrades had attacked the enemy but not at dawn as planned. About midafternoon on a hot day, they moved forward for battle. They fought mightily, advanced to Bald Hill, and attempted to take it.

From his location on top of a northern hill, Sherman heard shots in Decatur that meant that the Confederacy had hit McPherson's troops from behind. The Federal strategy to cut the rails to the south was denied.

Fighting continued for two days, as the Confederates were able to hold back the Union troops. They even reached the level of hand-to-hand combat at times. Finally, the Federals asked for a cease-fire to retrieve and bury their wounded. During the battle, General Hood's friend, Union General McPherson, was killed.

Bodies arrived constantly by train, wagon train and ambulance. Every form of transportation brought the wounded to the hospitals, which were soon overrun. Men were laid out on the ground all over Five Points as far as the eye could see. Men's arms and limbs were chopped off, and gory pieces of bodies were delivered to the site. Moaning, groaning, yelling and screaming filled the skies of Atlanta. The smells were sickening. Strange sights that most had never seen before, such as entrails, were unbearable, and yet people walked through it all to get to the wounded. Curious onlookers retreated in horror.

Shelling continued for a few days along the lines.

Once the shelling in the immediate area slowed down, Mary, Amanda and Sarah knew that they were needed as nurses on Decatur Street. They defiantly walked out of the cellar and took their place among the madness.

The battles continued, though, as troops moved to the west side of town and had an unexpected fight. Sherman tried moving again to the south to cut off the southern route by rail but was defeated by a gallant group of Confederate horsemen.

✳✳✳

After the Battle of Atlanta, a sense of relief and a thrilling moment hung in the air after so much fear and anticipation. A surge in morale became apparent because they stopped the movement of McPherson and Schofield. Hood was viewed as an inspirational leader. Hood would later comment that the Georgia state troops fought gallantly under Major General G.W. Smith.

The people of Atlanta were determined to not give up. A beaten and battered town limped on.

Sherman was unable to break the hold on the city, so he tried a new strategy. He began to move to the left of Atlanta with the intention of cutting off the West Point railroad going southwest. Southern Lieutenant General Lee met them at Lickskillet, and they had a battle at Ezra Church.

On July 29, Federal troops destroyed telegraph lines in Fairburn and Palmetto.

The same day, Sherman shifted to Jonesboro, working hard to destroy the railroads and roads, but Johnny Reb was soon on their trail, very comfortable in his own backyard. Jackson's troops were there in three hours to meet them. The Feds were surprised to see them and retreated.

Jackson's men worked to repair the damage.

Sherman continued shelling all around Atlanta. Bombs damaged several homes, but people began to leave their homes and take shelter with others. They became experts at dodging the shells and running for cover when necessary. Running to a stranger's porch was not uncommon; they were welcomed and made a new friend.

THE PROMISED LAND

Raiders and smaller bands of Union soldiers also spread their wings and hit smaller towns, plantations and homes around Atlanta. One of those plantations belonged to Thomas Maguire. He heard from scouts that the Yankees were at Stone Mountain around July 18, and he reported a couple of days later that he was behind enemy lines. At midnight, the yelling and commotion of Yankee soldiers breaking down the door of the house awakened him. Thomas got up and let them in. They pushed their way in and started knocking him around. They forced their way through the house, grabbing everything they could carry or breaking it. They went through each room, looking for valuables, opening trunks and drawers, and taking away keys to them. Thomas wrote in his diary, *They must have practiced roguery from their childhood up so well they appeared to know the art.*

The next morning, when Hood and his defenders of Atlanta were preparing for battle, the Yankees at The Promised Land left early on their way to Covington, Social Circle and back to Lawrenceville and Monroe. A few made their way back to The Promised Land and Durand's Mill. Thomas heard later that they set Rockbridge on fire.

That day, he recorded a list of items that were stolen — about seventy items, including flour, meal, wheat, baskets, salt, butter, soap, soda, sugar, fruit, black pepper, lard, pieces of bacon, syrup, fodder, one match, a pocketbook with money, eighteen dollars in silver, coffee, books, and one farm journal, among other items.

✳✳✳

A conversation at Five Points later in the month:

"What I wouldn't give for a good cup of coffee and a cigar right now."

"You really learn to appreciate the simple things when everything is gone."

"I'll buy you a drink, my friend, and we can toast to better times."

At Kenny's Alley, two men at the saloon talked it over.

"If Sherman takes Atlanta and heads on south from here, he could go down to Andersonville and release all of those prisoners, and then what?

They might kill us all!"

"But we are not letting Atlanta go to ole Sherm. No sir, we aren't going anywhere," and they lifted their glasses.

✳✳✳

Mary had to run to town to get some supplies for the hospital. She knew that shelling was dangerous, but the trip was necessary. *I'll get Mack's help when I arrive*, she thought. The shelling had been going on for a couple of weeks now. Surely she could make it through. One of the men had harnessed a horse and buggy for her to use, but she felt that walking would be safer.

She began cautiously but became more confident with each block she traveled. As she turned the corner at Decatur and headed toward the store, she noticed how odd it was that people were walking around town as if no war was going on. She became a little more relaxed as she approached the store. She heard the shelling in the distance and heard something hit about a block over. She moved more quickly and then, *BOOM*. She hit the ground and covered her head. Holding her breath, she looked up and around. Other people had also dropped to the ground, and they began to get up. She jumped up, brushed her skirt hurriedly, and continued to the store. She walked into the store and asked for a bag of flour. "For the cause," she told the clerk. She made her way back and made biscuits for the wounded.

On July 28, the governor declared all to defend or leave in ten days.

Mayor Calhoun called on all capable males to report for induction into military units, adding, "All male citizens who are not willing to defend their home and families are requested to leave the city at their earliest convenience as their presence only embarrasses the authorities and tends to the demoralization of others."

That day in the newspaper, a statement was printed that those who would not sign up would have their names printed in the paper daily to embarrass them until they signed up or left.

✳✳✳

On July 28, the *Atlanta Appeal* newspaper wrote, "The progress, which the enemy has made toward the heart of the Confederacy, and the enterprise he has manifested by his raids upon our railroads and undefended points, ought to convince our people that there is no security from danger but in active, energetic self-defense. The people of the Gulf States have so long lived remote from the actual theater of the war that they have flattered themselves with the belief that their homes would never be visited by the relentless invader. The events of the last few weeks will serve to disabuse them of this fond delusion and teach them that if they would continue to live as freemen, they must arm and rally to the front in their own defense.

"The guns of the tyrant foe are now thundering at their very doors, and supineness and inaction now are criminal; yea, suicidal. No one will for a moment deny but there are able-bodied men enough in the State of Georgia and Alabama either to annihilate Sherman and his army or to drive them howling back to the Ohio River. Will they not, at a crisis like this, come promptly to the rescue and aid our veteran soldiers in the good and holy cause? If those living south of us would defend their homes, their property, their liberty and the right they have inherited from their heroic ancestry, now is the time and Atlanta the place to make that defence ..."

✳✳✳

The heat of the Union troops was not the only heat on Atlanta citizens. It was in the high nineties in late July, and irritations were building as stores were looted and drunken soldiers hit the town. Citizens continued to create bombproof areas. Trains headed south, evacuating hospitals in Atlanta according to Hood's orders, and some weary doctors began to retire to other areas.

Sherman ordered firing on Atlanta all night long.

The wounded were transported to Newnan, about thirty-eight miles south on the Atlanta and West Point Railroad, as well as Macon and all points south. In Newnan, cots were all over the courthouse lawn. Refugees had poured into Newnan from all over as well. While they were trying to accommodate the influx of people, the Yankees arrived. Not much later, Fightin' Joe Wheeler arrived and defeated the Yankees. It was a terrible sight. Ninety-six were killed, and about eight hundred Yankee prisoners were taken.

Confederates were excited and high on the idea of holding Atlanta.

✳✳✳

On Sunday, July 31, no Protestant churches were open, but the Catholic churches were. Mary insisted on going to church. They knew they would be taking a chance on their safety as other churchgoers did that day. Mack harnessed his warhorse and old friend, Storm, to the buggy and lifted Mary into her seat. They gave a ride to two other neighbors who were also going to church that day. As they rode down Butler and took a right onto Decatur Street, Mary was taken aback by the desolate appearance of the town overnight. The shelling was worse, and neighbors were outside actively trying to assess the damage. Some were attempting repairs. One homeowner was boarding up the windows as if a huge storm were expected.

Mack tried to stay calm for Mary's sake but still felt anxious to reach their destination. Shells were ringing in the distance, and he felt they were taking an awful chance with their safety. Since the Catholic church was much closer to the center of town, the possibility of being hit by shells was much greater. As they reached Market Square and turned south onto the Broad Street Bridge, shells began to hit nearby and struck a house on Alabama. The horse moved more quickly. Again, another shell, another shell. Mary and the neighbors lowered and covered themselves with their shawls as they approached the church.

Mack stopped abruptly as a few shells landed in front of them on the street. He yelled for them to get out and run for the church, which was about fifty feet away. He watched them run to safety. Just then, he saw three other citizens walking to church a few blocks away. Without hesitation, he snapped the reins and, by horse and carriage, ran to their rescue.

Shells and cannonballs cascaded around them as he arrived. He waved to them and yelled, "Get in!" Cowering their heads in fear, the two ladies and the gentleman jumped in the buggy, and Mack headed back to shelter. They arrived safely but distraught.

One of the neighbors commented when they arrived, "Can't those Yanks stop even for Sunday services?"

CHAPTER 21

"Death tugs at my ear and says, 'Live. I am coming.'"

~ Oliver Wendell Holmes, Sr.

AUGUST

During the endless summer of siege, life became tedious as the bombing continued day after day. It was maddening. People stopped talking about it and decided to go on with their lives. Mack came home, and Mary was cooking. They didn't talk about it.

At a saloon in Kenny's Alley, men were gathered around the bar shooting the bull and causing a ruckus. As they stumbled outside and looked down the street, Humbug Square, located on Alabama Street between Peachtree and Pryor, was a circus of sorts.

"Real gold, or just like gold, rather." A man under a tent was holding up his jewelry with a twinkle in his eye.

"Over here, the best medicine that will cure what ails ya, mental or physical," another man yelled. "Only one dollar per bottle," he said, waving the bottle in the air. "You don't need anything else. My formula is the best, proven time and again." A shell landed right in the middle of the square. "Ahhhaahaahaha." He laughed hysterically.

"Find a little happiness, buy a balloon here!"

"Master of the universe!" a muscleman yelled and flexed his muscles.

Muscle men, masters of the universe, Doctor Good, tricksters, magicians, wild shows, freak shows, prize pigs, human and otherwise.

Stumble along, on your fantasy ride. Forget your troubles today.

The ultimate flimflam … and yet, people were clamoring to believe and lining up to see the madness to escape the madness. What is real? What is an illusion? On with the show!

They decided they were going to live. Until they died.

✳✳✳

Sherman had cut off lines going north to Chattanooga and east to Decatur, but he couldn't break through the lines going south to Newnan or south to Macon, so he decided to bombard Atlanta relentlessly.

On the first day of August, he ordered shelling from 4 p.m. until dark. The clear skies of dusk showed brilliant lights bombarding the city as the campfires began to heat up the night.

Sandbags were built on Marietta Street to guard against the shelling. It was common to see sentinels keeping watch over the city and surrounding area. A request to hire men to guard shops was not readily answered. "It appears nobody is interested in making an honest buck to guard shops," one citizen commented. Scavengers seized the opportunity to take what they could with most men in the fight.

Homes were being hit by shells along the Decatur road.

There wasn't much to eat in Atlanta, but the railroad was still in service to carry goods. Many people had gardens in their backyards with corn, tomatoes, and beans, but most of it had been given to the soldiers, churches or others in need. Coffee had become a new recipe — roasted cereal with a hint of coffee bean — that many said tasted like sawdust.

✳✳✳

By the first week in August, prices had skyrocketed. Mary and Amanda went to town to get a few things. "Look at these prices," Mary said.

Amanda was shocked as she read the prices in the store window. "Flour at $1.25, bacon at $500/lb, salt at $100/lb, molasses at $20/lb."

"Flour bread $2.50-$3.00/dz. This can't be right," Mary said in shock. "I can't even afford to write a letter. Look at the price of paper!"

"$5 for 25 sheets of paper," Amanda looked at Mary and shook her head.

"Let's keep looking, but we definitely need to talk to Mack about this," Mary said.

On August 2, big changes came for the Confederacy. Hood sent Wheeler and Iverson to Nashville.

A couple of days later, Sherman's impatience caused him to attempt another break in the Confederate lines, so he sent troops to the southwest side of Atlanta again. This time, he ordered his troops to a post office about six miles southwest of Atlanta at East Point. At that juncture, the Atlanta and West Point rails split with the Macon Railroad to move southwest to Newnan and Lagrange. The Macon Railroad moved more southeast toward Macon and Savannah. If he could cut the rails at this point, he could cut off Atlanta. The location where they rendezvoused was called Utoy Creek, located along Cascade Road. After a couple of days of effort, his men were not able to break the stronghold.

Newnan continued to see trains rolling in with prisoners from the railroad city due north of them, and the shelling continued in Atlanta, destroying homes and killing civilians.

THE PROMISED LAND

At the plantation, Maguire could hear cannonading all evening. They hid everything left of value and did the best with what they had. The Yankees were all around them, and Maguire's scouts led him to believe that they would be there soon. Maguire's son John E. took off on a beaten old mule to find out what he could.

Maguire's slaves were demoralized and had lost hope. Some had run away but had been retrieved along with a few others, one wearing a Union uniform. The other slaves belonged to someone else. The next day when Maguire woke up, he heard more cannons in Atlanta. He determined that if the cannons were still going off, then Atlanta was still in the hands of the Confederacy. He found out that the farmhands had gone to Atlanta to fight for the Confederacy.

✳✳✳

A group of spirited fools stood firm at Kenny's Alley at Five Points while the night sky rained bullets.

"Go on, fools, run scared. Not me!"

"Nor I, mate! We shall stay right here and have another brew waiting for ole Sherm to arrive. Hehehe. Not Atlanta, boys. I will be sitting right at this bar waiting. Hey bartender, another round for my friends." Guffawing and sniggering exploded and could be heard outside the saloon.

Atlanta was being bombarded all over the city, from Marietta Street to the cemetery, from Spring Street to Rawson Street, and all parts between.

Peachtree, Ivey and Pryor streets were hit repeatedly. Minie balls were flying. They hit the Western and Atlantic Railroad roundhouse.

The firemen who were in battle a few days earlier had returned to Atlanta for supplies, and Mecaslin sent back-up supplies down to East Point at Utoy Creek. Some men remained in Atlanta to fight the heavy artillery and fires that resulted from the bombardment. Some firemen from the Tallulah Engine #3 had run to get their equipment when a barrage of shells hit the firehouse, and the men had to run for cover. They went back when they could to grab their gear and then sprinted over to the next fire at the depot.

THE PROMISED LAND

On August 7, a passerby stopped at the farm and told Maguire that he had just been in Atlanta, and everything was all right. Maguire was struggling to thrash wheat with the few mules, an old horse and oxen that he still managed to have. He was trying to work during difficult times.

ATLANTA

The next day, the telegraph was running around the clock at the American Hotel at the corner of Alabama and Pryor as shells continued to pummel the town.

A huge fire exploded when a cotton warehouse on Alabama Street was hit, and it spread to businesses and houses nearby in no time at all. Mecaslin and his men arrived and fought the mighty demon all day and were so gallant. The shells continued throughout the day, and they couldn't contain themselves. "Ha, let's see you dodge another one of those," said Rodes as he handed another bucket to Kidd.

"That's my business over on Whitehall. Let's make sure it doesn't get that far. They've already bombed it pretty badly," yelled Kidd, pointing east toward Whitehall Street.

"What kind of hell is this?" smiled Mack. His comrades laughed and shook their heads. "It's like a nightmare putting out fires while you're still being hit."

"Look out!" yelled Rodes as they dodged another shell.

✳✳✳

The talk in town that night was nothing but praise and cheers for the mighty force of firemen who never stopped fighting fire until the last ember was out. They never left the scene until all agreed that they had done all that they could do. Then they were instructed to return to their troops for further orders because they knew Sherman was moving.

In the meantime, a powerful force was chugging in from Chattanooga. The train delivered two thunderous siege guns called Parrott guns for the Sherman team, capable of demolishing buildings.

Mary was at home getting items for the soldiers, then *BOOM! BOOM!* She fell to the floor. She got up and ran as fast as she could over to the Barnes' house, and Amanda was on the floor. "Oh my, dear Lord, come with me." They ran back to her house. Mary grabbed the birdcage, opened the secret cellar that Mack had built, and they crawled in. Ole Mack followed. An emergency lantern, blankets and goods had already been stored, and they sat and stared at each other.

"What was that? They must be really close to us. I am so worried about Mack and Charlie. Oh no, where are Sarah and Mary E.?" Cannons pounded one after another.

"We need to stay here for just a while," warned Amanda, "then we will find them."

They emerged later to find holes in the ground and houses that were blown down. No one was in the streets. As they ventured out, they found that a couple of people had been killed, and most people appeared to be in shelters.

They found their friends and decided to go to the church again for shelter. As the pounding continued, houses a couple of blocks away on Peachtree Street were destroyed. Many Atlantans were in shock. Some were sitting on the ground sobbing, and others were wandering, going through the rubbish and looking for things to pack so they could leave. Some citizens simply ran away.

Amanda had decided that it was time to leave. Her husband was in the field, and her house had been shelled. She hadn't heard from Bill in quite some time. The mail was taking weeks to be delivered. She wanted to pack up and go to Augusta. If she didn't go now, she was afraid of what might happen. "Go with me, Mary. I can't bear to think of you here right now."

"I have to stay with Mack. If you stay, you know we will be here with you."

"I've had enough."

She had heard that she had to wait for one of the less frequent refugee trains to go to Social Circle and then south to Macon, but she was worried about how to get home from there. *I just have to try,* she thought.

Mary and Sarah helped her pack her things and saw her off at the station. She left with other neighbors, and it was one of the saddest days they could remember. She was treated with great dignity as the wife of Atlanta's own Lieutenant Bill Barnes, but she had made a great reputation for herself as a woman of great grace who had taken in all the wounded that she could house and treated them as her own. Mary, Sarah, Mary Ennis and other ladies were there to see her off. Shells exploded nearby and another one hit a house, which burst into flames.

They cried and hugged each other and then waved forever as they watched the train move down the tracks and disappear.

✳✳✳

Women with children were running errands, taking care of themselves and learning how to move quickly. Many had moved into houses together and abandoned those that had been burned or hit with shells. Soldiers walked through town, beaten and hungry.

Shelling was the worst yet as Sherman increased the assault on Atlanta and its people. One hundred guns fired fifty shells each, or five thousand cannon shots. His troops continued to move to cut off the Macon rail.

On August 12, Sherman was held in check by the "stubborn defence of Atlanta" and ordered increased firing.

The *Intelligencer* had relocated to Macon and reported, "The armies in the vicinity of Atlanta seem to have remained very quiet … we retain the advantage of position at every point, and the indications are that we will hold Atlanta. Atlantans still have hope and are determined to stay the course."

The scene in Atlanta was unrecognizable. It had changed greatly since Sherman arrived a few weeks earlier. No fruit. Very little food. The soldiers had taken it all. Fire after fire continued to be ignited, and the brave souls of the fire department worked endlessly to protect their Atlanta and its people. The guards of the city were truly that.

Three trains arrived from the south soon after, carrying boxcars and freight cars loaded with more soldiers and supplies for the Confederate front.

That Sunday, a major movement of revivals occurred in Atlanta in all of the churches. People from everywhere went to church. Rock of Ages could be heard in the streets. Soldiers lined up at the churches and on the lawns, waiting to be baptized. General Hood and General Slocum were baptized.

A spirit of hope and faith was revived, and peace was felt for a moment.

THE PROMISED LAND

Maguire and his family continued to hear shelling throughout the land and were nervous for themselves and their family in Atlanta. Several Gwinnett County cavalry visited and shared news and moved on. Militia were also present in the area. Elizabeth baked biscuits and sent them out to the soldiers. Thomas finished wheat thrashing, which yielded 281 bushels.

On August 22, Maguire's scouts delivered a message that the Yankees attempted another raid and tore up the tracks at Jonesboro. They were in despair at the thought that the Yankees would take control. The Yankees felt confident that they had done enough destruction to cut supplies for days, but the next day, glorious news was delivered to Maguire that, miraculously, supply trains came chugging through Atlanta from Macon. Those relentless Confederates had repaired the damage overnight to get the trains through. What news!

Maguire sent his son to get the mail. He had to go to Conyers, Lithonia and Lawrenceville to pick up a backlog of some 150 letters, old news and old newspapers. The mail had been arriving only every few weeks, and one never knew what kind of news they would get and from whom.

ATLANTA

Mack had been working nonstop for days, even the entire summer, putting out fires and commanding the Thirty-fifth. He was in touch as much as possible with the Confederate commanders to make sure that he knew where they were and what their plans were. However, it was all very confusing. They went where needed to back up the troops throughout the surrounding area of the town. The men were exhausted.

People had become resilient and well-practiced in the dance with the shells. Shelters were widely known and frequently visited. When someone needed to go out, they knew where to go and what to do in an emergency.

While rumors at The Promised Land were that the Yanks had left Atlanta, it was far from true. Sherman's men had abandoned the works and moved to the southwest along Fairburn. The Union cut the lines at Red Oak, a few miles north of Fairburn, and began to move toward Jonesboro on the Fayetteville road. One more supply line and Atlanta would be theirs.

At the same time in Atlanta, Hood was stationed on Peachtree Street, waiting to give commands to the couriers standing nearby. Some of his troops took over Sherman's abandoned works. As soon as he heard where Sherman was, he sent word to General Hardee to move quickly to Jonesboro, and Lieutenant General Lee would follow that night. Hardee would make an unexpected attack at dawn.

Hood's plan was that a successful attack would send Lee south to the town of Rough and Ready, and the Georgia State Guard with Smith and Mecaslin would form a line to Lee's right near East Point. The whole force would move forward the next morning. The cavalry would check the enemy at the Chattahoochee River at Peachtree Creek, and Hardee would advance at Jonesboro.

Hood stayed in Atlanta on Decatur Street with his leaders, Stewart and

Smith. Major Mecaslin waited for orders to board the train southward to East Point. Both teams were heading for a showdown.

CHAPTER 22

"Our sweet illusions are half of them conscious illusions, like effects of colour that we know to be made up of tinsel, broken glass and rags."

~ George Eliot, The Lifted Veil, 1859

SEPTEMBER 1864

They waited for dawn. Then at dawn, they waited for the sound of battle, something to indicate that Hardee attacked by surprise. Nothing. Mecaslin waited to hear. The silence was as loud as one hundred cannons. You could cover your ears to try not to hear the silence.

No one wanted to think beyond the moment to speculate what would come next. Each moment in the moment brought hope. Prayer kept them in the moment.

Idle hours that felt like days went by for the troops on Decatur Street. This was their last chance, their final hope for the Gate City because all other supply lines had been cut. The pounding of gunfire that the Confederates had so long hoped would stop was now what they longed to hear. Hood knew. By the time he heard the gunshots late in the day, he knew it was too late.

Lack of timing and communication kept the Rebels from rendezvousing at the ideal time. The Federals cut the telegraph that prevented timely communication to Hood, and they took Jonesboro that day.

Major Mecaslin's men didn't move to East Point; their orders changed.

Two hours past midnight, Hood gave orders to Mecaslin to set fire to all military operations and ammunition as he prepared to evacuate the Gate City, the grand railroad center of the South. The firemen, whose job it had been to protect all from fire, had to go against everything they believed in. Mack felt sick with dread as he torched the very property that he had worked so hard to save. They were instructed to blow up the arsenals and let them burn but prevent the fires from spreading. The fires got out of control and damaged much more than they expected. Atlanta was on fire.

Mack sent word to Father O'Reilly about the events. He said to make sure that Mary and the others stayed at the church until they heard from him.

Lieutenant General Lee marched to Rough and Ready in the middle of the night, not to back a successful fight, but to protect the Confederate army while they marched out of Atlanta at 5 p.m. that day on the McDonough road toward Lovejoy Station.

✳✳✳

Mayor Calhoun of Atlanta met with several city councilmen, including Major Mecaslin, to discuss the fate of the city. They sent a message to the Federals to meet to ensure that persons and property were not destroyed. The Confederates had not surrendered to the Union, and Calhoun felt that he needed to act on the matter himself. He and his band met with Brigadier General W.T. Ward, Third Division, Twentieth Corps of the United States Army, who sent a message on to Union General Slocum.

Was it the morning fog, or was it the gun smoke lingering? A scout appeared through the haze at Sherman's headquarters. He was allowed to enter. Sherman, weary from a long battle against a resistant Atlanta, was ready to hear his words. He was informed that his officers had met the Atlanta mayor north of the city to discuss terms. The message conveyed that Slocum was asking Sherman for permission to enter the city.

Northern troops occupied the city. Sherman's army of 106,000 had been held back from Atlanta for 46 days by 45,000 Confederates. He entered Atlanta around noon.

A federal officer was appointed as provisional fire chief. All of the firemen who had been destroying property and checking the fires met back at Five Points with Major Mecaslin and his mighty crew. They stood together in a formed line, standing proud with honor as Mack stepped up to hand over the position of Atlanta fire chief to the Federal authorities. He was removed from his position as president of the Fire Department and major of the Third Battalion, Georgia State Guards.

The men saluted their commander and were dismissed. But they felt the job was not finished, and they all returned to various locations and continued to fight fires.

Major Mecaslin met with several of the men of the city to determine what to do next and how to look after their interests. He talked with Peters and Moore about the flour mill and Rodes, Kidd and others about the businesses.

Several Union soldiers came in and destroyed the Confederate flag and put up the Union flag. Union troops filed in and began to take over. They had agreed not to harm the women and children. They found their way to the post office and the newspaper office and went to work. Supplies were beginning to enter the town before the end of the day.

Firehouse #1 was taken over immediately and used as barracks. The new building across the street was used as a feed and hay depot. Firehouse #2 was used as a prison for Confederates, and Firehouse #3 was used as stables.

"Get your paper here!" yelled a young boy on Peachtree Street. "Yankees in Atlanta!"

The Federals had decided that Sherman's new headquarters would be at the Neal home at the corner of Washington and Mitchell.

***

Late that night, Mack found Mary at the church. She saw him and knew it was over. They were in a moment of time with no past and no future. He ran to her and held her as if he would never let her go. Tears streamed down her face.

"Thank God, you're alright," she said.

They turned and instinctively walked toward home, over the Georgia Railroad tracks, disregarding the ruins around them. They went into the war weary house and closed the door.

The world was falling around them, and they could only see each other. No rhyme or reason. A desperate need for each other led them upstairs, and they shut out the insanity. They made love as if there were no tomorrow.

CHAPTER 23

"A mind that is stretched by a new experience can never go back to its old dimensions."

~ Oliver Wendell Holmes, Sr.

Mack got up early the next morning, moving slowly, still exhausted. He started coughing.

"Are you feeling well? That sounds terrible."

"I'm fine, just a dry throat," said Mack.

"You aren't going anywhere, are you? You should rest," urged Mary, but she knew it was of no use.

"I have to see what needs to be done, for your safety and for the town. Get dressed. I will take you to the church. I don't want you to stay here alone."

Mack walked Mary to the church. He checked on Father O'Reilly and everyone in the shelter and then went to see the status of the town. The Union flag was flying. A large number of Union soldiers occupied the town. He went straight to the Fire Department and saw they had occupied the building. The fire equipment — the pride of the town that had saved so many people and property — was out in the street. Some of the equipment was in a ditch and had been torn to pieces. He found Kidd and some other men to secretly try to stop the burning buildings and destruction. Since their equipment was destroyed, the firemen were limited in what they could do. He met with the businessmen to discuss the next steps. They had heard rumors about Sherman's plans to evacuate everyone, but surely not; he had agreed that the citizens of the town would not be harmed and were of no concern to him.

A great deal of angst and uncertainty prevailed for the next several days. Nobody was sure what was going on.

"Who is going to save us now?" said one neighbor to another as they sat on the front steps of his home in ruins.

"God only knows," said his friend. "I am afraid we're done for."

THE PROMISED LAND

On September 2, Thomas Maguire wrote, *A great fire in Atlanta last night. It is said that Atlanta has given up and our army is falling back. All the public stores are burned that could not be got away. This is a great misfortune to Georgia but it cannot be helped. We are now in a bad fix.*

The following day, no news came from the army. Maguire wrote, *Two sick soldiers came by to eat. They live in Walton County. We heard the Yankees are coming, and the two sick soldiers headed for the woods. On September 5, two more sick soldiers were here at The Promised Land.*

The plantation continued to be a refuge for sick soldiers and weary travelers. Sometimes they were charged for their food and lodging, and sometimes not. The residents of The Promised Land were always eager to hear the news that the travelers brought. They took turns scouting around the area to see if any Yankees were approaching.

ATLANTA

By September 6, Sherman had finally moved his army into Atlanta and declared that they would remain there until they were rested and ready to move. The town was more than half depopulated of Atlantans and many abandoned homes were looted or destroyed.

The next day, Sherman made a statement that shocked the townspeople. "What is he saying? I thought we had an agreement." Such murmurs were heard around town.

Sherman communicated to the mayor that for those people going north, he would provide rail transport and rations to wherever they wanted to go as long it was Tennessee, Kentucky or Ohio. He agreed that they could take whatever they wanted, including furniture, luggage, and trunks. If the slaves wanted to go with their masters, he would allow that as well. But if they wanted to go south or elsewhere, they were on their own.

This was upsetting news to the town. People were sick, exhausted, injured, and dying, and many were already homeless with nothing to eat.

Chaos ensued. Sherman agreed to allow people to take as much luggage and furniture as they could carry, but in the madness, much was left behind.

Some family valuables were heaped so high in their wagons that they fell off and were left sitting in the street. Helplessness and despair were magnified.

Mack went home to Mary.

"You look exhausted," she said. "Are you ok?"

"We have to leave," he said despondently. He sat down at the kitchen table and stared off into space.

✳✳✳

Mack woke up the next day with a fever and couldn't get out of bed. It was as if he had waited until he could do no more before he collapsed.

"I'll be fine, I just need to rest, I'm sure," he told his wife. "But we should talk about our plans. I want you to go to Augusta as soon as possible."

"No, I am staying with you."

"No, Mary. It's too dangerous. Everything is too uncertain. At least you will have passage and can get back to your family."

"You know I'm not leaving you like this. Rest and don't worry now."

"We should still make plans."

"What are we going to do with our things? What about Ole Mack?"

"I don't know. Why don't you write your family and tell them that we need to send them some of our things? We should start packing right away."

"I'm really worried about what will happen to Ole Mack because he could get hurt, or they may tell us that we can't take our sweet dog with us. I couldn't bear to think that he would be left behind here with no one to comfort him."

"Let me talk to Charlie and see if he can send him with friends to Rough and Ready with the hope that we can get him to family somewhere."

✳✳✳

Atlantans waited for further instructions. Finally, a week later, they received an update.

On September 15, Sherman's order required all persons going south to be transported to Rough and Ready, a town south of Atlanta.

"Sarah, are you sure you can manage all of these parcels?" Mary asked.

"Mary, please go with me. This is not a fit place for a woman anymore, or for anyone. Please," her friend begged her earnestly.

"I can't leave Mack like this. I can't leave him," she shook her head. "He's not well right now, and I won't leave him. We will be fine, and God's grace will carry us through. Now don't you worry." She smiled a weak smile. "I don't know what I will do without you."

The men loaded several bags and trunks belonging to the Mecaslins, including valuables and family treasures. Mack sent flour and salt, which were in dire need in Augusta.

Along with the other items, Mary handed Sarah a letter. "Please deliver this to my mother if you can and give her a special hug for me."

"Of course," Sarah said with tears in her eyes. They hugged each other. On September 15, Mary wrote:

Dear Father and Mother, Brother and Sister:

I write this in hopes that it will find you in good health. We are quite well, thank God, but somewhat troubled as to what to do. All citizens will have to leave this place. We do not know where we will go but I must follow Mr. Mack wherever he goes. We may go to his people. It looks hard for me to leave you both in your old age, but if I do it will be for the best and you must not fret about us. We can get along, and I hope we will meet soon. God grant that we may. If it was not for you I would not care where I went but it will be a hard trial for me to go and leave you both. I hope God will spare us to meet again and in peace. I fear we could not live here even if we were permitted to stay. It looks hard to have to leave our comfortable home and go among strangers we know not where but we will trust in the Lord and all will be well. I will send this by Mrs. Rodes. She leaves in an hour or two. As soon as we decide what to do I will try to write you by flag of truce, and hope you will not fret about us. I s'pose it is the fortune of war that we have had to undergo all this. Give our love to James and family and to all inquiring friends.

Hoping that we may all soon meet again, I remain

Your daughter,
M.A.M.

P.S. You must use that flour and salt just as you see fit. If you want to keep it do so, and if you want to sell it, do so and use the money just as if it was your own. If Mrs. Barnes wants flour or salt let her have it. You may need other things more than flour, so you can either sell or swap-just as you see fit, and tell James he must not want for flour while it lasts. You must not think it won't do to use because it is mine. You have free control of it now, and if there is anything in the box that you can use, do so but take good care of my Maggie's toys. Everything of hers is dear to me. So now good-by again and God grant we may soon meet again is the prayer of

Your affectionate daughter,
Mary

The Federals inspected everything that went, including the letter that Mary sent to her parents via Mrs. Rodes.

This refugee train was supposed to go to Rough and Ready, and from

146

there, Hood's troops were to assist them to Macon and other points south, but truly the passengers knew that their destination was unknown.

Ole Mack the dog was right there in the mix of things as he always was. Mary looked down at him at her side and was overwhelmed with sadness. She stooped down to pet him and hug him. Everyone hugged and said their goodbyes with solemn faces. Mary gave Ole Mack another big hug and a loving pat, then walked him to the train car. Mrs. Rodes called, "Here, Mack." He playfully hopped up to the train, and as the train was leaving, tears streamed down Mary's face. Mrs. Rodes held onto Ole Mack in the train car, waving to everyone, especially her husband, Charlie, not knowing if she would ever see any of her friends again.

Mr. Taylor, the freedman, returned to his home that day to find a sack of flour sitting on his front porch. He looked around but saw no one. He gratefully picked it up and took it in the house. He could feed his family and friends for a little longer.

When they returned from the station, Mack went back to bed, and Mary made dinner. He didn't eat much. For the next couple of days, he stayed in bed.

Mary called for the doctor to check on him, and it took Dr. D'Alvigny several hours to arrive at the house. He went into the room and Mack looked terrible. Mary was worried as she put cold compresses on his head.

"Mary, he's just exhausted. He's been fighting those fires and working late hours, gone for days at a time for so long that his body was waiting to rest. Try to get him to eat."

Hour after hour, she watched and waited. Day after day, he was the same. Fever, moaning, sleep. She stayed with him.

That certain first shock is a terrible blow to the physical system, then gradually an extended exposure to stress becomes accepted by the body and mind, and you function with that level of stress. Then if another factor of stress or fear occurs, the body takes another beating. Gradual adjustment to an extended level of stress causes the body systems to lower, and you don't even realize it. In times of extreme difficulties, like the end of a battle, with no food, shelter, or comforts, you became numb. Mack couldn't allow himself to stop defending, stop trying, stop fighting the fires and held on until he finally turned over the reins to the enemy, and then he just collapsed. His body could take no more.

Mary called for Dr. D'Alvigny again. The doctor was overwhelmed with the sick and dying throughout the town. When he finally arrived, his diagnosis was different.

"Mary, he has the fever. He's very ill, and he has to want to live. It's in his hands and God's hands now. Pray for him and for all of these unfortunate people. You must also take care of yourself. You have worked hard and must rest as well, or you'll get it, too."

"Mack, wake up. Please."

Friends would come to visit but only for brief periods of time. The doctor said that he needed quiet. Rodes and Kidd came over every day.

"Any change, Mary?"

"No, Charlie. Do something. Go and talk to him."

Nothing worked.

✳✳✳

Days went by. Mary was exhausted and worried, and she would lay down next to Mack, talking to him as she had done so often. She told him of her dreams and hopes for the future.

"What will I do without you? Don't leave me, Mack. I can't make it in this world without you." She drifted off.

I dreamt of you in my peaceful slumber. It was as if the darkness enveloped me and lifted me to some airy cloud of no concern. We were weightless. Like angels. We met in midair, translucent as we twirled round and round each other, our hands grasping each other until we merged as one, and then we drifted off ...

Suddenly, Mack jerked around in his sleep, waking Mary. Tumultuous, feverish dreams absorbed his thoughts.

Gunfire, smoke everywhere. I can't see you. I can't see anything, it's so hot next to this fire. I can't seem to put it out, it just keeps burning ... inhaling smoke, coughing. The smoke is clearing, and I see dead and sick soldiers everywhere, amputees, gangrene, people going hungry, calling for help. "Help me, help me," then silence.

"Son, I miss you," Mother's voice echoes.

Little brother George, age six, walks along the water with me. "Here's a good fishing spot." I grabbed a worm. "Here's how you bait a hook, George. Watch me now. This is how you cast your line."

George cried out, "Where are you, brother? I need you."

"Keep piling the flour sacks, then take 'em down to the docks. Attaboy. You're a hard worker, and it will pay off someday," Dad says as he pats me on the back.

"You're it. It's your turn to walk the plank!" My friend says, standing on the dock.

Aye, she was a grand vessel. Aye, she was.

"Daddy, watch me run!" little Maggie called out.

A flood of emotions sent Mack tossing and turning.

"In fellowship, love and trust, brother — F.L.T.," I can hear my dear friend Lieutenant Barnes and see a huge smile on his face.

"Mack, wake up, I can't do this without you."

CHAPTER 24

"Not knowing when the dawn will come, I open every door."

~Emily Dickinson

A cool breeze blew gently through the window as mid-October winds arrived. Smoke covered Atlanta all the time now as the Yankees had been burning and destroying things for several days. Looking out her upstairs bedroom window to the left, Mary could see the Federal camp set up along the railroad tracks by the Georgia Railroad. She could see many things she couldn't see before because the soldiers had cut down many of the glorious trees to build fortifications, and those that weren't cut down were blown to fragments during the bombings and battles. In fact, to the east toward Decatur and to the north, the trees were gone. Somehow fate had gracefully left a shade tree here and there, and the leaves were starting to turn. It lent a strange beauty to a scorched and barren land. Funny how the Georgia red clay became a stronger reddish orange because there seemed to be more of it. Only a branch or stick was a reminder of what was there before.

Mary sat down in the bedroom chair. *Poor Atlanta*, she thought. She remembered the night she first arrived in the small town. The stars were so glorious and spring was in the air. How exciting the future was. What a wonderful place to be newlyweds and to start a family.

Now to look outside at night was haunting. The evening before, she had seen the Federal campfires burning all around town. Few Confederates went out at night. A ghost town.

✳✳✳

She heard a hoarse whisper. "Mary."

A chill ran through her, and she turned toward the bed in a start. She ran over to him, leaned forward, and grabbed his hand. His eyes were open. "Mack, can you hear me?"

He nodded.

"Blessed Mary, Mother of God, you came back to me!" She held him in her arms. And she sobbed.

Kidd and Rodes had stayed close by during Mack's illness. They wanted to be near in case something happened and to keep Mary secure.

"Charlie and Will, Mack's awake. Hurry!"

The men rushed up the stairs and stopped at the door.

"Come in, please."

"Well, you have given me a reason to smile that I haven't had recently. How are you, my friend?" Kidd said.

"Sight for sore eyes, brother," Rodes said.

Mack nodded.

The bird sang sweetly in all of the excitement.

News traveled fast around town. Dr. D'Alvigney arrived later that day as a surprise to Mary. He said, "Dr. Beach has refugeed north to Indianapolis to be with his family. I'm afraid it's just us now." He looked over Mack and reached for his shoulder. "The worst is over now, son. You need to rest and heal." The doctor left to go back to the soldiers. Mary gave him a biscuit on his way out the door. She continued to watch over Mack as he rested.

Mack began to recover slowly. She felt nervous. *I need to tell him,* she thought. *No, I'll wait.*

Many changes had happened while Mack was ill. Mary felt that it would be best for his friends to discuss the changes. They came upstairs to visit. Mary sat quietly while they told Mack the news.

"The Union troops have been civil to us, but they have completely taken over the town. I don't want to worry you right now with everything going on."

"No, go on, Will."

"Federal officers now live in most of the homes, and they have torn down homes to build cabins for the troops. They say there must be eighty thousand troops here. You know, mostly everyone who was going south has left, but people are waiting to go north. Sherman has promised passage and rations north as far as Ohio to anyone wanting to go, but there have been skirmishes all around the area, and we're not sure which way to go or what Sherman will do next. Trains have been trying to leave daily for Chattanooga, but since both sides have been tearing up the tracks, some

150

make it and some don't. It's very confusing. It may take a long time just to get to Chattanooga. Once in Chattanooga, the word is that it may be weeks before another train goes north.

"It's a pretty dangerous ride, I think. There are probably going to be more battles north as the Confederates try to retake Georgia and Tennessee. Word says that Hood has headed to northern Alabama. We haven't heard anything lately. We're hoping that the Yanks will leave soon so we can take care of things," Rodes stopped for a moment.

"I'm not leaving, I'm telling you, boys," Kidd said.

"Hundreds of families — men, women and children — have evacuated because of Sherman's orders. Many went south by train. Some walked away," Rodes said and shook his head.

Mary could tell that Mack was getting tired. "Dear friends, I think Mack needs to rest now. Perhaps you can call on him again tomorrow."

They nodded. "Of course. We will see ourselves out, Mary."

She couldn't wait any longer. "Mack, I need to tell you something." She held his hand.

"What is it, Mary? Is everything ok?"

"We are going to have another baby," she smiled.

"Oh, Blessed Mary, I can't believe this. How do you feel? Why didn't you tell me sooner? I have to get you out of here!"

"You need to rest and get well, my dear. Don't worry. We can talk about it more later." She stayed with him until he fell asleep.

The men came back to visit the next day with a couple of other friends, and Mack was able to sit up and talk. "We don't know what the Feds are going to do next," Will began. "They may continue further south, or they could head over to Augusta and then Charleston. If you think of it in terms of army terrain, the road to Augusta isn't bad, and they could really do some damage to the homes, plantations and tracks along the way."

"Oh, I believe that our army can put up a good fight," Rodes said optimistically. "We could really make it tough on them if they head to South Carolina and over to Charleston. They will never get through Augusta and over the Savannah River bridge. They couldn't survive that Carolinian swamp land."

"What I am worried about is that they could camp here for the winter, rest, regroup, and then continue to tear up our town and leave in the spring for who knows where," Kidd continued.

"If they go south, they will probably head for Macon and Milledgeville, and who knows, maybe even Savannah. That would be a long march in winter, but it's warmer in the South," Mack said.

Nobody knew what would happen next. So they waited. One thing that they didn't talk about was what had happened. Because they knew. And how to recover some of the things they hid. Not a word. They just waited.

CHAPTER 25

October 21, 1864

Mary wrote a letter to her mother stating that they were to leave soon. They were ordered to go.

My dear Father and Mother:

I have written to you a great many times and hope you have received some of my letters. This leaves us quite well. Mr. Mack has had a spell of fever but thank God he is over it, but is not very strong yet. We are getting on tolerable well. A great many people have left here for the North and a great many are now waiting for the State Road to be fixed to go north. The Rebels have cut the road several times, and this keeps people in a continual excitement. Sometimes we think of going to see our relatives and friends in Maryland and it may be that we will go this winter. I would like so much to see you both and all the rest of my friends in Augusta, but that is impossible just now. I hope the time will soon come for us all to meet again. Mr. and Mrs. Bryson are here with me. They are waiting for the road to be opened to go north. They are quite well.

Father, I want you to take that piece of jeans in that box and have a suit of clothes made of them. There is enough for a coat, vest and pants, and you must use that shawl and everything else that you can use, but please take good care of my poor Maggie's toys. I wish I had sent all her things to you, to take care of. I would like to hear from Uncle Thomas, but cannot. You must give my love to Mrs. Barnes and Joe and Angie and all the rest of them. Tell Mrs. B. to go to see you often and tell her I say to make your caps and I will do as much for her if we ever meet again. I do pray to God that we may all meet again and that before long. We have been well treated by the Federals up to this time. I try to treat all as well as I can and some of them have been very kind to me during Mr. Mack's illness. The greatest trouble that I have been in was on Mr. Beach's account. I would rather see anyone else in Atlanta leave before him. He has gone to Indianapolis, but old Dr. D'Alvigny is here and we call on him. I hope, however, that we will have little use for doctors.

You must give my love to James and Amanda and Jinny and Mamy and Joe, and to all my friends.

Mr. Mack joins me in love to you all. If you should have an opportunity to write do send me just a line or two to let me know how you are. I trust in the Lord that this will find you all quite well and may we all meet soon again is the prayer of

Your affectionate daughter,
Mary A. Mecaslin

CHAPTER 26

"Fear is pain arising from the anticipation of evil."

~ Aristotle

THE PROMISED LAND
1864

At the end of September, hard times wore on. The little children went to school, and everyone struggled with the thought of work. A challenging atmosphere continued as people heard rumors about the slaves running away to find the Yankees. The Rebel scouts of the countryside searched for them. Some of the slaves were caught, and some who resisted were shot.

A few days later, Maguire awoke to news that his slaves Isaac, Merritt, Lewis and Peter were missing. Maguire thought it might happen and thought they had gone to the Yankees. This was bad news, but there was nothing he could do about it. Elizabeth went over to David Anderson's to see if Isaac might be there. *What will turn up next, I do not know,* Maguire thought. *The times have not got to their worst yet. If nothing worse befalls us, we can make out.*

On October 5, scouts brought news that the Yankees were falling back from Decatur, and the Confederates were almost over the Chattahoochee River. A few days later, he believed the Yankees were out of Atlanta, and their nearest pickets were at the rolling mill on the east side of town. The rumors said, "Our army is across the railroad in their rear, and Sherman's headquarters are in Marietta. If that's true, things may soon be right."

A week later, he received big news. The Rebels had retaken Rome and three thousand black prisoners. All of the Federals were out of Decatur and might soon be out of the state.

His son, John E., straggled up the walk to the Maguire dwelling late after dinner. He had walked all the way from Social Circle with several papers in his hands, anticipating the look on Maguire's face when he told him. "Look, look at the news."

Thomas read, "The railroad from Big Shanty to Kingston is torn up, and the army has taken all Yankees from Big Shanty north to Kingston. At Lake Allatoona, they grabbed four thousand prisoners and supplies, and stores have been recovered."

The next few days were hopeful as they thought that the Yankees would soon leave Atlanta.

"I am curious and nervous about what's going on, Pa. I think I should go to General Iverson's headquarters and find out the details."

"Ok, John. I hope you can send us some good news."

Mid-October work was pleasant and cooler. With a more buoyant spirit of late, Thomas and his hands cleared the yard of cane and almost finished working on making syrup for the neighbors. A farmer's work is never done. As he worked in the field, he remembered that someone at the station was talking about General Sherman burning Atlanta before he left it, and he wondered if that was true as he looked west to Atlanta and saw all the smoke that continued to rise from that location. He looked forward to tomorrow, when he could work on the Henly patch.

That Sunday, October 16, when returning from church, a friend commented. "Look at that smoke coming from the west. That must be Atlanta. I hope Atlanta is on fire. Then surely Sherm will be leaving there soon."

The following week, business continued for the farmer as a local citizen procured sixty-five bushels of wheat for the Confederacy. Maguire worked until he finished grinding up all of his cane. His farmhand Will hauled rails to burn.

The unknown made Thomas nervous as he spent time planning and hiding supplies in case an evil time should come. He and Will put two boxes, eighty bushels of wheat and some barrels of syrup in the field. While they were working, they noticed something moving behind a tree.

"Look, there. What's that? Those two women, see if you can catch 'em." Thomas ran wildly after Will as they gave a good chase and a scare but couldn't catch them or the syrup they dug up. "Well, we didn't hide that so well, did we?" They both laughed and shook their heads.

They continued to hide salt, syrup and wheat.

John E. left for his post in the buggy with Dick. A few days later, he returned with alarming news. "I just saw some Yankees at Lithonia, and scouts say they will be heading this way in the next day or two. Have you finished storing things?"

"I have been hiding supplies all week, but not enough, I guess."

John E., the farmhands and Maguire put the hogs in Mill Field, finished preparing the wheat and loaded it on the carriage wagon. They worked another day or so to hide the supplies, sheep and cattle to stand trial with the Yankees.

On Sunday, a beautiful day was dawning as several scouts moved through and shared the news of the Yankee movement. They continued to move back and forth, scanning the fields and river. Maguire, anticipating the arrival of the Yanks at any time, hid things around the house and lodged some valuables and his ledger book safely in the chimney. The day became chillingly quiet and still as no news arrived.

"Maybe they won't come this way. Maybe they'll go off in another direction," John E. said aloud.

"I expect we will have to drink the bitter cup as others have done," Maguire spoke in a cautious tone as he prepared gear in case they needed to leave quickly. He then made a bed for a neighbor who was spending the night.

The next morning, Maguire woke to the sound of cannons going off in the direction of Flat Shoals toward Atlanta and to the south at East Point. Scouts came by to share the news that four thousand Confederate troops were in Conyers the night before. That was exciting news, but they continued to play the waiting game to see if the Yankees would come. Even though he was hoping that the Yankees were gone, not to come back, he decided to be cautious and sent Will, Dick and David Anderson to head all of the hogs, all of the sheep and almost all of the cattle way out to the mill, and some were sent over the creek. David took his cattle as well. Several of the hogs came back, and he had to send more folks out to the mill with them.

John E. ran into the house. "The Yankees were driven back!" he yelled. "They won't be coming around here anytime soon."

"Ah, what a relief, great news," said Thomas, although doubting anything for sure. "Hard to hear the truth even from the other side of Yellow River."

Several older boys from eleven to fourteen years old came galloping up late in the evening, very animated. "The Yankees are after us, sir. Can we stay at your house and hide out?"

"Get in here, boys, and tell me what's going on."

They dismounted from their horses and ran inside, greatly relieved. "We were at our posts and got spied on by some Yanks," one of them said. "I think they've been eyeing us for days. Anyway, Sam here sent a whistle for a warning, and we skedaddled. They came after us, but we had a head start, and besides, we're much quicker." He looked around confidently and his mates nodded. "They finally slowed down, and we took a different trail to lose them."

"Why, you're just in time for dinner. You boys hungry?"

They ate corn, beans, bacon and biscuits until they were full. They stayed for several hours and calmed down. After dark, they were on their way.

Within minutes of their leaving, a Confederate lieutenant arrived with eight soldiers and fourteen horses, looking for shelter for the night. Elizabeth reset the table for nine more to eat a late dinner. Everyone had news and shared their stories.

"Do you know of any Yankees around here, sir?" asked John E.

"We believe that they are over at Indian Creek, due west toward Decatur," the lieutenant responded.

"How about any other direction, maybe from Athens?" Thomas asked.

"No, not that we know of. We sure do appreciate your hospitality, sir. It has been a long day without food."

"We're so glad that you are here, and we thank you for all you are doing for us," the owner of the homestead replied. It was always a comfort to know that soldiers were near, and it gave them the hope to keep going.

Maguire escorted the men to the stables where they fed and watered their horses and hid them away. He made room for nine guests throughout the house, and everyone had a peaceful sleep.

Early the next morning, Thomas said goodbye to his guests and soon after, twenty-one Confederate cavalry members passed by on the way to Social Circle and Lawrenceville.

"Who are they?" Thomas asked one of his hands.

"Well, I asked him, sir, and one of the soldiers, he tipped his hat and said, 'Dibrell's,' and kept moving."

"Odd. Why would they be going in that direction when we heard from the soldiers last night that the Yankees are just south? That means they could come on through open country. I don't understand this."

✳✳✳

As he had predicted, about thirty Yankees showed up soon afterward. *Oh, no, what will befall us now*, Thomas thought.

The Federals made themselves comfortable and took what they could manage. He thought they were about to leave when one troop went over to his son's saddlebags and grabbed them and whatever was in them.

✳✳✳

A neighbor walked up the next morning.

"Good morning, neighbor," Maguire said. "Are you staying well?"

"Have they been here?"

"Yes, they were here yesterday right after some of our cavalry passed by. What a confusing sight."

"They were at my place, too. They even had their forage wagons and pulled up at my fields and loaded those wagons full of corn."

"They raided us pretty well," Thomas continued. "They took a wagon and both horses. They went through and found our meal and flour and took all of it, plus a keg of syrup. They rummaged through the house as if they couldn't find anything at all but managed to take everything they could and the last bushel of grain that we had. I guess they got their corn at your place." Thomas grinned.

"That appears to be the case this time." The neighbor shook his head and waved as he went on his way.

Maguire felt the need to find whatever he could and hide it. *I need to do something,* he thought. He hid his old carriage and tried to think of what he could do to prepare for another hit. Nobody felt like working because they were worrying about the Yankees. Some of the women were spinning to keep from fretting.

Another scout came riding up and yelled, "Yankees at the neighbor's house, Mr. Maguire!" He wondered if David Anderson's house had been invaded. He sent Will to check on him before sundown. Some of his scouts notified him of the whereabouts of his slaves that night.

"This is a very troublesome life to lead. Tomorrow I suppose will bring our fate and probably our destruction with it," Maguire mumbled to himself.

✳✳✳

The next morning brought early news to the homestead. "Go wake up Mr. Maguire," Elizabeth told a slave. "Tell him that the Yankees are at Haines Creek." Haines Creek was about ten miles east of them. Maguire woke up, quickly dressed and went outside to find what news he could.

Standing on the front porch, Maguire noticed Will coming up to the house, waving urgently with a serious look on his face. "Everything was taken from Mr. Minor and David Anderson, and Merritt was with them. The Yankees are on the other side of the Yellow River."

"Is this true? Will, this is bad. And you saw Merritt?"

"Yessir, and Mr. Anderson say that the Yankees gone back now. He say they done served him bad enough."

"Come on, then, let's go see if we can help them." They left immediately.

More Confederate cavalry, including Lieutenant Hight and ten men from Williamson's brigade, stayed all night. They remained for breakfast, and Maguire had a chance to find out what was going on around him.

"Sir, can you tell us anything about the surrounding area? We have been hit hard several times and would love to see those Yankees on the road to someplace else."

"I saw some men down the way a bit. We will be happy to reconnoiter and swing back by to give you some news," one of the soldiers said.

After breakfast, they rode down to the river, crossed over and looked around. They returned to give a report to the neighbors as they promised. Several people had gathered at The Promised Land by that time. News passed quickly that the soldiers were going to bring them news.

A crowded porch anxiously awaited the news.

"Sir, the Yankees are gone," one said. Maguire recognized the soldier from earlier. Wild yells and hurrahs erupted from the group. "They were last seen going down the Covington road."

"Thank you, thank you, kind sir, for such welcome news. We're grateful for your attention. Please come in and stay a minute," Elizabeth said, standing next to her husband.

"We must be on our way. Thank you for lodging and breakfast. It was much appreciated."

A busy road continued as seventeen cavalry passed the house heading south toward Jonesboro. They hailed from Dalton.

In the early evening, the advance guard of three Confederate brigades came up to get food for their troops. Maguire generously gave them three fields of corn.

At dark, they heard some rumbling in the distance, and all ran out to the front yard. "What's going on?" Maguire asked one of the hands.

"I'm not sure."

"Oh, my, the earth is shaking," said Elizabeth, and she began to cry.

The rumbling of a hundred horse hooves and the shuffling of feet gave way to the sight of torches held high that lit up the night sky. Maguire's heart was pounding. All of the members of the plantation clapped and yelled, "Hurrah!" as they saw a grand sight of Confederate troops coming to their rescue. Maguire put his arm around his beloved wife, Elizabeth, and others hugged each other. It was a glorious moment. Tears of joy!

An exciting time began with a bustling of activities. It was amazing to see how the men were so organized in setting up camp and beginning campfires in this cool weather. All of a sudden, the feelings of fear and worry were replaced by peace and security. Everyone around began to laugh and cry with sighs of relief.

Colonel Dibrell took a moment to meet Thomas, shake his hand and thank him for his hospitality.

"Thomas Maguire," Maguire greeted the colonel.

"Colonel Dibrell from Tennessee," he held out his hand.

"May I ask, sir, what area have you come from and what action have you seen?"

"We are traveling south from Saltville, Virginia, where there was a battle. We have orders to find our way to General Wheeler and truly complicate Sherman's path." Dibrell smiled wryly. "Colonel Anderson is out there with the troops. You should meet General Robinson in the morning."

"Well, it sure is a relief and providence that you're here. You're welcome to whatever forage you need. It's my pleasure to support the Cause. You are truly our heroes," Thomas said.

In late October, Hood and Sherman turned their backs and went in the opposite direction. Hood went to north Alabama, then to Tennessee in hopes that Sherman would chase him and evacuate Atlanta.

November 1

Exciting and grateful feelings soon gave way to concern.

Thomas told Elizabeth, "There are so many soldiers here now that they will soon eat me out of house and home. They have taken nearly all my corn from the Little Creek Field, the Little Bottom, most of the Large Bottom, the Lee Bottom and the old ground."

"We must be thankful that they are here because that likely means that the Yankees will stay away. I'd rather *our soldiers* get our food than the Yankees."

"That's true, I guess." He looked out the window at a plantation full of troops who were waiting for orders as they were eating and storing food. "I don't know what to do."

"There's not much we can do."

A few hours later, Colonel Dibrell's brigade received orders to go to Hood's command. They moved out quickly, but the other two brigades remained for some time.

Thomas continued to provide them with what they needed.

Finally, the other brigades moved on to another plantation and placed scouts at the river and beyond. Maguire was thankful for that. He instructed his hands to gather as much corn and other forage as they could from what the troops had left behind. They grumbled at the thought and began to work.

"This is war time and worse may be coming, but we must try and bear it as best we can," he said.

***

On November 3, a ruckus drew Maguire out to the front porch.

"Mr. Maguire, sir, we have two wounded men here. We need help," Will said. Two men were hunched over an old mule.

"What? What happened here? Get them in the house."

"Sit here," Thomas said once they were inside. "Elizabeth, bring me some water and bandages." She returned with the first aid and tried to nurse the wound. She called for a worker to help her with the other injured man.

"Now, tell me what happened."

"We was down at the old store, and that fool right there," one said, pointing to another who arrived with him, "started shooting his mouth off and wouldn't stop. So I shot him and his horse, too. That'll fix 'im."

"Yeah, and I shot him right back. You killed my horse!" the second man shouted. "Nobody has a horse anymore. That's worse than killing me." He stood up and lunged toward his old friend.

"Ok, back off, now. That's enough," Maguire said and pulled him back.

"Do you happen to have any whiskey, sir? I sure could use it for medicinal purposes," the wounded man said and looked around.

"It looks as though you may have had enough already," Thomas said, but motioned to Elizabeth to bring him some brandy. "Seeing's how you don't get along, maybe one of you should go to another place."

"Yeah, I can't stand the sight of him. I'm leaving. I've friends in Social Circle." The wounded man got up and stumbled toward the door. Over his shoulder, he commented, "Much obliged for your hospitality, sir. What was your name?"

"Maguire."

"Yes, Mr. Maguire. Thank you. And good riddance to you, you sorry horse killer." And he left.

Maguire noted in his diary that night, *What will become of us? God only knows.*

***

On November 4, a scout ran up the hill, yelling, "The Yankees are leaving Atlanta! What if they come this way? Our boys have left the area. They aren't at any of the farms around here. Where have they gone? We need them now."

"Well, if we knew where they were and where they were going, we would be alright, but we just have to be patient."

"I'll go to Weaver's and see if I can find out anything," Anderson said. "I'll leave right after supper."

Worrisome thoughts crowded Maguire's mind. *This news may not be pleasant, I fear. I don't feel much like getting out and looking around the property to see what damage my crop has seen. It's so cold right now, my bones are creaking. Maybe if the weather is better tomorrow, I may try then.*

Three days later, buoyant feelings reappeared as one hundred infantrymen and cavalry, clad in comforting grey, passed by the plantation going to Zoar Church for duty.

"This will be some protection, being so nearby," Thomas said. He felt his day brighten and felt like walking out back to check on things.

He saw his familiar slaves who had run away. He didn't talk to them and simply let them go. They stayed overnight and ate some meals but were gone again before Maguire knew it.

"We should let them decide what they need to do," Elizabeth said. "They know they can come here if they are in want or need."

✳✳✳

On November 8, news spread far and wide that the election was over and Lincoln was re-elected. "Whether for good or evil to the South ..." Maguire mused.

Life went on as the plantations prepared for a possible visit from the Yankees as they left Atlanta. No one knew where they were going, and the uncertainty destroyed their energy. They pulled together and helped each other hide everything that they could.

"This is a bad state of affairs," Maguire told Anderson in the barn. "We must stick together at all costs." He packed up his tools in a box that would withstand the weather when he buried it.

"Good news I heard today," David said as he reached for the hammer. "They say that the Georgia Railroad is ordered to be up and running as far out as Stone Mountain as soon as possible."

"For the Yankees or the Rebels?" asked Maguire.

"God only knows, brother." David shook his head.

"Come on, let's go out and scout around and make sure that all of our treasures are still out of sight."

On November 11, rumors moved quickly that the Confederates got the better of the fight in Atlanta.

Maguire's thoughts traveled to Major Mecaslin and Mary in Atlanta, but he couldn't communicate with them and didn't know the condition of things in Atlanta.

CHAPTER 27

"Where we love is home — home that our feet may leave, but not our hearts."

~ Oliver Wendell Holmes, Sr.

Most of the Atlanta pioneers had only been living in Atlanta for ten to fifteen years or so. What caused them to be so loyal to stand by their homes and refuse to leave? There was a real attachment to the people here, to what they had built and what they accomplished. Those who were not attached or were afraid fled by the thousands. But many remained, determined to take a stand and do their duty to their land, country, and family and to preserve the lifestyle that they knew and loved.

During October and November, travel was uncertain as the Confederate army was north and west in Alabama heading to Chattanooga. There were rumors of the Confederates tearing up the rails and the Yankees fixing them, which made for an anxious and dubious discussion about when or even if they should leave Atlanta and in which direction.

Sherman provided one last train out of Atlanta on November 12, 1864, in which all remaining citizens were forced to leave. The Mecaslins had no choice but to board that train with the destination of Chattanooga.

✳✳✳

There was no food to pack because the pantry was bare except for the last few biscuits that Mary had prepared for the trip. As she cooked the food, she looked at the pantry and tried to recall the last time it was full.

Those were wonderful days of abundance when Mack had the produce store. If only.

She lost interest in preparing for their trip and wandered to the dining room and sat down. She began to dream about better times to recover from the pain. The reality was terrifying — they were walking away from their home and everything they'd owned and known for so many years. It had become the best possible place to live, "this place" being so nondescript because she couldn't think of words to describe the shocking truth. A sense of detachment set in because the thought of holding onto it was too painful.

Will the canary, her darling, colorful companion, chirped, and she smiled and shook her head as she thought of how that bird would survive. She told Mack that she couldn't leave him behind. Will had lifted her spirits when she was down and alone, and it reminded her of Bill Barnes and of better days.

"Aw, what would I do without you, darling little bird? You bring so much pleasure to my life. Look at how you flutter your little wings." She laughed. She reached into the bag and gave him some breadcrumbs.

"What should I wear?" she asked her husband in frustration. "It's cold outside, and we can't pack everything."

"Everything you've ever owned," he said and laughed as she made a silly smirk.

"It sure would make the trunks lighter. How much can we take?"

"I wouldn't take too much, although they say we can. It may be difficult to carry since we don't know what to expect in our travels. And if you're taking Will, well, he'll take up half a trunk." He smiled.

She laughed and said, "No, he will not go in a trunk. I'll carry his cage."

In her final decision, Mary put their valuables and necessities in two trunks and a suitcase. She included the little box where she had placed her daughter's blanket ages ago but which oddly seemed like yesterday. Tears welled up when she realized that she couldn't take Maggie's precious things with her. She walked from room to room and considered that their lovely home may not be here when — and if — they ever returned. The beautiful piano that offered so many happy times, what would become of it? She could feel the love of the family and friends who filled the space of these walls.

Mack was right behind her. "It's all at the mercy of the Yankees now." He put his arm around her. "Are you ready?"

She nodded.

Silent tears streamed down her cheeks as she took one last look. But she was numb to the pain. She stopped, looked ahead, and took the first step away from the house.

Most of their friends had left by this time, but Rodes, Kidd and a few other councilmen and firemen stood nearby and helped Mack load their things onto the train. They thought of their dear friends who were on the front somewhere, they knew not where, as they hugged each other goodbye in hopes of seeing them again someday. Mack thought about how difficult it was to leave, how hard they had worked to protect the city that they loved, and the families and friends that meant so much. He looked over at Mary and knew that, for now, it was best to leave, take care of Mary, and provide her with the comfort and safety that she deserved.

Mack looked at Will and said, "We fought the good fight, my friend. I will see you again on a better day."

Then he turned to Charlie. "I have never worked with a finer group of men, of whom you both are surely a part," he said looking back at Will. "In fellowship, love and trust — F.L.T." He smiled. "And thoughts and prayers for all of our friends in the field."

Will smiled a half-broken smile at his friend, remembering Bill Barnes. "We'll be back. I'll find you in Baltimore, and we will drink to old times," he said, and the men shook hands.

Mack nodded and reached for Mary, who was standing near him. Mary approached the men and smiled. She hugged Kidd and Rodes and promised to write when they arrived at their destination. "Please tell Sarah and Amanda hello, Charlie, when you see them. Will, you are such a wonderful friend. May God bless you all."

Mary and Mack boarded the train and looked back at their friends. When would they see them again, or would they? A sickening feeling swept over Mack, and he forced himself not to think about it. Then they looked out over the town.

It had changed dramatically over such a short period of time. Mack remembered when he first arrived and had so much hope for the future. Then he remembered when he brought Mary to see her home for the first time and how Atlanta had truly become their home. *We will return*, he thought, *and start over*.

The train was packed with people of all walks of life who were starving, dirty, penniless and desperate. Many people didn't know where they would go once they reached Chattanooga. Mary looked around and clutched her bag, not knowing how they would reach Baltimore. All had a look of uncertainty about the next moment in their lives.

The desperate tone turned worse as Mary looked sadly at the destroyed town that had been burned and bombed beyond recognition. Carcasses were everywhere, and the stench was unbearable. Wild dogs fought scavenger birds for the pickings.

Mack saw the horror on Mary's face. "Don't look back, Mary. Don't look back," he said as the train started to move. She dug her face into his chest, feeling physically ill. She wasn't sure if it was because of her condition or fear of the unknown or the visions that she had just witnessed or saying goodbye forever to her friends and home — or all of the above.

CHAPTER 28

"But O the ship, the immortal ship! O ship aboard the ship!
O ship of the body — ship of the soul — voyaging, voyaging, voyaging."

~ Walt Whitman

NOVEMBER 1864

The overloaded train chugged slowly north along the Western and Atlantic toward Chattanooga carrying a heartbroken South. The engineer was experienced with refugee travel and was therefore not optimistic. He knew how challenging it would be to reach the next station because the Yankees would tear up the rails to prevent Confederates from moving through, and then the Confederates would tear up the tracks ten miles down the road to prevent the movement of the Yankees.

Just as he was feeling a moment of relief, the engineer saw a gang of marauders on horses run across the tracks ahead. He made an abrupt stop.

One shot a gun into the air. Panic struck everyone in the cars.

"Oh no, it's the Yankees! They're going to kill us all!" The passengers began pushing and screaming, either trying to hide or get out. A few men pushed their way through the crowded car and jumped. Then they ran across the field, and as they reached the edge of the tree line, the bandits shot them. Horrified, the people still in the cars froze in place and waited. One of the bandits ran over to the warm bodies and took valuables from their pockets.

Mary stuffed the remaining food and money in her sock. Mack discreetly wedged some money and papers in a crack in the boxcar.

Meanwhile, other renegades told people in the cars to get out and throw their valuables in a pile. Mack put his arm around Mary as she was holding Will's cage, walked past the pile, threw his watch in it and kept moving with the crowd.

When the outlaws had all they could carry, they mounted their horses, yelled out "Yip yip" and "Yeehaw" and galloped away.

The freezing, horrified Atlantans stood in shock. The devastation and war that they had experienced in the past several months was not the end. They had barely begun the removal from their homes and had already witnessed murder and robbery.

The bandits had gone through the trunks and taken anything of interest to them. Clothes, broken dishes and other items were strewn along the side of the train. The passengers humbly gathered what they could, repacked broken trunks and torn suitcases, and continued on.

Once they reached Chattanooga, it was chaos. Thousands of people were there, many of whom had been waiting for days for a ride north. People wandered aimlessly, trying to figure out what to do next. Others were hunched in corners with whatever belongings they had. Some were weak, gaunt and sickly. People of all ages, creeds and colors. High society and newly freed people alike were represented.

Mack stepped off the train and shook his head. "Madness," he said.

"God protect us," Mary said aloud.

It had been raining for days, and it was horribly muddy everywhere. Ladies' skirts were covered in mud, and it was so cold that the mud was frozen in places as they crunched across the road.

Mack and Mary were told to get off the train and wait their turn for the next northbound transportation. They said goodbye to a few of their acquaintances who went off in their own direction.

After waiting for some time with no hope for a train, they decided to lighten their already light load. Mack stuffed as many necessities as he could in the carpetbag, and they started walking. Mary carried the birdcage. Several miles down the road, they saw a train stalled at a road crossing in the distance. They hid behind some trees and slowly approached. Mack saw what he thought was an empty boxcar with the doors off. Mary was so cold that she had wrapped her hands with her shawl. Mack motioned to Mary to move slowly. He saw the conductor moving toward the engine. He grabbed Mary's hand and they started running, with the birdcage in her other hand and the carpetbag in his. Just then, the train started to move.

"Oh no, hurry," he said.

They ran faster, and Mack threw the bag into the car. He grabbed the birdcage without thinking and threw it. For a moment, Mary thought *Careful with the birdcage*, instead of fearing for her own safety. Running faster than she had ever run in her life, and with all other thoughts removed from her head, she heard Mack say, "Jump." He grabbed the side of the car, and still holding hands, they jumped onto the train and pulled themselves into the car.

Out of breath, Mary could not feel relief. Mack looked at her and, putting his arm around her, said, "Are you alright?" She nodded, breathing heavily and coughing. She pulled the birdcage to her and saw that Will was a little flustered but moving.

Everything seemed to be going along smoothly for a few miles, and then the train started to slow down. It slowed to a stop, and Mack looked out to find that the tracks were completely gone. They were stowaways and couldn't let their presence be known. They also didn't know where they were going. Then they felt the train move in reverse. They couldn't believe their luck. The train had no choice but to go back the way it had come. Mary looked at Mack and started laughing. They laughed until they cried.

After making their way back to the Chattanooga station, Mary and Mack finally found space on a train going north and gratefully crammed in with the others. The silence in the car was unbearable. An old-timer in the corner whittling a pipe whistled the first line of "Dixie" in a long, drawn-out fashion and then paused. A man from another corner whistled the next line, and the whole car broke into song:

Look away, look away, look away, Dixieland
I wish I were in Dixie, away, away
In Dixieland, I'll take my stand
To live and die in Dixie.

And then they sang again in a more upbeat tone, smiled and cried.

Mary looked over and saw that a little girl about Maggie's age was cold and didn't have a coat. She glanced at her mother and pulled a shawl from her bag. She asked her mother if she could put it around the girl, and her mother nodded gratefully. Mary reached over and gently covered the little girl. Pulling the warmth gently around herself, she said, "Thank you, ma'am."

Days later, after Mack and Mary had been sleeping in the boxcar and traveling in deplorable conditions, shoulder to shoulder with strangers, the train pulled into the Nashville station.

They arrived worn and hungry to see thousands of people waiting — waiting to find a boat or a way farther north or simply someplace safe. They thought it was bad in Chattanooga, but it was even worse in Nashville.

It had rained for days, and a cold front had come through. It was the coldest winter that Tennessee had seen in years. The masses were not prepared for the cold and some froze to death. Elderly, young, babies — they camped out all over the area. There were too many to care for and not enough rations to go around. Mack and Mary looked around in shock.

Mack helped his wife from the train. The cold wind whipped through their bodies like a razor. The freezing rain went right to their bones.

Mary lifted her skirts from the mud as she walked. She felt the cold seep into her socks through the soles of her worn shoes.

Mack looked toward the river and noticed someone familiar.

"Look, Mary, it's Bill Sheridan and the Connellys. Come on!"

As they approached each other, Mack said, "Hello, dear friend." He shook Sheridan's and Connelly's hands. Mary hugged Mrs. Connelly.

"Have you seen anyone else?" Mack asked.

"No, we arrived just a while ago," Connelly said.

"How are we going to make it out of here? I can't even find out how long the list is for a boat," Sheridan said.

"Let's find a seat for the ladies, and we'll see what we can find out from the officials," Mack said. They took the ladies to some trees away from the group. The ladies stood together and pulled their shawls more tightly around themselves, trying to get warm. Bill stayed with them while the other two men explored.

"We won't be long," Mack said.

He approached someone who was giving food to a little boy. "Do you know how long it will take to get river transportation north?" The young man looked at him in desperation and moved on.

They asked another man if he could help them, and he pointed to a long line of people waiting in front of a tent. "You might as well get in line."

Mary told Mrs. Connelly, "It's so cold. I can't imagine going any further north. I can't imagine staying here either. What will become of us?"

"May God help us," Mrs. Connelly said.

The ladies looked around and noticed a small camp nearby where people were laughing and joking and passing around a bottle as they sat huddled among a couple of mattresses and trunks.

"They are making the best of the situation," Mary said.

Down the way from them, a group of newly freed men, women and children were singing gospel music, sometimes joyfully and at other times sorrowfully. A doctor was dashing around checking on the sick, while a preacher was delivering his sermon to whoever would listen. A large crowd began gathering around him.

Mack came back with a report. "The Federal official said that it could be days before a boat would be able to take us north. They are sending people out of the city as fast as they can."

Mary, Mack and their friends found a space way out from the crowded refugee station and sat down. They tried to pass the time by sharing stories. It was too much to bear.

After a while in the cold, when they could stand no more, it started to snow. They huddled closer and looked around in despair.

"Do you know of anyone here who might take us in for the night? Mary is with child and she can't stay out here in this weather," Mack said to his friends.

"Oh, Mary, honey, my dear child. We must take care of you," said Mrs. Connelly.

Just then, a fiddler played a favorite tune. Mary was miserable. Mack stood and bowed to her and asked, "Mrs. Mecaslin, may I have this dance?" Mary looked at him with a tilted brow.

"Come on," he whispered, "it will keep you warm." She stood up, and he held her closely. "We're going to get through this," he said quietly, and they danced.

Mr. Connelly asked his wife to dance, and they joined the Mecaslins. The fiddler noticed attention to his music, and he played another lively tune.

✳✳✳

A commotion broke out near a tavern, and they learned that it was opening for business. People were quickly moving in that direction. "You can't come in here if you don't have money," said the man at the door as refugees flocked to the entrance. Mack showed his money, and they entered.

Mary was reluctant to enter a place that she tended to strictly avoid but then realized it might be her only chance to get warm.

"Come in, little lady, and bring your cheery yellow bird," said the barkeep. "We could use a little song or two." Mary smiled shyly and entered.

Mack and Bill Sheridan made friends with the barkeep, regaling him with stories from Atlanta and their battles. Mack laughed and continued their talk. "I remember the first day that I arrived in Atlanta. I walked into the saloon, and immediately this guy named Bill Barnes introduced himself and his friend Will Kidd, and we have been friends ever since."

The bartender said, "Will Kidd. You know Will Kidd?"

"Why, yes, we're the best of brothers. Do you know him?"

"Yes, but I haven't seen him lately. Have you seen him? How is he?"

"I saw him when we left Atlanta. He's worse for wear, but aren't we all? He said he would be right behind us on his way north."

"Well, a friend of Will's is a friend of mine."

They were safe and warm, but it was getting late. "You need a place to

171

stay?" the bartender asked Mack.

"Oh, yes, we would appreciate any help you can give us and will be happy to pay for any assistance."

The man was taken by these charming characters and wanted to help them out. "The owner has a small mat in the back but not enough room for five."

"That's ok," Mack said, "I'll sleep on the floor or in a chair."

The other men looked at each other and chimed in, "I'll sleep anywhere."

That night, when the bar was closed and quiet and the friends were finally settling in for sleep, Mary whispered to her husband lying next to her on the floor, "Mack, remember the time at the parade when Maggie was standing up on the store rail so she could see everything and watching you proudly march through town in your gallant fireman's uniform? She yelled at you, 'Hey Daddy,' and you winked at her. She was so thrilled and loved you so much."

Mack looked down and quietly said, "Yes, I remember like it was yesterday," and he hugged his wife. "I miss her every day."

Mack became regretful and shook his head, realizing the reality of sleeping on the cold, hard floor of a tavern with his pregnant wife next to him. *How did I let myself get to this point?* After a while, he touched her hand. "I should have sent you to your mother's a long time ago."

"We're partners. I am not going to leave you. Wherever you go, I will go. We will get through this together."

"I'm so sorry, Mary," he said softly.

"It's shelter from the storm, my dear man."

He hugged her and said, "Let's get some sleep."

During times of difficulty when you are social with others and know the art of polite conversation, discussing the difficulties of the day, you may not really want to talk about it at all and won't talk about how it really feels inside because there are no words to describe it. Those feelings really are pushed down until late at night when thoughts that you wish wouldn't enter your mind pop out of nowhere. The fear and uncertainty arise about where your next meal will come from or if you will ever get home.

I'm almost out of money, Mack thought.

God protect us, thought Mary, and she held her belly.

✳✳✳

Mack and Mary had to wait two days to board a boat with the final destination of Cincinnati, Ohio, although there were stops along the way. Bill Sheridan and the Connellys were on the same boat.

The refugees had a difficult journey during the coldest December they had ever known. They had to stop at two locations due to the overcrowded and unsanitary conditions.

Sherman was to provide rations along the way, but they found that there were few rations and long lines when there was food. Once per day, the Federals would provide a cold hard biscuit or bread. Very little fresh water was available. Whenever they could get it, Mack would do his best to get more. For the baby. So much for the guarantee of rations.

The Southern population was not prepared for the cold weather and disease, and illness was common. Mack would often give his food to Mary with her objection, and he began losing his strength and coughing more often.

By the time they made it to Cincinnati, their friends decided to stay there, but Mack and Mary needed to soldier on.

They waited for another boat and had to pay a fare to go to the next destination at Parkersburg, West Virginia.

The journey to Cincinnati was too much for most. They had to stop there because passage was no longer free for refugees. They had endured so much, but Mary and Mack still found the strength to move on, through the travels north, the weather, hunger, only thinking of their destination at some times, other times only thinking of how to hold on until morning, through the darkness of night and the fear of not surviving. When she didn't think she could move, Mary remembered her baby, this new life. She found something new to hold onto, some hope and faith. From fear stems courage. The main thing, step by step, was food and shelter and love for her husband. She wanted to reach out to strangers sometimes, but it was difficult to communicate when she saw that glazed-over look of shock of those wandering lost souls.

✳✳✳

Starving, discouraged passengers disembarked at Parkersburg. A tedious, freezing, ongoing journey continued. However, Mack found strength and became almost giddy because he knew the train tracks would go straight to Baltimore. Now they seemed closer. *Just a little longer*, he thought. *We can make it.* As they left the boat, a stranger asked them where they were going.

"We're heading to Baltimore as soon as we can," remarked Mack.

"Well, man, you may have a time of it if you want to go all the way to Baltimore on *that* train. Confederates have been tearing up these tracks throughout the war. You'll never make it that way."

Mack's gut twinged, and Mary's heart sank.

We have to, thought Mack. *We have no choice and nowhere else to go.*

CHAPTER 29

"Through the ample open door of the peaceful country barn,
A sun-lit pasture field, with cattle and horses feeding;
And haze, and vista, and the far horizon, fading away."

~ Walt Whitman

Wasting no time and determined to continue on their journey, Mack and Mary found their way to the train station. When they arrived, it was closed. They had to spend the night at the station. The next morning when the office opened, the keeper said that it would cost eleven dollars per person to get to Baltimore, and there were no guarantees during war. Mack noticed a sign that said it was 320 miles to Baltimore.

"How long will it take to get there?" he asked.

"Like I said, no guarantees. Last I heard, it was taking maybe a week, depending on the damage done."

Mack reached for his money. It wasn't in his pocket. "Mary? What?"

He looked around and checked all over his body as if he may have misplaced it. *Somebody stole my wallet.* He looked in his bag. Someone had rummaged through it and taken everything of value.

"Mother Mary, help us," he said despondently. Panic ensued and an overwhelming feeling of helplessness arose. Mack looked around frantically but deep inside knew that it was of no use.

"NO more free ride for refugees. You have to pay for a ticket. Money or leave!"

"We have no money or anything to trade. What do we do now?" He paced around in a circle, waving his hands and sweeping his hands through his dark hair.

Mary dug out a few coins that she had stuffed in her sock and handed them to her husband.

He put his arm around her and said, "We can eat one more time."

Mack didn't have the money. So close but so far. The train could have taken them home to his family, a warm meal, and shelter from this awful storm. They started walking, not really sure where they were going. Mack had no hope, and Mary was on the verge of tears.

"I don't know how far I can go, Mack." He noticed how gaunt she was. She leaned over and held her stomach as if to get sick, but she could only gag. He went to the nearest place for food and spent the last of their money.

Even when you are beaten down, have lost everything, including friends and family — and you don't know where some of your friends and family are — don't know where your next meal will come from, having to take care of someone else, something happens deep inside. You keep going, don't quit, intestinal fortitude, as long as you can breathe, have faith, you will survive. Just when you don't think you will make it, someone reaches out, a sliver of blue sky, shelter from the storm. Berries in the field, a spring of water, a bit of shade. Relief!

✳✳✳

A short distance outside of Parkersburg, Mack and Mary noticed a farmhouse with a barn nearby. Exhausted and numb from the cold, they desperately needed shelter from the freezing, windy night. They hid in the barn until morning. The farmer went into the barn and began to milk the cow. He heard a cough in the hay. Mack and Mary both had colds, and Mary couldn't prevent her cough. The farmer looked over and was startled. "Hey, who goes there?"

Mack came out from hiding and apologized, "I'm so sorry to intrude, but we needed shelter." Mack tried to explain Mary's condition and, at once, the farmer gave Mary some milk and took them inside the house. He told his wife right away and placed them next to the fire. His wife quickly found Mary clean clothes and dry socks. The farmer found a clean shirt and pants for the stranger. He took the birdcage and placed it nearby in the dining room.

Before long, the kind innkeeper whipped up some eggs, bacon, bread, butter and milk, lots of milk. They ate and ate until they could eat no more. Finally, a warm fullness filled their sickly bellies. No one spoke. Most of the time, their eyes were cast down toward their food.

Mary began to cry.

"Are you alright, dear?" The farmer's wife asked.

"I'm just so grateful," she said.

"Why don't you come over here and sit by the fire?"

Mary moved over to the fire and soon fell fast asleep. The thirty-one-year-old Mary had seen more in her young life than she had ever dreamed or wanted. The kind wife handed Mack a warm quilt to cover his wife. His face showed unbridled gratitude for all they had done.

"How can I ever thank you? You have saved us."

"Where are you from, sir?" the farmer asked as he poked the fire.

"Atlanta, Georgia. We're headed to my family in Baltimore."

The farmer was quiet. He played with the poker in the fire a little more.

"I heard it was bad down there," the farmer said.

"Yes, we lost everything."

"I am so sorry to hear that." And more silence. "Time to heal. Then you will begin again. I want nothing more than to tend to my land and protect my family just like you. May we find that peace someday."

Mack nodded. "Indeed."

"My wife has prepared a bed for you for the night. Please stay and rest here."

"Thank you so much. We are grateful for your hospitality. My own family could not have treated us better."

"Our pleasure. Now don't you worry. Rest now."

The next morning, Mack asked if he could stay and help the farmer to repay him for his help. The farmer said, "We all can use a little help now and again."

They stayed another day, and Mary rested. She chatted with the hostess and enjoyed Will's songs. Mack fixed a fence and patched a hole in the barn roof. He cleaned out the chicken coop and chopped wood. He sat with Mary and the couple by the fire in the evening. They had books to read and stories to share. The kind lady gave Mary some yarn to knit booties and some crumbs for the bird. He began to chirp again so sweetly, and he brought a delightful aura to the room. They had a dog, and Mary said, "We have a dog, too. His name is Ole Mack. We had to send him south on a train. We didn't want him to get hurt. We hope he's found a good home like this one."

Mack and Mary decided that it was time to go. They were saying their goodbyes, and as Mack shook the farmer's hand, he felt something. The farmer was trying to give him money. "No, sir. I did the work to repay you."

"Look, son." He covered Mack's hand with the money and looked him in the eye. "You've got to get your wife to your people. Take it and get tickets for the train. It's got to be."

Mack was dumbfounded and speechless. He shook the man's hand again, and said, "What a kind Christian brother you are. God bless you. I hope I can repay you someday."

The farmer said to Mack, "Maybe this is all we've got right now, brother, helping one another. You better be going while you've got daylight."

The farmer's wife hugged them both and gave Mary a bag of food.

"God bless you, dear people, and may God grant that we meet again," Mary said.

The farmer nodded his head and said, "May God be with you. I just know you're going to have a fine baby."

The farm couple stood in the doorway and watched as their new friends walked down the road and turned and waved.

They were on their way, finally.

"What beautiful country this is!" Mary exclaimed.

Mack was pensive. A moment of uncertainty now clouded his thoughts as he realized that he was returning to his family as a failure. As the oldest in the family, he had helped to take care of the younger ones when he was at home. He felt that he should be strong and successful and a leader. But he was returning in rags, weak and penniless. *What will they think of me?*

BALTIMORE

They arrived at dusk, exhausted and hungry, dirty and in rags. Mack carried the carpetbag and the birdcage. He soon saw a friend.

"Mack, hey, Mack," Patrick ran over and hugged him. "It is so good to see you. It has been so long."

"It's good to see you, too. We've just arrived on the train. Been traveling for weeks now. This is my wife, Mary."

"Hello, well, let me give you a ride." Mack helped Mary into the buggy. "I'll take you straight home," Patrick said.

Soon after, Patrick pulled the buggy up to the house and yelled, "George, everybody, Mack's home!"

George came running out the door. Their eyes met and the pain was understood. Mack was surprised to see George, though, not knowing if he was still at the front. He helped Mary from the buggy and ran to meet his brother. They shook hands. A brief memory of childhood was whisked away by the realization that his brother had fought and struggled in the war. Years of worry and waiting for both of them were relieved in that moment.

His mother stepped into the doorway with her apron on. "Oooh my, John. John, you're home." She ran down the steps and flung her arms open, and he hugged her. She cried and wouldn't let him go.

His father approached, held out his hand, and looked him in the eye. "Welcome home, son." They shook hands. Mack turned to blink away the water in his eye. Everyone gathered around Mary and Mack with hugs and kisses and ushered them into the house.

✳✳✳

After a warm dinner, they all sat around and visited.

"I've written letters that I had hoped would reach you, but I've also written letters that I never sent. George, how long have you been home?" Mack asked.

"I was mustered out in October," said his brother, who was now much older than his years.

Mack looked him over and remembered a much skinnier, innocent boy of sixteen when he last saw him.

"How are our sisters, Rebecca and Catherine Marie?"

"They are well, and we can send for them tomorrow."

"We're so happy that you're home," his mother said. "You and Mary must be tired."

"I haven't been able to tell you that Mary is expecting."

Everyone in the room lit up. "Well, how wonderful!"

Mack's father said, "That calls for a celebration!"

"That's so nice. We haven't really had time to celebrate."

His father brought out the brandy and set up glasses. "To Mary and Mack and their exciting news! We can use some good news around here."

They retired early that night due to exhaustion and were happy to be in Baltimore in a safe and loving home.

✳✳✳

After about two weeks of sleeping in a warm, comfortable bed, being provided with good food and being surrounded by a supportive family, Mack and Mary were recovering nicely.

Mary wrote her mother a short letter with not much to say. She had been through so much that she couldn't put into words and was careful about what she told her mother.

Holidays with family and weeks of rest left the couple feeling grateful to be safe and warm, but still they had a sense of incompleteness. Leaving Mary to rest and recover in their room, Mack joined George and his father at breakfast one morning. Mack was becoming stronger. They could see he was unsettled.

"What can we do for you, son?" his father asked.

"I would like to travel north and see if we can find some people who might have news or information about our Atlanta friends and neighbors. It would be great to know that they arrived safely."

178

"Say no more. I can see why you're concerned," his father said. They planned the trip.

Soon after, the men set off to New York, Philadelphia and other towns and ran into friends from Atlanta who had also refugeed north. He ran into the Lynch brothers. Mack and John Lynch agreed that they would return to Atlanta as soon as they could. They exchanged addresses and how to communicate with each other so they would know where each other would be. Lynch told Mack to look in the *Baltimore Daily News* each Friday under Rooms for Rent. He was instructed to look for Lynch's name and remember the code that they shared to be aware of news of friends and updated information.

✳✳✳

The Mecaslins attended many churches during their stay. One of their favorite services included a sermon that was delivered in Danish. "That was the best sermon I have ever heard," Mack declared, and everyone laughed.

Mary spent some time at Mack's sister's house and relaxed while reading and knitting as much as possible to recover from the trip. She wrote many letters, including some to her uncle Thomas. She didn't receive a letter from him and was concerned.

✳✳✳

On April 9, 1865, General Lee met General Grant to surrender at the Appomattox Court House in Virginia. The soldiers began going home in droves.

Mack learned the location of many of his friends, and some were returning to Atlanta. Captain Kidd was in Philadelphia but was on his way back to Chattanooga and then to Atlanta in May. Mack was hoping to hear from him soon. They learned that John Ennis was killed at the fight at Weldon Road. Jim and Peter Lynch were in Nashville. Mack saw John Flynn and Hayden, both dear friends and involved citizens of Atlanta, in Philadelphia. Mary and Tom Malone and family were in Louisville, Kentucky. He found no mention of where Charles Rodes was. Henry Gullatt, brother of Amanda Gullatt Barnes, had died, but Mack found no other information. He didn't know where many of their other friends were, including friends in the field such as Bill Barnes. Mack and Mary had not received any word about Thomas Maguire either. Southerners were scattered in many places.

Mack and Mary longed for home.

"Thank goodness for your mother and father and family who took us in," Mary said. "I don't know what we would have done without them. I

179

know you are so happy to visit with your family. But as the war is now over, and Lee has surrendered, everyone is going home. I'm so heartbroken about our damaged country, feeling the victory from the North. But I have been longing to get back home. I need to go, Mack. I'm sorry. I have lasted with good spirits as long as I can, but now I have to get home." She lowered her head, buried her head in her hands and sobbed.

Mack knew it was time. He was mostly waiting for her to say something. He was concerned about her condition but knew where her heart was and how much it meant for her to be in Augusta with her parents when the baby was born. She had only received a couple of letters from her parents. He knew they had been worried about Mary's safety and, getting on in years, wondered when or if they would see her again.

He also yearned to get back to Atlanta. He would, of course, be with Mary in Augusta. Atlanta would be no place for her right now, not knowing what was taking place there, but their home was good ole Atlanta. So much unfinished and so much unknown. Mary, too, was anxious to get back to see how their home and town had fared since they left. They had heard rumors and reports from people, but they didn't really know.

"I'll make the arrangements, my dear. Let's go home."

Mary was elated. "Thank you, thank you." She cradled her belly and said, "We're going home."

CHAPTER 30

"There was no dignity in fighting this war, no celebration. No glory in this war, just necessity."

~ Unknown

THE PROMISED LAND

On November 16, four days after the last train of refugees left Atlanta, the families at The Promised Land were on constant alert. Maguire and David Anderson sat up by the fire all night keeping watch over the homestead. "After burning Atlanta and Decatur, they are surely on the way to destroy us next," Thomas told David.

A scout knocked on the door. Thomas wearily wobbled over to the door and opened it. The worried young man said, "They've burned more houses at the mountain, sir. I must move on to tell the others."

"Come on, David, we have more work to do." David and Thomas and the hands scurried to hide all the items in view such as the toolbox, horse and buggy. "Back in the house."

"I need to head on home and make sure all is well at my house," said David. "They will be here by nine o'clock if they are coming this way." He moved off in the direction of his house on Rockbridge Road. Thomas looked at his watch. It was seven o'clock.

"He's right about that," he said. He walked back in the house and told his wife, "We are now waiting for the worst to come, still hoping they will not come this way."

After some time, Thomas couldn't wait, and he walked over to the Anderson homestead.

When he was walking down the road, he heard the sound of hooves and hid behind some trees. Moments later, he was shaking in his boots as he saw Yankee troops on horses and on foot, spreading across the land like a wave of locusts. Thomas ran as fast as his legs could carry him, dodging the trees and looking back in fear, hoping that none of those evil bugs were after him.

"David, they're here." Thomas huffed and puffed as he arrived at the door. "I just saw them on the road. They're heading to my place."

"Do you want to go back?"

"No, I think we're safer here."

"Who was it? Could you tell?" David asked.

"No, I saw them and took off. There were Yankees as far as I could see."

Slocum's corps were the troops that Maguire had seen. Henry Slocum commanded the Twentieth Corps and, on September 2, had occupied Atlanta. Sherman's "March to the Sea" included Slocum's group barreling their way east of Atlanta and preying on the Southern countryside, including The Promised Land.

Thomas and David crept close enough to watch the show. The Union troops came in droves and camped all around the house. He saw them slaughter hogs and sheep. "Look at that, skinning my sheep to regale their Yankee palates," Thomas said bitterly. The destruction continued as they made themselves at home. Thomas and David stayed in the woods all night but didn't get much sleep. "Not very pleasant for either body or mind, David, not knowing what is going on at home."

Where are Dibrell's corps when we need them? Where are they, anyway? David wondered.

They awoke suddenly the next morning after a fitful sleep to some stirring in the woods. A wandering sheep had made its way into the woods. David ran him back up to safety and headed back into the woods, dodging about and trying to see if he could spot any Yankees. A few stragglers finally left around eleven o'clock, from what they could see from their hiding place.

A sleepy Thomas finally came wandering up his walk around 2 p.m. He checked on all of the folks at home and was happy to see that they were not abused. He shook his head in horror at the destruction of property that he found. The gin house and screw were burned, and the stables and barn were in smoldering ashes.

"Gone, all gone," he said. The fences were burned, and the demolition continued as far as he could see. The carriage and big wagon were burned up. Everything was gone — corn and potatoes were gone, and horses and steers disappeared. Sheep, chickens and geese were nowhere to be seen.

As he moved around the property, it was too much to take in. He slowly wandered over to the ashes of the barn. He noticed that the syrup boiler was damaged, and one barrel of syrup was smoking and ruined. Saddles and bridles were in pieces and burned.

He gathered his farmhands together and said, "Help me try to salvage some fragments of the spoils. It is useless to try to record the destruction of property. Still, I hope we can live."

The discussion was somber at the dinner table that night.

"I think we have plenty of corn and wheat and syrup hid out," Maguire said. "Some twenty bushels of wheat burned in the gin house. Some were ours and some were Mr. Minor's and others'. We have much to do to save the corn cribs. The gin house and the straw piles are still burning. Three bales of cotton were burned, and the others were cut open to make beds for the soldiers. All of those bales belonged to a local. The gin thrash and fan were burned, and parts of the machinery are in ruins. It's the destruction of Jerusalem on a small scale."

The next day, they awoke to the scene of plunderers who arrived in droves. The family did all they could to save their goods from the thieves. Still, there was a sense that the Yankees were finally gone, hopefully forever. Several dead horses and mules were scattered here and there. One horse was limping along, and a hand ran to fetch him and patch him up.

A scout came to the plantation, shouting, "Yankees left the Georgia Railroad below the circle and turned off towards Monticello. Wheeler's group is on their trail."

"Any news from Atlanta, son?" Maguire asked.

"Yes, sir. Not good news, sir. Atlanta is in ruins, but there are a few houses left."

Maguire thought of Mary and Mack. "How about our people? Do you know anything?"

"Oh, they're all gone from there now, sir. Forced to leave."

Maguire took a breath and looked off into the distance.

✳✳✳

December found the plantation folks working the cornfields when they could. They had little wood to make fire to stay warm, but they had enough to eat so far.

The Yankees were nowhere to be seen. A few soldiers came by and Maguire charged them two dollars each to stay.

He wrote in his diary on Christmas Eve, *Little or no preparations for Christmas are being made. No stockings filled with candy, no turkey, no pies.*

The next day, he wrote, *Not much fuss on Christmas morning by the little ones about Christmas. Not like it used to be in other years.*

Maguire rocked on the front porch, sewed shoes and aimlessly looked out over his desolate land, wondering how he was going to pay his taxes. "What will happen to us now? God only knows."

CHAPTER 31

"I will go back to the great sweet mother,
Mother and lover of men, the sea."

~ *Algernon Charles Swinburne*

Mack and Mary left Baltimore on June 21, 1865. When they arrived in New York on that Thursday morning, they unloaded their baggage and, of course, Will the bird. Mack told Mary to sit on a bench with their baggage, and he went to secure their place on the ship.

Mack couldn't get a stateroom on the steamship *Chase* because all of the rooms were occupied. Mary was quite distressed, and Mack was upset because they didn't know what they would do.

Why did I not make previous arrangements?

Mack began to talk to some passengers but couldn't find anyone who would help him. Finally, several hours later, having had nothing to eat and feeling frustrated, he found two people who were willing to share a stateroom, and he paid them well to do so. Thank goodness Marshall and Lynch were there to help and see them off.

"Remember to stay in touch," Mack said.

"I'll see you in Atlanta," Marshall smiled and shook Mack's hand.

Mary and Mack boarded the ship along with their darling bird. Mack was comfortable on the ship and loved the adventure and excitement of it all. He had not traveled by sea in recent years, but the familiar feeling returned.

The trip seemed well until Saturday when the weather was rough and the wind was unbearable. Mary could barely hold on in her uncomfortable state as the ship was knocked about. Mack worried that this trip was not in her best interest and thought for a moment that they should have stayed in Baltimore. She became dizzy and seasick, and the minutes seemed like hours. The birdcage was by her bed but had become unstable and began to roll to and fro on the floor. Will was being tossed about. Mary was horrified and called Mack to get the birdcage and find a safe place for Will.

The storm continued for days. Their faith was again tested during the torrential wind and rain.

"Hang on, Mary. Just hang on. I love you so much. We are going to get through this. I will be right here with you." Mack held his wife's hand. He did not show the deep concern he felt for his fragile wife.

✳✳✳

Two o'clock Monday morning found them off the bar at Savannah. They stayed anchored there until daylight, when a pilot came aboard and took them over the bar and up the river to Savannah around 10 a.m.

When they arrived in Savannah, they disembarked and went directly to find passage on another boat that would take them up the river to Augusta. Only one boat was available at the time, and Mack knew his chances were slim. Still, with great focus and grit, he determined that this was the only way. He found a bench for Mary and placed the small amount of luggage and Will the bird next to her.

"I will return soon," he said.

When he boarded the *Amazon*, he found the captain on deck and spoke to him. "Sir, I need passage as quickly as possible to get my wife to Augusta. She is with child and may give birth at any time. Please, sir, do you have a room for us?"

The captain replied, "No, absolutely not. This is a freight steamer, and I don't have accommodations or provisions for you, and I can't take care of her. I would recommend that you go elsewhere for your transportation."

"Please reconsider. I will take full responsibility."

The captain could see the weariness and desperation in Mack's eyes. He had no time to argue. "Very well, sir. It's your decision. We leave in fifteen minutes." He shook his head and walked away quickly, waving his hands in the air.

Mack ran frantically down to the dock and saw a man sitting in a chair smoking a cigar behind a produce stand. He approached the man and startled him by saying, "Hello, sir, may I buy your chair? And please allow me to purchase a few of your fine peaches there." The man stood up. Mack shook his hand, gave him some money, grabbed the chair and ran over to Mary sitting on the bench. He gave her the peaches and said, "Come on,

Mary. We have to hurry."

Mary smiled at her thoughtful husband and was so grateful to have some fruit. "Georgia peaches. We're almost home." She got up slowly and took some time getting to the ship. Mack put the chair down among some boxes and barrels of whiskey and told her to sit down. Mary looked up at him inquisitively.

"It's the best I can do right now."

Speechless, she looked around.

"Mary, I don't know when another boat will be available. It could be days, and I don't know where I can get medical help for you here. I don't ever want to find you in a state that we were in before."

"Well, sir, you know how I feel. Let's go home."

Mack wasn't satisfied with the situation. His wife seemed so uncomfortable. He doubted it would be long before she was miserable. The heat of the day was starting to wear her down. He began wandering.

He started talking to a member of the crew. They talked about the days gone by and the current status of the Confederacy. Mack interrupted and stated that Mary may have her baby on the freighter. "Well, sir, the captain and the clerk both have staterooms up by the pilot house." He pointed in that direction. "Perhaps you should talk to them."

"Hmm, thank you, kind sir!"

Having already bothered the captain enough, Mack thought it best to approach the clerk and find out what he could. After checking on Mary, he looked for the clerk. He approached him in a friendly manner. "Hello, my good man. How goes it?"

"Well, sir, and you?"

"Fine, thank you. I was wondering, would it be possible to borrow your stateroom for a while for my wife? She is with child and seated over there among the crates and barrels. She's being knocked about quite a bit. I would be happy to offer you some monetary compensation for your generosity."

"I see. These are difficult times, and what kind of a man would I be if I didn't allow comfort for a fine lady? You may take my stateroom if it will help."

"It is gentlemen like you who remind me of why we are here. I am forever indebted to you, kind sir." He shook his hand.

Mack took Mary to a room that was six feet long, six feet high and four feet wide. A storage space, really, and so stifling hot. But it did have a cot that she could lie down on. It was a relief.

"Oh, this will never do," he said, disappointed.

"This will have to do," she said in a tired and weak voice. She began to sit down.

Mack sat down next to her on the floor, and they both slept for a while.

The next day, it was so hot that it was unbearable. *Why is the freighter moving so slowly? It's so humid and stuffy in this little room*, Mary thought. She fanned herself with a piece of thin board. She pulled her handkerchief from her sleeve and wiped her brow.

As the day wore on, Mack tried to cool her with rags and did his best to comfort her. *Just get us to Augusta in time*, he thought.

"Mack, what if we don't make it to Augusta? I need to get home."

"We will get there. Don't worry, it's going to be fine."

Mack had a lot of time to wander around and visit with people. He had a lot of time to think. He couldn't help but ponder what awaited him in Atlanta. He kept getting updates about what was going on. *I can't think of that now*, he thought. He kept pushing feelings back down to that space within that allowed him to move forward.

He started talking to a Confederate soldier who said that he was trying to get back home to Alabama. "Everyone who can is heading home. Why, I was at Saylor Creek, and it was just awful," the soldier said.

"Oh, I heard that a close friend of mine was at Saylor Creek. Do you know Lieutenant Bill Barnes?"

"Sir, I am sorry to give you this sad news, but he died in a hospital where I was working as a surgeon a few weeks after he was wounded."

Mack hung his head. He wiped his brow. *It must be 100 degrees out here*, he thought.

"We were best friends. I promised him I would take care of his wife and family."

"I am so sorry to hear it. War has no mercy."

"I don't know how to tell his wife or even my wife."

Mack told him about Mary.

"Can I be of assistance?" the surgeon asked.

"What? Ha! Please come by and visit my wife. She seems fine but a bit weary. We have been traveling by sea for many days now." Mack was relieved.

The surgeon went to see Mary.

"I am grateful to see you, sir, although I plan to make it to Augusta. My mother and family will care for me," Mary said.

"I am sure that's true, ma'am. But allow me to check on you, and please call on me if you need me." He said his goodbyes.

"What is it, Mack? What's wrong?"

"Nothing, just worried about you." *I can't tell her now*, he thought. *I don't want to upset her.*

"No, what's wrong? What has happened? You look sick." Mary reached out to him. "Sit down, please. Now, tell me," she said calmly.

He knew he couldn't keep it from her. His heart was aching. "It's Bill."

"What? What have you heard?"

"That surgeon just told me that he didn't make it."

"Oh, Bill. Poor Bill. Did he suffer?" She began to cry. Mack shook his head and shrugged his shoulders.

"I didn't want to tell you because you don't need to be upset right now," he said with a worried brow.

"You couldn't keep that from me. I wonder if Amanda knows. Dear, sweet Amanda. Amanda and the family. We have to get to them."

"Not now, Mary. Just rest. You need your strength." Mack held her hand and sat quietly in his own pain.

After some time of sitting together, Mary fell asleep. Mack felt the need to check on the condition of things on the ship. He recognized some acquaintances that they knew from Atlanta who were also desperately trying to get home. A few people went to visit Mary and wish her well.

"No need to worry," she said. "I will be home soon."

✳✳✳

However, Thursday morning around 7 a.m., opposite Burke County, Georgia, about fifty miles from Augusta, they had one more passenger than they boarded with.

The surgeon was on hand to deliver a healthy little girl amidst the bags and barrels and sea life aboard the ship. All rejoiced mightily for this new life. Mary was weak and frail, but she was happy. The doctor handed the newborn to Mack, and he looked down in awe.

He looked at Mary and said, "I hold the future in my hands."

Will the bird sang sweetly.

Their daughter was dubbed Mary Amazon, as the sailors would say, in honor of the ship. Her given name was Mary Catherine "Kathleen" Mecaslin.

✳✳✳

The *Amazon* landed at the wharf at Augusta around nine o'clock that evening. Mack looked around for help, and a worker named Harrison asked, "May I help you?"

"Harrison, do you know Augusta well?" asked Mack.

"Yes, sir. I've lived here all my life."

"Please go to 12 Fenwick, the home of my wife's family. Ask for Mr. Mullin and tell him we are here. Thank you. Hurry, won't you?"

Harrison jumped on his horse and galloped off. In no time at all, he knocked at the home of Mr. Mullin. "I have a message from Major Mecaslin. They have arrived at the wharf, and Mrs. Mecaslin has had her baby. She's doing well and has asked that you visit as soon as you can."

"Aye, sir," Mullin said as he reached out to shake his hand. "God bless! God bless! Saints be praised! Come in, please! Everyone up, good news. Good news! Margaret, Mary's home!"

Margaret tore down the stairs and stood at the landing with her hand over her mouth as tears welled up in her eyes. She was speechless. James Jr., Amanda and Jane all ran quickly to the parlor and yelled, "What? Really, Dad? Where is she? Mack, too?"

"Yes, they're at the wharf. All right then, hitch up the horses. Let's go!"

When they arrived at the dock, they found Mary still on the ship in the stateroom. Mary cried with joy when she saw her mother and father. She couldn't speak, only tears and smiles. It had been more than a year and many lifetimes ago since she had seen her family. Her heart was full. "What a blessing, what a blessing!" she said. Her family surrounded her with hugs. James hit Mack on the back, and they shook hands.

Ole Mack jumped off the wagon and ran to Mary, his tail wagging. Mary looked up and smiled, a tear running down her cheek. "Mack, Ole Mack!"

The dog licked her hand and ran to Mack and jumped happily around him. Mack stooped down and petted his dog and said, "Hey, old buddy, how have you been? Here to welcome us? Good dog!"

Mack spent one more night on the floor of the stateroom next to Mary as they decided that she was still too fragile to move. They made arrangements to transport her home the next day.

An omnibus arrived to take her home early the following morning. As Mary and the newborn were waiting to board the carriage, she looked back at Mack and realized that the birdcage was not with her. She reached for Mack and said, "Mack, where is Will? Please ask someone to go back to the ship and get him."

Mack looked over at one of the sailors who heard her request, and he went back for the bird. He looked all around the deck, and when he located the birdcage, he ran over and noticed that the door was open. In a panic, he quickly looked around to see if he could find the bird. He noticed that it was perched on the railing nearby. Then in a flash, it flew up to a rope and then to the top of the sail. He yelled, "Sir, the bird is out of the cage! Quick, the bird, it's getting away." There was much commotion and excitement as sailors and others looked up and wondered how they were going to get the canary back. Mack told Mary to look up, and he pointed at the bird on the top of the sail. She gasped and held her breath. Then they shaded their eyes as they watched it fly up and against the sun. With her newborn in one arm, Mary reached for Mack's hand with the other. She sighed and smiled all at once. *Goodbye, sweet Will. You will always sing in my heart. You were there for me when I needed it most.*

Her mother warmly said, "Let's go home."

ACKNOWLEDGEMENTS

I would like to thank my daughter, Carolyn Crist, without whom I could not have finished this novel. She provided never-ending support, encouragement and editing throughout the years and was the final editor.

First readers: John Crist, Linda Gathings, David Gathings.

For assistance in research: The Kenan Research Center at the Atlanta History Center, Augusta Historical Society, Georgia Archives, Georgia Heritage Room located in the Augusta-Richmond County Public Library, Maryland Historical Society, and Oakland Cemetery in Atlanta, Georgia.

For their research and preservation of history: Kathleen Rafferty Harrison Gegan, Charles Bearden, Reverend James L. Harrison, John "Pops" Mecaslin Harrison, Sr., and other keepers of the family treasures.

For support and encouragement: My brothers and sisters John Crist, Cathy Berggren, Sharee Crist and Kevin Crist, and friends Hugh Allen, Rick Broome, Lane Ritch, and Robin McDonald Steel.

I am also grateful to so many others who inspired me along the way.

ABOUT THE AUTHOR

Janine Crist, born in Illinois, has lived in the Atlanta area for most of her life. She's traveled up and down the roads mentioned in this book many times, commingling her own memories with the stories of the Mecaslins, the Mullins and the Maguires.

Her favorite aspect of writing this book has been the moments where she could stand and "be" in the places where these characters lived their lives — Mecaslin once held land where the Grady Memorial Hospital campus now sits, as well as the produce market on Decatur Street where Georgia State University exists. She's hunted for and found likely sites of the railroad amidst concrete slabs and new buildings and looks forward to finding more.

She has degrees from the University of West Georgia and Georgia State University in counseling and kinesiology. She taught middle school in Georgia and worked for the Department of Defense in North Carolina. She's currently a learning specialist in metro Atlanta.

This is her first novel. Janine welcomes visitors to her websites at janinecrist.com and maryamazon.com.

Made in the USA
Columbia, SC
14 November 2019

83263420R00124